ONE

UNFORGETTABLE

FAVOR

A MORGAN BROTHERS NOVEL

NICOLE VIDAL

COPYRIGHT

TABLE OF CONTENTS

KEEP IN TOUCH WITH NV

Visit me on social media or online to learn about my newest releases:

Facebook (http://fb.me/NicoleVidalAuthor)

Instagram (http://instragram.com/nicolevidal_author)

My website (www.nicolevidal.com)

Goodreads (https://bit.ly/NVGoodreads)

Amazon (https://amzn.to/2XCLSlR)

Pinterest (http://pinterest.com/NicoleVidal_Author)

CASSIUS

This city, the Big Apple, is electric. It has always been. As long as I can remember, the bustle of the city was an enigma to me. As a child it enthralled me. As an adult, not so much.

"Good evening, Mr. Morgan."

"Good evening, Arthur. How is your family? Did Ella have her baby yet?" Arthur is the concierge at my high-rise apartment building. He's been a constant in my days since I purchased my condo here.

"They're doing well. Still waiting on our newest granddaughter. And you, sir?" Arthur and his wife have three grown children. A new grandchild seems to be born each year lately.

"I'm well, also. Thank you. Have a good night." Entering the elevator, I slide my key into the slot and select the top floor. A diminutive blonde with piercing blue eyes steps inside the elevator as well.

"What floor?"

"Same as you," she replies.

I can readily admit, she's beautiful. However, I've realized in the last few years, my forever woman is not in this city. I'm ready to settle down—not that my social life is crazy; it isn't anymore. I've had my fair share of wild nights in the big city. Now I spend my days looking for amazing investments for my clients, and I moonlight as a private pilot on the weekends. When I'm not working, I'm home.

"There's only one unit on my floor. Who are you?" I ask, wondering what kind of prank is going on and who is pranking me. Likely Sam, only because he thinks I have a type, but Mina is a dark horse in the prank game.

"I clean the unit. I was tied up at school and haven't gotten there yet today."

"Beatrice?" I'm utterly shocked by the appearance of the woman sharing this elevator with me.

"Yes. You must be Mr. Morgan." She extends her hand to me. This woman cleans my home, but she's so young and has perfectly polished fingernails.

"I am. I'm sorry, I was expecting someone older and, well, dressed to clean."

"I was expecting someone older too. I have clothes in my bag." The door opens into a small alcove outside my door.

"Beatrice—"

"Mr. Morgan—"

"Ladies first."

"I can come back at another time. If I recall correctly, you prefer to be out while your home is cleaned."

"Thank you. I'm sure it can wait another week. Why don't you join me for dinner instead?"

Surprise crosses her pale features. "I appreciate the invitation, but I'm engaged." She lifts her left hand, showing me her ring. Classy, not flashy.

"My apologies. I didn't notice. Please take this week off," I say, pressing the down button for her.

"Are you sure?"

"Of course. Good night."

"Good night, Mr. Morgan." She steps into the elevator.

Once the doors close, I strip off my tie and head inside. I bought this unit for a few reasons. Primarily, it's the penthouse with an outdoor terrace that rivals most suburban backyards. With entrances off the living room and master bedroom, I have a large patio with two seating areas, a firepit, and a four-person jacuzzi. Second, the privacy it affords me has been a blessing and a curse. My family is well-known in this city, as am I. Very few people who aren't related to me by blood know where I lay my head at night. It's much easier that way.

I exchange my suit for some shorts and a T-shirt. Pulling out the pans, I start cooking some dinner. I'm not a chef by any means, but I get by. Someone with my means could eat out daily, but I prefer to cook at home. Flicking on some national news for background noise, I make a masterpiece of chicken and veggies. White wine and plate in hand, I walk out onto the private terrace to enjoy my dinner alone.

I would love to spend this time with a partner, but I haven't found her yet. Frankly, the women in my social circle aren't right for me. My parents, Warren and Margaux Morgan, for lack of a better term, have an arranged marriage. My grandfather offered my mother up in a business deal similar to how my father attempted to offer up my sister last year. My father didn't realize Mina is much stronger than Margaux.

Margaux is the epitome of a corporate wife and mother. She handled the house, business events, and carried the four of us with grace. Along with my three siblings, I never wanted for anything, except our mother's attention. Instead we had a gaggle of nannies to care for us. When we were of appropriate age, they shipped us off to boarding school. To be fair, I see both sides of that coin. We were out of the house, but we received the best education money could buy.

As the classic literary tales would suggest, my parents are old money and new money combined. My father started making a name for himself in his own right in the mailroom. He worked his way up to the top of a Fortune 500 company, making sound financial decisions along the way. Marrying my mother was a business deal, a smart financial decision. Just like Mina didn't want an arranged marriage, neither do I.

Mina is blissfully happy with her fiancé, Peter, in Maine living her dream of taking on the fashion world. When I learned about my sister's fiancé, I needed to check him out myself. Not only is Peter a stand-up guy, but he extricated my sister from my father's business deal—a deal that would have my sister marry someone for my father's gain. Technically, she's my half sister, and the bidder for my father's shares learned that fact and tried to leverage it. He failed, thanks to Peter's quick thinking and my sister's strong backbone and sharp tongue. He stood next to her as she went toe to toe with our parents and won. Rarely do my parents fail. It was epic.

As odd as it may sound, I want the fairy tale. Yes, it's abnormal for a guy to want a fairy-tale marriage. Nonetheless, I want a partner who challenges me to grow with her emotionally as well as professionally.

I spend my days investing other people's money. On my own time, I search for investments for myself and fly planes. Tonight, though, I plan to enjoy my solitude. Tomorrow, despite my objections, my mother has set me up on a blind date. No doubt, it'll go up in flames, but I assured my mother I would have dinner with Miss Templeton. If anything, I'm a man of my word.

The closer I get to this blind date, the more I want to cancel. I won't, but deep down, I want to. Brittany Templeton attended a fine boarding school in Connecticut, then earned her bachelor's degree in business at Harvard. I see why my mother thinks we have some things in common.

As I approach the hostess, I'm greeted by name. "Mr. Morgan, a pleasure to see you again. Miss Templeton has already arrived. Right this way." The curvy, blonde hostess leads the way.

Our table is near the back of the restaurant in the corner. I appreciate not only the privacy but the ambiance the table will afford, even though I have no intention of seeing Brittany past tonight.

"Cassius, so good to meet you." Brittany rises from her seat, kissing both of my cheeks.

"It's Cash. Good to meet you as well," I reply, taking in her dress, or lack thereof. Unlike most men, I don't have a type, despite what Sam thinks. That isn't to say physical attraction isn't important, just I don't have a thing for only blondes or curvy women. Her dress leaves little to the imagination. I'm all for a woman being comfortable in her own skin, but there is a line of how much skin should be showing. Brittany vaulted over it with her deep V-cut wrap dress. It's surprising, considering her upbringing.

Our server shares the daily specials and drink with us.

"Why don't you order for us?" she says, closing her menu.

"Are you sure?" Not only is that an odd request, but I don't really know her at all.

"Of course, my father always orders for our table."

I order our dinner, and we chat about her job as the Director of Giving at a charitable organization. Reading between the lines, I determine she makes phone calls to her parents' wealthy friends asking for donations and throws parties for a living. Nothing wrong with philanthropy; it just doesn't take much work when you have a Rolodex stacked like her parents. Outside of our parents' social status and tax bracket, we have nothing in common. No common interests or mutual friends. We eat in silence. When our server offers us dessert, I request our bill.

"Can I walk you to your car?" I offer, hoping she declines. She's nice, but not for me. I kept my word. That's all Margaux could ask for.

"I was hoping you would walk me to your place," she replies in a sultry tone.

"I appreciate the offer, but I'm not interested." I hold her coat for her as she slips into it. I'm not sure what type of reaction I was expecting, but I certainly didn't peg someone with her background to cause a scene. She begins shouting and making a fuss, disparaging our server and the restaurant in general. Everything about our meal was perfect until I turned her down for a one-night stand. An hour later, after the police took my statement, I walked home . . . alone.

NOELLE

Rays of sunlight filter through my blinds. That could only mean one thing, it's the weekend. I rise before the sun during the week to open the center. Just two weeks ago, I watched my oldest brother and Hollywood's Sexiest Man pledge his undying love to one woman. On a private overlook in Aspen, Nicholas and Kelly got married in an intimate ceremony that I almost missed. Thankfully, my brother's private pilot was able to finagle another plane to get me there on time. I was so overjoyed, I kissed him. Embarrassed doesn't even begin to cover it. It's still impossible to set aside the butterflies I felt when I was in his arms. With chocolate eyes, flawless skin, and dimples, drop-dead gorgeous doesn't do him justice. He's remarkable and unforgettable. I shake that delicious thought away.

My older brothers and I have an understanding. We agree to get together for weddings and at least one major holiday each year. Our pact originated a few years after our parents died in a horrific car accident. We were born and raised in Colorado and lived there until our parents' deaths. I came to California for college and never moved back home. Nicholas has a home in Colorado and now Maine where his wife is from. Noah never left.

I hurry through the shower and dress. I have a date with my bestie for moral support for her sister's baby shower.

"Noelle," Kate shouts from the foyer, "I'm here."

Only Kate and Nicholas have keys to my cute condo. I bought this home solely for the outdoor sitting area. There's a private patio with a pergola. The remodeled kitchen is clean and modern, and the bedroom is huge. My décor is simple and cozy. The couch is perfect for cuddling while watching movies on a rainy day.

"I'll be right out. I'm looking for my sweater." I scour the drawer again, trying to recall the last time I had it. To no avail, I grab another that somewhat matches. "What is the theme? Did you tell me the gender of the baby yet?"

"Evie doesn't want to know the gender, so we're going with a forest-theme shower." Kate follows me out the door.

My phone vibrates, but I ignore it for now. "Where are we headed first?" I settle into the passenger seat of her car. As she drives, I watch the scenery fly by, wondering if I should expand my job search horizon to include Colorado or even Maine. I put in applications at local daycare centers after the first issue with my boss about six months ago. A few weeks ago, she and I had another discussion. Even though my title is director, as the owner, she makes the decisions. While developmentally, my curriculum change was perfect, the child's mother didn't agree. Hence, the sit-down with my boss.

Kate pulls into the spot and takes out her phone. I check mine as well.

Unknown: Are you free tonight? I'm in town for work.

I consider who this might be. I don't recall giving anyone my phone number recently. Generally, I add a name. I check the history and see I have talked to this person before.

Me: Who is this?

Unknown: You forgot me already? I'm crushed. I guess that kiss wasn't as memorable for you as it was for me. It isn't everyday a stunning woman kisses me.

"Holy fish sticks!" I blurt out. Even though I'm an adult, I've trained myself not to curse because of my job. Apparently kissing Cash made more of an impact than he let on. He *was* being gentlemanly about it. What did he just call me? The stupidly handsome pilot thinks I'm stunning. He needs to get his eyes checked. Wait, don't pilots have superior vision?

"Noelle, who are you talking to?" Kate breaks into my thoughts.

"I'm not sure yet, but I think it's Nicholas's pilot."

"Can you text and walk? I need to get this done before my date with Kellan tonight."

I nod before opening my door and following her into the party store.

Me: Cash?

Cash: Yes. Were there other kisses I should know about?

No, not even close. My stomach is knotting up as I type.

Me: Maybe. Yes, I'm free tonight.

Not sure why I teased him, but….

Cash: I'll be there by six. Does that work?

Me: Yes.

Cash: Text me your address. I'll escort you properly.

I reply with my address and hurry to catch Kate in the store. I'm stuck on the fact that he wants to see me while he's in town. Did he really call me stunning? In my teenage years, "awkward" and "lanky" were more the words that guys would use to describe me. Even now, stunning is a stretch.

"Here's the section for the forest theme. What do you think?"

I hear Kate talking, but I'm not focused on her words.

"Earth to Noelle."

"Sorry, forest theme right here. What is your question?" I look toward her, yet still not affording her my full attention. I'm a horrible bestie right now.

"What happened with the pilot that you aren't sharing?"

"Nothing happened exactly. When he figured out a way to get me to the wedding on time, I might have kissed him."

"You're seriously holding out on me," she says.

"I was grateful, and I kissed him in my excitement." I hope my face isn't blushing. The memory of that brief but amazing kiss is fresh in my mind. "He just asked me out for tonight."

"Sweet, let's focus so we both have time to get ready."

I fumble along with Kate, nodding when appropriate while she makes so many choices for the decorations. I'm more focused on the fact I just agreed to go on a date with one of the sexiest—no, hands down the sexiest—man I've ever seen. And kissed.

"Where is he taking you?"

"I didn't even ask."

"You probably should so you know what to wear." Kate checks out of the party store.

"Where to next?" I ask before pulling out my phone to text Cash.

Me: Where are we going?

I chuck my phone into my tote.

"The florist next, which will be quick, then the bakery. After that, we're done for today. Thank you so much for coming with me. I want details tomorrow after your date. When is the last time you went on a date?"

I consider her question before answering. "I go on dates. The issue is the men around here are uber rich and arrogant. They don't warrant a second date. I want the fairy tale. I don't want to be a corporate wife, K. I love my career, perhaps not where I do it, but... I'll find the guy eventually. I'm just not sure he's here in this ritzy part of California." In short order, Kate chooses flowers and we're on to the cake tasting. My tote vibrates a brief time later.

Cash: It's a surprise. Casual clothes will work. It's not fancy.

Me: Okay. See you later.

After a few too many tastes of yummy cake samples, Kate and I choose a vanilla bean with a fresh strawberry filling for the shower.

There will be a single-layer, round cake for her sister to cut with cupcakes for the guests. Well after three, Kate drops me off, reminding me she wants details of my date tomorrow. I sigh after waving her off.

Strewn around my room is almost every top I own. As the clock strikes five, the doorbell chimes. I don't receive unannounced guests. I throw on an oversized sweatshirt to hurry to answer the door. As I round the corner, I see his profile in the sidelight. Dear God, he's hot, and he clearly doesn't know it.

I open the door. "Hi."

Dressed in dark jeans and a thin, fitted hoodie, he looks dangerously sexy.

"Hi, I'm a bit early. I hope you don't mind."

"Not at all. Come in. I just need to finish getting dressed." I close the door behind him.

"These are for you."

He hands me a bouquet of mixed flowers, including camellias, roses, lilies, and a purple flower I've never seen before. I'm sure my face is a perfect shade of pink.

"Thank you." I take the flowers into the kitchen and search for a vase. I don't remember the last time I received flowers from someone other than my brothers. Maybe that's one problem with the men around here. "Would you like a drink? I just need ten minutes to finish getting ready."

"No, thanks. I'm fine."

"Make yourself at home." I motion to the living room before disappearing into my room. I need to pick a top and calm my heart rate. I love that he's tall and I can almost look him in the eye barefoot. I almost never wear heels. Most men don't like their dates to be taller than them; plus, preschoolers require flats or sneakers. After selecting an emerald, cold-shoulder top to pair with my skinny jeans, I spray my favorite perfume and return to my living room. Yet I don't see Cash anywhere.

CASSIUS

When she answers the door, I'm taken aback. She isn't even ready, and she looks gorgeous with her long, auburn hair cascading around her face. Nerves don't usually play a role for me when I'm about to go on a date. In fact, I haven't been nervous in years. Yet with her, I am. Her lips on mine was like fireworks exploding on the Fourth of July. It was amazing but impulsive, yet I felt heat.

While she finishes getting ready, I wander onto her terrace. It's a gorgeous space like mine. Well, it's a perfect outdoor space for her condo. My wealth affords me a bit more space, but her home tells me she likes the outdoors, or at least fresh air.

"That was quick," I say when I see her standing in the doorway.

"I just needed to pick a top. Your arrival just sped up the process. You should see the mess in my room right now. Generally, I'm neat, but I couldn't choose." As I move closer to her, jasmine and orchid tickle my nose.

"You look beautiful and smell amazing." I'm just a half step away from being able to kiss her.

"Thank you. I'm ready when you are." She takes a step backward.

I'm not sure if it's because I'm too close or she's ready to leave. "It's perfect out here. Do you sit out here often?"

"This is my favorite spot. I bought this place for the terrace and proximity to the beach. The whole area is beautiful. The people, well, that's a different story."

After locking the sliding door, I follow her out. Her hips sway just enough as she walks. The bottom of her locks skim the curve of her tiny waist.

"Are you up for walking, or do you want to drive?" It doesn't matter to me.

"Walking is fine." She takes my arm.

We walk the first few blocks in silence. I glance over at her occasionally to make sure this is really happening. When I'm working, I don't go out. Normally, I leave the airport and immediately crash at the hotel until the return flight. On rare occasions, I research investments for my day job while I'm in another state.

We start speaking at the same time.

"Noe—"

"Cash—"

"Ladies first."

"Tell me something few people know about you." She looks over at me.

That's an odd question for a first date, but we spent twelve hours talking before her brother's wedding.

"I'm a homebody. When I was younger, I had some wild times with my classmates and friends. Now I prefer to be home."

"That's surprising considering you wanted to go out tonight," she observes.

"It would have been a bit forward to assume you would be willing to cook for me."

She laughs softly. It's a wonderful sound.

"What about you?"

"Most people don't know that my brother Nicholas was my guardian for about a year after our parents died."

"How did he pull that off?" I interlace my fingers with hers.

She inhales sharply, as if hesitant to answer.

"You don't have to share."

"It's easy to share with you. I feel like I've known you longer than one day." I nod as she continues. "Even though it's been almost a decade, it's still hard. Nicholas refused to let me go into the system for any amount of time. Mabel was our nanny, for lack of a better term. She helped my parents around the house. She was there when we got home from school and left just after one of my parents arrived after work. Mabel was instrumental in Nicholas being able to keep me out of the foster care system. He petitioned the court to become my guardian and moved back to Colorado until I came here for college."

"Is that why you're so close to your brothers?" She fiercely loves her siblings like I do. Her adamance about attending the wedding made that noticeably clear.

"They're all I have. Even though Nicholas is well-known, he's always there for me. Noah is a bit prickly, but he's my brother. What about you? What's your family like?"

I release her hand to guide her across the street, retaking it after we cross. Her delicate hand with long, slender fingers fits in mine perfectly.

"My parents were distant and absent during my childhood, even though my mother didn't work. My father worked insane hours to provide for us. He still does, even at his age. I have two brothers and a sister. Sam is my older brother; he works in insurance for high-end art. Mina, my younger sister is a designer who just got engaged. My younger brother, Auggie, is finishing up culinary school in New York."

"It's amazing to have a bunch of siblings. I gather those are nicknames, right?"

"They are. My parents chose unique names for us: Samson, Wilhelmina, August, and Cassius."

"Cassius. I wondered where Cash came from. I love it. I suppose you don't like it."

My full name falling from her lips is exquisite. The way she pronounces it makes me shiver.

As we arrive at our first destination, I reply, "You can call me anything you want." The hostess escorts us to a table immediately but not because of my family name. I pull out her chair before taking a seat.

"Thank you." She places her napkin in her lap. Nodding, I grab my menu.

As we eat our dinner, we chat about several topics, straying away from our families. The food at the quaint café is delicious. The conversation and the company are even better. I've never met anyone like Noelle. She's easy to talk to, fun, and gorgeous. Too bad she lives in California. Although, I'm here at least twice a month, usually more.

"Ready for our next stop?" I ask her as our server gives me back my credit card.

"Are you going to clue me in?"

"Nope, not at all." I guide her outside, but leave my arm resting on her waist while we walk. As we get closer to our destination, I feel her energy tick up.

"I haven't been here in a few years. Thank you." She leans over and kisses my cheek.

We stroll hand in hand along the pier, stopping occasionally. The sights and smells surround us as we walk. As we pass the carousel, I raise an eyebrow. A huge smile spreads across her face. We hurry to purchase tickets and stand in line. While we wait, I pull her close to me, not only to feel her in my arms, but to make it clear to her two admirers that we're together—at least we're on a date. Together is a far-flung dream right now. As I clasp my hands around her waist, I hear a small inhale and her gaze shifts to mine. Holding her in my arms makes my heart race.

"Tickets," the teenage girl asks, interrupting the moment. I hand her the tickets before following Noelle as she chooses a horse. The sheer joy on her face is amazing to see. She opts for the only unicorn on the ride. I take the horse next to hers. Around and around we go. I should be taking in the scenery, but instead I'm watching her. Only her. As the ride slows, she glances over at me and leans in.

"I'm having a wonderful time. Thank you." She lightly kisses my lips.

"I am too," I manage to reply. The warmth of her lips on mine is a heady feeling. I dismount my horse and offer her my hand. As she turns, her foot slips, causing her to fall into my arms. Her curves feel perfect in my grasp. "Are you all right?"

"Yes, thank you," she replies in a shaky breath. I'm not sure if it's from falling or me. Just like before, she inhales. The next group of riders is already moving around us. Taking her hand, I guide Noelle toward the exit. As we step through the gate, a tiny blonde girl with a cherub face tugs on her shirt.

"Hi, Miss Noelle."

Noelle releases my hand and crouches down to her level. I join her at eye level of the little girl.

"Hi, Annaliese. How are you?"

"I'm great. I rode the carousel and the Ferris wheel. We ate ice cream, and is he your husband?" She looks over at me, her words staccato like.

"He's my—"

I wonder how she will answer her student. How would I answer her student? There are maybe three options: friend, date, boyfriend.

Boyfriend certainly doesn't apply, but it would be a clear explanation for the little girl.

"Annaliese, leave Miss Noelle alone. You'll see her on Monday. I'm so sorry," her mother states, rushing up to collect her daughter.

"It's no problem. I'll see you Monday," Noelle replies as Annaliese throws her arms around Noelle's neck.

"He's cute," she whispers with a giggle.

"He is," Noelle whispers back. Noelle stands and waves to her student. I rise too. Taking her hand, I lead her back to the end of the pier.

"You think I'm cute, huh?"

"Maybe. Maybe I was just agreeing with my precocious student. I'll never tell," she replies with a smirk.

"Do you want to sit here or go onto the sand to watch the sunset?"

"Sand." She takes a seat on a nearby bench to remove her shoes. I join her, doing the same. She's a breath of fresh air. No woman from home would even consider stepping onto the beach without all the necessary accoutrements. The beach isn't crowded right now, so there's plenty of empty sand to choose from. We walk side by side, stopping just above the wet sand. Taking a seat, I set my shoes beside me.

"May I?"

I'm unsure what she's asking but nod anyway. Noelle drops her shoes with mine before sitting between my legs, facing the water. I wrap my arms around her waist and hold her close. She sighs softly as she relaxes against me, and I kiss the top of her exposed shoulder.

The sun is showing off tonight. Glorious colors streak across the sky. Reds, pinks, orange, and some yellow dance on the horizon. Generally, silence, especially on a first date, would concern me.

"Are you always this quiet?" She cranes her neck to look at me.

I want to kiss her to see if the sparks from our friendly, impulsive kisses were real or if they were in my head. "Not exactly. I carefully choose my words. Right now, I don't have words to sum up everything that's going through my mind."

Her eyes drop to my mouth as she licks her perfectly pink lips. "Start small," she whispers, twisting so she's facing me, her legs bent over my thighs.

I rest my hands on the curve of her hips. "This is by far the best date I've ever been on."

NOELLE

"That's small?"

I agree with his assessment. However, the bar is terribly low.

"It's a small part of what I'm thinking. My recent dates haven't made it past one. I haven't been on a second date in a few years," he replies, searching my face for a reaction. How on earth do his dates not see this sexy-as-sin man as he is?

"Same for me. The men here are arrogant and presumptuous. One fancy dinner doesn't equal sex, at least not for me. Where do you live?" I ask softly.

"That's another part of what's floating in my head. I live in New York City. I have a day job in the city, and I fly most weekends."

Undeterred, I ask, "How often are you in California?"

"Are you asking me on a second date?"

"Maybe, if you're interested."

"I'm interested. I've never met anyone like you. I feel like I've known you much longer than I have. This may be the second time we've been together, but we were talking all night while we waited at the hotel the first night."

"True. You're a great listener." The breeze picks up as the sun falls below the horizon.

"Are you cold?"

Not this close to you, not at all. Warmth rolls off him in waves.

"Not even a little, but maybe we should start walking back."

Cash slides his thighs out from under me. The loss of body heat makes me instantly cold. He offers me a hand and assists me to my feet. I brush the sand off my jeans. After grabbing our shoes, we return to the same bench and put them back on.

"To answer your question from before, I'm here at least twice a month. One of my clients from New York visits her grandson every other weekend. Those are on my schedule indefinitely. The rest of my flights are at the whim of my clients."

After sliding on my flats, I take Cash's hand and he leads me back toward my condo. His hand moves to rest on the small of my back to guide me across the street, and I notice he makes sure I'm on the inside away from the street. He's gentlemanly. It's refreshing considering how my recent dates have gone.

"When will you be here next?' I ask as we round the corner on my block.

"In two weeks. Are you free?"

"I think so. I need to check my schedule when I get home."

I notice he hasn't checked his phone since he arrived. That's rare. We arrive at my condo, and Cash follows me inside.

"Would you like a drink?" I ask, grabbing a water out of my fridge.

"No, thanks. I'm fine. Are you free for a second date in two weeks, Miss Barnett?" He steps close to me, resting his palm on my hip.

"Bothered you just a tiny bit that I asked you first, huh?"

"Maybe a little," he replies with a smirk.

Those dimples, oh my!

"So, you're a bit traditional."

He shrugs.

Grabbing my phone from the counter, I check my schedule. "Yes, I would like to go out with you again. What time do you need to be at work tomorrow?" I don't want this amazing date to end.

"I need to be at the airport by eleven. Mrs.—my client likes to be home in the early evening east coast time."

"Will you sit outside with me?" My voice is shaky.

"Yes. I'm not ready to leave yet."

Why am I nervous? I've already kissed him, but the heat from that friendly kiss was a lot to handle. I follow Cash onto the terrace, grabbing a throw blanket off my couch as I pass. He takes a seat with his back against the arm of the rattan couch. As if he sensed my desire to be held, he opens his arms to me. I curl up with him, covering my feet with the blanket.

"The view here is nice. It's surprising you can see so many stars considering you're in the city."

"It's relaxing out here," I reply, internalizing his fingertips running up and down my upper arm. That feels nice. We chat about varying topics as well as Nicholas's wedding after I thank him again for going out of his way to stay with me.

"I'm glad I was able to get you there in time. Like you, I would do anything for my siblings. Sam doesn't like to rely on anyone. When he asks for help, it's usually big. My sister was in an awful car accident a few years ago. Mina ran away to follow her dream of fashion designing. Sam and I were sending her money each month to make sure she had everything she needed."

"That's generous."

"I needed to make sure she was okay. Auggie is the youngest. He'll finish the Culinary Institute in the spring. He plans to open a farm-to-table restaurant after graduation. I don't know if that's feasible in the city, but I'll help in any way I can. You mentioned that Nicholas took care of you before college and you grew close. What about now?"

"I can take care of myself. I don't need Nicholas's money." Just when I thought this was going well, he acts just like the rest.

"Whoa, that isn't what I meant. I can see you're independent. It's an attractive quality. Let me try again. Is it hard to spend time with your brother due to his profession?"

"I'm sorry. Not many people know that he's my brother. I don't tell anyone that Ellis Barnett is my big brother. I say my brother's name is Nicholas, which it is. Most people don't pry or put together that they are the same person. As I mentioned when we talked before the wedding, we agree to get together for at least one major holiday and weddings. We text every few days and video chat at least once a month. Noah, on the other hand, we text occasionally, but that's it. I think part of it goes back to after our parents died, Nicholas chose to take care of me, but Noah was already out on his own. My bond with Nicholas grew a lot during that time."

We trade basic getting-to-know-you questions after talking about our siblings. He loves football but hates baseball. I'm not really a sports fan in general. I've been to a few games here and there, but I don't seek them out. I'm more of a concert goer. That's something we have in common.

"Who would you go see in concert, living or dead?" I ask him.

"Dead, definitely the Beatles. Alive, I would say Billy Joel."

"Interesting."

"Why is that interesting?" he asks, mocking my voice.

"Did you just mock me?"

"Maybe. It's not like you're going to do anything about it."

Before I think better of it, I turn to face him and reach under his arm to tickle him. Unfortunately, he isn't ticklish, at least not there. Pushing aside his shock, Cash grabs my wrists in one hand, pinning me to the cushions.

"Don't. Please don't." I narrow my eyes at him. "I don't want to hurt you by accident. I have no control when I'm tickled."

"You started it." A devilish twinkle glints in his eye.

"That's a response one of my students would give. Try harder," I reply, not really knowing what on earth he'll do. The weight of him of top of me is inviting. Releasing my wrists, he drags one hand down my arm, raising goose bumps along the way. Anchoring himself with that arm near my waist, he cups my cheek with his other hand while moving closer to me. Inhaling sharply, I slide one hand to the curve of his neck and the other flat against his chest. Beneath my fingers is a sculpted expanse of muscle. Slowly, he lowers his lush lips closer to mine. I search his eyes, trying to find why he's hesitating, but come up empty.

"Kiss me," I whisper.

The heat of his lips on mine is better than I remember. He's gentle at first, but then the tenor turns needy. I open for him, allowing his tongue to explore my mouth while mine explores his. The scratch of his facial hair prickling my chin. He trails a path along my jaw to my ear. After a small nip of my earlobe sends a shock down my neck, he moves outward across my shoulder and back.

When I kissed him at the hotel, it was friendly. This is something else. Cassius claims and consumes when he kisses. Holy hockey! The planes of his back are hard beneath my fingers as my other hand roams. He delves into my mouth before pulling my lower lip between his teeth. The hard ridge against my center only serves as a reminder that it's been too long since a man has been this close to me. No one has ever kissed me like this. His warmth surrounds me as he pulls back, looking down at me, his eyes pinned to mine. My breath evens out slowly.

"Was that hard enough?" He smiles, revealing those sexy dimples. All I can do is nod. I could kiss him forever. "I've wanted to do that since I arrived. When you kissed me at the hotel, I was surprised. I figured there was no way the heat could be that hot. I was wrong. It's so much hotter."

"Yes, it is."

Cash sits back on his heels and helps me to sit up. I settle back into his arms, and we cuddle under the blanket, staring at the sky for a while before realizing the time.

"I should go."

Nodding, I rise from the couch. I don't want Cash to leave, but I understand. I'm sure he needs some sleep before flying home tomorrow—a home that is so far away. This may have been the best first date I've ever been on, but the fact he lives on the opposite coast is disheartening. We walk to the door hand in hand.

"I had a wonderful time tonight with you. I'll talk to you soon."

"Okay." I slide my arms around his waist and look into his eyes. Threading his fingers into my hair, he tilts my chin upward slightly and presses his lips to mine. I revel in my feelings. I've only wanted to turn back the clock one other time, and that moment was life changing. Perhaps this one is too.

CASSIUS

Walking away from her door is harder than it should be. Overall, I've known Noelle for less than a weekend, but there is something about her. She's fiercely independent, kind to her students, and gorgeous. She's markedly different from the women in New York. After a few hours of sleep, I return to the airport for my flight home.

Me: Good morning, beautiful. How did you sleep?

Noelle: Morning. Fine, and you? Did you get enough sleep?

Me: I did. Thanks. I just checked in at the airport. There is a sweater here. Is it yours?

Noelle: Beige, super soft?

Me: Yes.

Noelle: Yes, it's mine. I have been looking for it. I misplaced it before the wedding. Thanks.

Me: The crew put it here after the plane was repaired. I'll keep it until I see you. Gotta go. TTYS.

I grab Noelle's sweater, resisting the urge to smell it only by the slightest of margins, and continue my preflight checks. After greeting Mrs. Waller, I point the plane back toward New York. There's an uncomfortable tightness in my chest I've never felt before as we lift off the runway.

After spending much of my day on the phone nailing down details for my latest deal, I leave the office for the gym. I would like to rush home and talk to Noelle, but she won't be out of work for another few hours I suppose. My desire to talk to her again is high. I want to hear about her day with the kids and see if Annaliese planned our wedding yet, especially since Noelle didn't dispel the notion that we're a couple at the pier.

My gym is ultra-exclusive and caters to men with means like me. I have no concerns about who I might see or if photos will be taken of me during my workout. Stacy, Kip, and Danny are in the locker room. After two nods and a bro hug, we move on to our workouts. Men are different in their interactions with their friends or gym mates. We don't talk. We're here to sweat out our problems, not use our words. If words are necessary, so are beers.

I receive a nod from my trainer as I enter the ring. Evan kicks my ass regularly to help me stay in shape. We circle each other, throwing punches and body shots. Jab, cross, body shot. Thirty minutes into sparring, Evan lands a strong uppercut. I drop to the mat, rubbing my jaw.

"C, are you okay?"

"Yes," I reply from the mat. Perhaps I should focus on Evan's gloves rather than the feel of Noelle's curves in my arms, the taste of her on my lips, and the ease of our conversations, even though talking about my family is typically a no-go zone for me.

"Where is your head? It's clearly not here. What's her name and does she have a sister?" Evan offers me a hand up.

"How do you know there's a woman?" I inhale a few times, taking the reprieve his questions give me.

"C, I've known you since college. We shared an apartment. I saw the revolving door that was your bedroom. I don't think you ever slept alone. I know that look well on other men's faces. You met someone, and she isn't a one-night type of woman."

I guess we will be using our words without beers.

"Her name is Noelle. I met her a few weeks ago through a client. It's a long story, but I went out with her on Saturday."

"She's still got you tied up in knots. I need to meet her. I've never seen you like this. Ever. Not once." Evan smacks his gloves together, indicating he's ready to continue kicking my ass. Instead of answering with words, I spend the rest of my hour turning the tables on Evan. The last thirty minutes are hard. My time at the gym has done nothing to clear my head of my auburn-haired stunner. *My?* Luckily, Evan has another client right after me, so he can't grill me more. I hurry through the locker room, gather my clothes, and head home.

As I walk, I consider whether I could pull off a trip to see Noelle this weekend instead of waiting. Unfortunately, I can't. I promised Auggie I would go over his business plan with him and offer support at my parents on Sunday morning. I dread trips to my parents'; there's always an ulterior motive—typically, one that includes me finding a wife before I'm old, gray, and impotent. Just because Margaux had all of us by my age, twenty-eight, doesn't mean that I need to do the same. Plus, my attempts to explain to her that her idea of a suitable wife doesn't match what I desire in a partner have been ignored.

"Good evening, Arthur," I say as I enter the building.

"Mr. Morgan. Here is your mail and a package. Have a nice evening," he replies with a smile.

"You too." I step into the elevator.

After a boiling shower and a quick dinner, I settle on the terrace to call Noelle. It's a gorgeous evening to sit outside. I need a way to jump into a novel and borrow Hermione's time turner. Just hearing her voice isn't going to be enough. How I know that already is surprising.

Me: Are you free?

Noelle: Yes.

I call via video chat so I can see her beautiful face. Not only am I rewarded with her face, but she's wearing a low-cut tank top and a thin cardigan. It must be warm today.

"Hi. How was your day?"

"Meh. I had another issue with a parent today. It will probably be the last straw at this job. I've been looking for another one since her first complaint about me."

"What happened? Start at the beginning." I don't like that she had a crappy day, but hearing her voice relaxes me.

"About six months ago, I noticed that a student, I'll call him M, was falling behind. He's almost three years old. I suggested to the owner that he should have a screening to check his development. Was her consent necessary? No. I could have done it on my own, but it's her company, so I felt I should ask. Instead, my boss decided to bring it to the parents' attention herself. The owner and I had a lengthy discussion with the parent who decided against having the screening." She pauses, taking a moment. Her brows furrow with frustration. I hate that she's bothered by this.

"What do you think is wrong with him?" I hope to pull her back to the reason she wanted the screening.

"I think he's autistic. He doesn't like when people touch him. He doesn't always respond when we call him and can't put words together like he should. A few weeks ago, the mother complained that the center is failing because M can't do some of the things his peers can. My boss pulled me in again, asking what can be done."

"You're correct that M is behind?"

"Yes, I am. I'm sorry, we should talk about something else. This is boring."

"Absolutely not boring at all. If I tried to explain my job to you, it would be boring. You're genuinely concerned for M and want him to thrive. There is nothing boring about that. It shows you care about your students. What can you do?"

"Are you sure you want to listen to all of this drama?"

"I want to talk with you about whatever is bothering you. If you need to vent about your boss and ways to help M, I'm here to listen. Plus, I want to know about our tiny date crasher, Annaliese."

"He needs to have a screening to see how far behind he is. I estimate he's about eight months behind where he should be. He'll need support for the rest of his schooling life. Enough about me, tell me about your day."

"As you know, I'm a venture capitalist. I connect investors with entrepreneurs who are looking to start a new business or grow their current business. Basically, I spend my days looking over reports, prospectus, and business plans to find a good fit for my client's or myself."

She leans forward to grab her drink inadvertently offering me a glimpse of her lacy bra.

"What was the best project you ever invested in personally?"

My brain short-circuits for a minute. I need to gather my thoughts before answering her. Not only was the glimpse spectacular, but it was unintentional, which makes me feel slimy. I feel guilty, not only for looking but also for my physical reaction to her even thousands of miles apart. "There is a group home for veterans on Long Island that I invested in personally. They provide programs to get service members the treatment they need, as well as temporary housing if necessary. I still sit on the board."

"Any special reason you chose that project?"

"My college roommate's dad was a marine. He was severely injured while serving our country. Unlike me, Evan and his family didn't have the means to get him the support he needed. I couldn't help Mr. Arnold, but the home helps other men and women like him."

"That's impressive. You surprise me, Cash."

"Why?"

"You're aren't like most successful men."

"Is that a compliment?"

"Yes, it is. Most successful men, at least the ones I meet here, are self-absorbed, pompous, and don't pay attention. No way would they remember the name of my student. It's rare that someone who is successful and has means isn't a total jerk. I'm glad you're different."

"Thank you. So, tell me about our matchmaker. I think she had our wedding planned in her mind."

She smiles and fills me in on Annaliese and the rest of her evening at the pier. We chat a bit more before I turn in. Generally, I sleep well, but a tall, red-haired beauty stars in my dreams, keeping me up all night.

NOELLE

"I'm here, so the party can start," Kate shouts when she arrives at Kiely's Tavern, a local hole-in-the-wall bar. We've been frequenting the small bar every Thursday since college. Not only does the bartender, Keyton, still honor our college IDs, but he gives us half-off appetizers whenever we arrive. A Chris Hemsworth doppelgänger, the bartender has been courting Kate for years. He's good-looking, if you like insanely built, light brown hair, and piercing blue eyes. Keyton does nothing for me, but he's precisely Kate's type.

Now, tall, dark, and handsome Cassius does do it for me. Not only is he hot, but his mouth should come with a warning label. No man has ever kissed me like that before. If I were standing, I would have liquefied into a puddle at his feet. The heat was indescribable. He correctly classified our kissing as hotter than at the hotel.

"You never told me about your date. How was it?"

"It was nice, Kate."

"Nice. Okay, fine. The real question is are you going to see him again."

"Yes, I'll see him next weekend when he's back for work."

"He doesn't live here?" Kate asks, as if that should be a deal breaker for a second date.

"No, he doesn't. It's just a second date, Kate. It isn't as if we're going to get hitched—well, Annaliese thinks we will, but...."

Keyton makes a special trip from behind the bar to deliver our food. I don't miss the looks he's sending Kate, but she seems oblivious.

"How was your date with Kellan?" I ask after Keyton returns to the bar.

"Fine, he isn't the one. There's no... fire. I can take him or leave him. That isn't what I want long-term. There has to be fire."

"I agree. Maybe you should consider accepting Keyton's invitation."

"Maybe I will. Why did you say yes to a second date with Cash if you know he lives far away?"

With a sigh, I consider my words carefully, knowing Kate will twist them. "When I kissed him at the hotel, it was a friendly, thankful kiss. It was impulsive. I was grateful he was able to get me to the wedding in time. I took him by surprise. Even then, I felt something. When he kissed me on Saturday, the heat was impossible to ignore." I keep replaying every single delicious second over and over in my head, remembering the taste of him on my lips and the heat of his hands on my body coupled with his instant arousal. The combination makes for fitful nights of sleep.

"Can't say I have ever felt like that just from a kiss."

"Me either. Hence, the second date. He's here at least twice a month, usually more." I decide not to offer more information about Cash and his jobs. Even with my limited knowledge of the financial world, it's enough to know he's likely in the same tax bracket as Nicholas or close to it. His paycheck likely has three more zeroes each pay period than mine. It's surprisingly refreshing that he's like Nicholas in that he doesn't throw his wealth around. If he wanted to, he could have taken me to a Michelin-rated restaurant in a hired car last week. He didn't, and for that I'm grateful.

We've been texting often and talking nightly, usually via video chat. I like being able to see his expression when he answers me.

I'm a tad tipsy when I call him tonight after Keyton called us an Uber.

"Heeeyyyy, hot stuff! How are you?"

"Hey," he says hesitantly, concern marring his gorgeous face. "Did you drive?"

"No, of course not. I only had one drink with Kate, but my burger was too rare, so I didn't eat it. Hence, I'm a bit buzzed."

"Are you home?" I can still hear a bit of concern in his voice. It's sweet. He touches his jaw as if he's in pain.

"Yes, I'm home." I recheck the door before moving into my bedroom. I plop down on my bed, lying on my belly.

"Noelle, baby, I need you to either shut off the video or roll over." His voice sounds strangled. Heat rushes straight between my thighs.

"Why?" I look down. "Fish sticks!" *At least my bra is sexy.* Generally, my workday lingerie is more comfort than anything else. I need to do laundry, so today's is a bit sexier than normal for a school day. I grab a fluffy throw pillow and put it under my chin to block his view.

"Thank you. That view was way too tempting considering how far away you are. Do your panties match? Did you just say fish sticks?"

"Yes, I match. I can't curse at work. I have a bunch of substitutes: fish sticks, holy hockey, croutons, fire truck, and shitake. If I do curse, the situation is extremely good or extremely bad."

"Was work that bad today?" Apparently, he's still reeling from the accidental glimpse of my breasts. His face has a tight expression. Even though the video isn't great, I can see his eyes are dark with lust.

I want you too, Cassius, more than I should at this point, especially given the distance between our homes.

"No. Yes. Sort of. Kate and I have drinks at Kiely's Tavern every Thursday after work. We've been going there since college. Plus, Keyton, the bartender has a thing for Kate. She hasn't given him the time of day yet, but he still tries every single week. As far as work, it hasn't gotten any better with M's mother. She threatened to leave the center if my boss doesn't fix her son. Newsflash, your son doesn't need fixing; he needs support. Plus, career day is falling apart. I had six different careers set up for the last Friday of this month, and two bailed earlier today." Surprisingly, it felt better saying all of that out loud. A small weight lifted off my chest by sharing my problems. "Thank you, Cash."

"For what? I didn't do anything."

"Of course you did. I only have Kate here for the day-to-day stuff. Thank you for listening."

"Anytime. You can call me even if it's the middle of the night." He rubs his jaw.

"How was your day? What happened to your jaw? That's the second time you touched it tenderly since we started talking."

"Work was fine. I negotiated a deal for one of my investors to buy a large farm for a nonprofit animal rescue. Generally, those don't make money, but it's what she wanted, and I found the ideal angel investor for her. And my jaw hurts because of you."

"That's wonderful. What is an angel investor?"

"An angel investor—"

"Me? What do you mean your jaw hurts because of me?" I interrupt, my voice laced with angst and my chest tightening. I would like to learn what an angel investor is, but I'm more concerned about his jaw.

"*Tesoro*, I appreciate your concern, but I'm fine. My trainer and college buddy, Evan, landed a strong uppercut at the boxing gym after work. I wasn't in the ring; I was thinking about you. I know better."

I feel my skin heat up. I've driven this sweet man to distraction. What did he call me?

"An angel investor is a person with capital who is looking to invest in someone else's project like a new small business. Usually, the angel takes an ownership stake in the new company. Sometimes, he or she wants to start their own venture capital firm. Other times, the angel just wants to share his or her experience or wealth with a new entrepreneur."

"Are angel investors the norm, or is that just the beginning?"

"That is just one portion of where the capital could come from. Are you sure you want to hear all of this? Some people think my job is boring and repetitive."

"Yes, I want to hear all of it. You clearly love what you do, and you didn't make me feel dumb for not knowing what an angel investor is. Do you prefer investing or flying? Plus, your voice is sexy. I like listening to you talk."

"I have a strong urge to set some of your past dates straight. No one should ever make you feel less than because you don't know about a subject, especially something complex like venture capitalism. I have an exceptional aptitude for investing, but I prefer flying."

"Why do I sense some underlying issue with preferring flying?"

His eyes soften, and his shoulders relax even more. "How? I love how you see me. Truly see me. Flying is not an acceptable profession as far as my parents are concerned. Any service job is beneath a Morgan. To them, being a pilot, even if it's a private pilot, isn't good enough for their son."

"Please excuse my bluntness, but why do you care? If you're happier in the cockpit of a private plane than in an office on Wall Street, make a change. I know firsthand that life's too short to be unhappy in anything. While I don't remember as much as Nicholas, and even Noah to some extent, my parents were blissfully happy. We didn't have a lot, but we had each other for a tragically fleeting period. With your knowledge of investing, I'm sure you could manage whatever assets you have to take the massive pay cut I assume flying would be. I'm sorry this conversation just turned heavy."

"Nothing to be sorry for. Your view of life is refreshing in its simplicity. Losing your parents so young has impacted your world view for the better, and it's heartening to meet someone who believes that life is meant to be lived not bought."

I try to stifle a yawn but fail. I imagine he's ready to sleep as well.

"Go to sleep, *tesoro*. I'll call you tomorrow."

"Good night, Cash." I end the call wondering what that means, set an alarm, and snuggle under my covers wishing he were here.

CASSIUS

The sound of my front door opening jolts me from my bed. I overslept. Normally, I'm up with the sun even on weekends.

"Cash? Are you up?" my younger brother calls presumably from my living area. Auggie is the youngest of my siblings. My brothers and I look alike—tall, dark complexions, dark eyes. Auggie is a tad skinnier than Sam and me but only because he doesn't have as much time to hit the gym while he's in school. Apparently, becoming a chef is a grueling educational endeavor. Our sister, Mina is our antithesis. She has light eyes, long blonde hair, and is tiny.

"I'll be right out." I roll over with a groan. Not only does my jaw still hurt, but my muscles ache from yesterday's workout with Evan and Kip. I grumble as I sit up and climb out of bed. Pulling on a shirt, I trudge to the kitchen.

"Bro, you look like hell. Late night with a guest or too much booze?"

"Neither. I was up late on the phone." I busy myself making coffee. "Do you want a cup?"

"Sure. We can do this later if you want. I have the entire day free."

"I can't. I'm going out with Evan later. The time difference is rough."

"Wait, the person you were talking to lives in a different time zone?"

I set a cup in front of him and turn to make my own. "Yes," I reply, foaming the milk.

"She must be something special," Auggie observes before downing half his cup and pulling a stack of papers out of his backpack.

"She is. What did you bring for me?"

"That's it? That's all you're going to share," Auggie asks.

"There isn't a lot to share. I just met her a few weeks ago. She was a passenger on one of my flights. There were some mechanical issues with the plane, and my client asked me to do whatever was necessary to get his sister to his wedding. After some negotiating and making a few promises, I was able to secure another plane to get her where she needed to be. When I was back in her area last weekend, we went out."

"You like her," Auggie states pointedly.

"Yes, I do. Not only is she gorgeous, but her take on life is refreshing. Due to the hand she was dealt, she believes a person shouldn't do anything that makes them unhappy."

"Good for you, bro. I hope it works out for you. Didn't Mom fix you up with Brittany a few weeks ago too?"

"I do too. And yes. That was a train wreck. Not only is she boring and not my type, she caused a scene requiring police intervention at the bistro on Fifth."

"What on earth did you say to her that required a call to the police?" Auggie asks, hoping for something juicy.

"When I offered to walk her home, she said she wanted to walk to my place. I turned her down, and she lost her mind. I've never seen a woman act like that. The maître d' called the police immediately. What about you? Any relationships over three weeks I need to know about?"

"I have no words, especially since Mom supposedly vetted her. There are only two women who have lasted more than three weeks, Mina and Caro. Our sister is fine. She's happy with Peter and her new life. Caro is my best friend. We have a standing weekly dinner and talk daily. Otherwise, everything is the same as it has always been between us."

"Does she know you want more?" I inquire, seeing the longing in my brother's gaze. Presumably, that's the look Evan saw on my face before he landed his punch.

"No. She tells me repeatedly she isn't interested in ruining our friendship even if the sex were magnificent. Her words. I'm not in a place where I can fight for her like she deserves. Someday I'll tell her."

As the second cup of coffee wakes up the rest of my neurons, I grab his business plan. We spend the next few hours making some small tweaks in the mission statement and a substantial change in the five-year-plan projections before upping the initial capital investment he's seeking. The business plan is in great shape. I hope Margaux and Warren are willing to give him access to some of his trust account early to open his dream restaurant.

After finishing our changes to his plan, Auggie takes off. I have a few hours before meeting Evan for a few games of hoops at the club. I decide to text Noelle.

Me: How is your day so far?

I set my phone aside to catch up on some sports news on my terrace. Surprisingly, she answers immediately.

Noelle: Not too bad. I'm getting ready to hit the beach with Kate and her goddaughter.

Me: Not fair. You tempt me with my own imagination.

After hitting send, I push away how I think Noelle would look in a bikini. "Smoking hot" are the words that come to mind. Full breasts, smooth belly, and long, toned legs. All the blood rushes south as I picture her in my mind. Instantly I'm rock-hard. Her next text puts my imagination to shame. At the photo of Noelle wearing a black bikini, I'm painfully aroused. Arguably, it covers everything it should, but my brain is going wild with the ways I could untie the strings set on her curvy hips.

Me: Holy hell. You look hot!

Noelle: Thank you. What are you up to today?

Me: Playing basketball later with Evan and a few other guys.

Noelle: Make sure you pay attention. No more injuries on my account.

Me: I'll do my best, but you don't make it easy. Have fun at the beach.

Noelle: Call me tonight when you get home.

Me: I will.

I focus my energy on something nonsexual to calm myself. In my mind, I formulate ways to explain my job to Noelle. My job isn't boring to me, and she seems genuinely interested in learning. Slowly the strain against my boxer briefs lessens. Thinking about my job brings me back to our conversation last night. Is she right? Do I need to make a change? Do I want to?

I prefer flying to my day job—a fact I have only admitted to her. It isn't lost on me that she makes me rethink things and dig for deeper meaning. The fact that she's an orphan significantly impacts the way she views the world. It's clear she has a strong connection with her brother Nicholas and her bestie, Kate. She's selective with whom she spends her time. I'm grateful to have a chance to become someone she trusts.

After thinking about Noelle and her observations, I decide to shift my strategy to create an exit plan that decreases my hours in the office with an eye on resigning by the end of the year. I beg off basketball and begin my research immediately. Who do I share with next that ensures my privacy? It's probably my brother Sam, but I hold off on that call for now.

Five hours and a food delivery later, I have a plan for my work life. I haven't really thought how Noelle might fit into this, but at a minimum, I feel lighter and my outlook is genuinely more positive.

She calls me back after I send her a text. She divulges the details of her trip to the beach with her bestie and that she's lounging on her terrace soaking up the evening breeze. We chat for a bit before choosing

Shawshank Redemption to watch together from afar. For both of us, this movie is one of the all-time best. Every now and then while we're watching, I hear her sigh. I can picture her curled up in the corner of her couch with a cozy blanket. An increasing part of me wishes I were there with her.

"Good night, Noelle," I murmur into my phone near two in the morning East Coast time.

"Good night."

I imagine her burrowing deeper on her couch until morning. Stumbling to my bed, I fail miserably to sleep a wink. By seven on Sunday, I'm already on my second cup of coffee while preparing myself for brunch with my parents.

Their penthouse is located on the Upper East Side of the city. The skyline views are spectacular. Their home is overly big for just the two of them, but moving isn't an option. The address is indicative of their status in the New York social elite, and Margaux would never agree to give that up.

"Good morning, Henry. Nice to see you again." Henry has been with my family as long as I can remember. He's a portly man who serves as the house butler for my parents. He taught me and my brothers how to play pool in the servants' quarters while my parents traveled. The best times we had in this house were when our parents were gone.

"You as well, Master Cassius. Your parents are in the front parlor. Your brothers have already arrived," he replies.

"Thank you." I walk to the parlor, attempting to center myself as I get closer to my parents. The last time I was with my parents was at the Salvatore wedding last year. It appalled me to learn that my father was attempting to marry my sister off to a business associate like my mother was to him. The same night, we learned that Mina is my half sister. She's working on her relationship with her bestie turned half sister, Della, and her biological father. She refuses to see our parents, and I don't blame her. I'm only here today to support Auggie.

As I step into the room, both Sam and Auggie nod.

"Cassius, thank you for coming." Margaux remains seated, dressed in a tailored lilac suit with matching pumps. Even for brunch in her own home, Margaux dresses like she is dining at the Waldorf.

"Mother." I take a drink from Salma, their housekeeper and cook. She and Henry came to work for my parents as a couple. I have only seen one other couple as deep in love as them: Arthur and Eloise. They give me hope that my fairy-tale marriage is a possibility.

An image of Noelle floats quickly through my mind. To keep her out of this meeting, I shove the gorgeous image away. I have no intention of mentioning her to my parents, and I'm sure Auggie won't either. "Father." Warren is an investor through and through and dresses the part as well. He's tall with salt-and-pepper hair, fit, but it's obvious sweets are his weakness.

"Cassius. Nice of you to join us in a timely manner."

I let his dig roll off my shoulders. I'm not late. My father believes that to be on time, you must arrive at least fifteen minutes early. We were set to meet at ten; it's five minutes before, and he still chastises me. I'm a successful businessman, and my timeliness has never been an issue.

Salma indicates that our meal is ready. We move into the formal dining room. I'm sure Auggie wants to talk about his proposal, but I assume our father will push him off until after brunch. After Salma serves our food, the only sounds in the room are from silverware touching the plates or polite requests to pass the cream.

We return to the parlor after brunch, and Auggie sets out his plan for early access to his trust fund. Surprisingly, my parents listen intently to his presentation. Before Mina's discovery of her parentage and my parents releasing her entire trust in an attempt to reestablish a relationship with her, I would have said this meeting was futile. In the end, my parents agree to allow Auggie to use half of his requested amount to capitalize his farm-to-table restaurant upon successful graduation from the Culinary Institute. Thanks to me, Auggie will have about 20 percent more than necessary from the amendments we made to his business plan yesterday.

As soon as I can, I excuse myself from the depths of my childhood nightmare. After the ride home, I still need to decompress, so I pull on some running shoes to run a loop around Central Park.

NOELLE

As each day passes and the weekend is in sight, I get increasingly giddy. The early part of the week has moved along at a decent pace. Cash and I have exchanged texts or video call each night. Midweek the owner decides that I need to rearrange the entire center to appease M's mother. I'll do it, only because it will help M. My boss, Sheila, is doing it to maintain her reputation with the elite clientele of the center. Her attitude regarding the status of her students' trust funds gives me pause.

Luckily, I have a phone interview set up for this evening. I spent the entire day restructuring the math, reading, dramatic play, and sensory areas of the classroom today. I'm exhausted. Thankfully, this interview is by phone. My tired eyes might reflect on my ability to keep up with preschoolers.

The phone interview goes well. The director indicates that she's looking for her replacement and has a few more candidates to interview. Afterward, I hastily throw together some dinner. After setting my dish in the sink, I change into shorts and a cami. I snuggle into my bed with a book and promptly fall asleep. Near midnight, I wake to my sheets soaked with sweat with the urge to vomit. My muscles ache, but I'm sure it's from moving fixtures around all day today. I barely make it to the bathroom before losing my dinner. With maximum effort, I plod to my couch and promptly fall back to sleep.

Near eight the next morning, I summoned the strength to text Sheila, letting her know I'm ill. That was hours ago. Rays of hot sun are streaming in through my sliding door. I push up to sitting, attempting to ignore the spinning in my head. The next thing I remember is Cash carrying me to the bathroom.

I hear water and feel something running up and down my back. Kate. Kate is here too.

"Here, take these." Kate shoves some pills into one hand and a sports drink into the other. Someone is taking off my clothes and washing my hair. I'm so weak, I don't have it in me to figure it out.

Wakefulness seeps in slowly, but it doesn't appear to be morning. A heavy arm curls around my waist. I tense up and strain to find a clock.

"Relax, *tesoro*. Kate let me in. It's crazy early. Go back to sleep."

Everything is fine. Cash is here. I snuggle deeper into his warm, hard body. My inner most thoughts take over as I drift back off to sleep.

Hot, my arm feels hot. The sun from the skylight is hitting my arm. Hearing Cash must have been all in my head. Cash isn't here. It's just me in the big, cold bed. That dream was vivid—right down to his rock-hard arousal against my ass and the feel of his breath against my neck. Pushing up to sitting, I dangle my feet off the side of my bed. Rising, I wobble a bit and sit back down.

"Hi, sweetheart. How are you feeling?" Cash stands at the threshold of my room.

"You're really here?"

"Yes, I'm here."

"It wasn't all in my head. How? Why?"

He sits next to me, pressing his lips to my forehead. "I'll fill you in. First, how are you feeling?"

"Dizzy and weak."

He nods before rising and offering me his hand so I can stand. "Let's get you something to eat. I'll catch you up afterward."

"Okay." I slide my fingers into his hand and stand slowly. The moment I waver, his free hand grips my waist. It feels protective and possessive at the same time. It feels perfect. Once he's confident I won't keel over, Cash guides me into the kitchen for some food.

After making sure I'm seated, he sets a sports drink in front of me and some crackers.

"If you can keep those down, I'll make you something else in a little while." Bottled water in hand, Cash sits alongside me.

"What is going on? Why are you here?" My memory is foggy at best.

"What is the last thing you remember?" Concern mars his gorgeous features. There's a small crinkle near his eyes. It's downright sexy as sin. He's impossible to ignore.

"On Wednesday, Shelia instructed me to rearrange the center for M, and then I had a phone interview for a new job that evening. What day is it? What time is it?"

"It's Friday near eleven."

Sheer panic courses through my veins.

"Croutons, I have to call Sheila. She's going to fire me!" I twist in my chair, moving to stand, and I'm instantly dizzy.

Cash's strong arms encircle my waist, holding me up. Despite how I feel, being in his arms is heavenly.

"Kate texted Sheila last night before she left," he murmurs near the shell of my ear. "Why don't you sit back down, and I'll tell you everything."

I nod, pulling back slightly. With Cash's assistance, I retake my seat.

"When I texted you late on Wednesday, you said you would call me after your interview. Admittedly, I fell asleep waiting. When I woke up on Thursday morning, I sent you a text first thing. I waited a few hours because I know it's earlier here. When you didn't respond by noon, I started to worry. I reached out to my client to see if she was interested in coming a day early. She agreed. I flew here and knocked on your door as soon as I could. When you didn't answer, I considered finding the building manager or whatever, but then I recalled your standing Thursday date with Kate." He's rubs circles on my arm while he's talking.

"You flew here for me?"

"Yes, I was worried about you. I went to Kiely's hoping to find you there with Kate and there was some issue with your phone. I talked to Keyton, who said that neither you nor Kate arrived like usual. Keyton called Kate, and she met me here."

"Did you wash my hair?"

"No, it was Kate. I didn't think it was appropriate. When we arrived, we found you curled up on the floor. It seems like you were trying to get back to your bed. I carried you to the bathroom, and Kate cleaned you up and helped you get redressed. I replaced the linens on your bed and threw them in the wash. Then I carried you back to your bed. Kate stayed with you while I went to the store for supplies."

"You flew here for me?"

"Yes. If we lived in the same zip code, would it bother you that I came?"

"Well, when you put it that way, no. Thank you for coming."

"Of course."

"Can you get my phone for me?"

He stands and fetches my phone from my bedroom. He moves gracefully despite his tall, built frame. When he returns, he hands me my phone. There are seven texts and two missed calls.

Cash: Good morning, beautiful. How was the interview?

Nicholas: Hey, sis. How was your interview?

Cash: Are you okay?

Kate: How was your interview?

Kate: I'm running late to Kiely's.

Kate: I'm not going to make it. I'll call you later.

Kate: Are you home?

I review the texts while Cash grabs some fruit from the fridge. "I've ruined our date," I whisper to myself, apparently loud enough for Cash to hear me.

"No, you didn't." He takes my hands as he sits facing me. "We can curl up on your terrace or your couch to watch movies. I'll take you out the next time I'm here if you're up to it. First, you need more food." He prepares some toast for me and replaces the sports drink with a fresh bottle.

Is this what it feels like to be part of a couple? I realize it's early, but he came here to check on me and is taking care of me.

"Don't you have to work today?"

"I have to clear my inbox and return a call, but otherwise, nothing pressing. Feeling better?"

"My stomach is less queasy, and I'm not dizzy anymore, so that's a plus." *Dizzy that you're here, but not from my illness.* "Why don't you get some of your work done while I rest some more?"

"Okay." He clears and washes our dishes.

This is a first for me. The last person who took care of me while I was sick was Nicholas. Never someone I was interested in. I reply to Nicholas and send a thank you to Kate.

Kate: Glad you're on the mend. You failed to mention that the pilot is HOT!

Me: Did I? I'm going to take a nap.

Kate: Rest up. Love you.

Me: Love you too.

Standing before my bureau, I take in my current state. I look like death warmed over. My skin is pale, my eyes tired, and my hair is a knotted mess. Sighing, I pull out the hair tie.

CASSIUS

Even sick, she's beautiful. When I arrived with Kate last night, I was concerned. She looked fragile curled up on the floor. Noelle is a lot of things, but fragile isn't one of them. After Kate cleaned her up, I felt a little less concerned, but still not enough to sleep on the couch. I'd been smart enough to know bathing her was inappropriate. Sidling up to her while she slept seemed okay under the guise of making sure she didn't fall again. My arm curls around her tiny waist perfectly. Her curves securely against me feels amazing.

I grab my bag and move toward her room. As I approach the door, she's tugging a brush through her hair.

"Did you need something?" She turns in my direction.

"Yes, but it can wait until I'm done." I extend my hand to her, asking for the brush. A glimmer of pain shoots through her eyes as she hands it to me. She sits on her mattress near the foot of her bed facing the headboard. I split her locks into three sections, pushing one over each shoulder. Goose bumps rise on her skin as I draw my hand away. Starting at the bottom of the section to her right, I pull the brush through her hair. A soft sigh escapes her lips. Methodically, I move through the sections until her gorgeous hair is a sheet down her back.

When she turns, a single tear falls down her cheek. I lean forward, kissing it away. She inhales sharply.

"I didn't mean to upset you. My sister loved having her hair brushed, especially when she didn't feel well. She roped the three of us into it as often as she could."

"My m… Only my mom ever did that for me. Thank you."

"You're welcome." Wrapping my arms around her, I pull her against me. Her hands wind around my back. I feel her inhale and exhale a few times to calm her nerves.

"What do you need?" she asks against my chest.

I need to sort out my desire to be here with her against my other responsibilities. She doesn't need to hear that right now. She asked some tough questions the other night, making me question my priorities. Flying is my passion. I need to find a way to channel that into a paycheck—well, expand what I already have into a bigger paycheck. "Your Wi-Fi password."

"It's JosieB1012." She spells it out, indicating the characters that should be uppercase.

"Will typing bother you if I sit in here?"

"No, not at all." She stands, rounding the bed and sliding under the duvet. The furniture looks old, like it was her childhood bedroom set. Her décor includes bold colors. The walls are teal with a lighter-colored stripe on one wall. The bedding has a white background but large flowers in teal, gray, black, and purple emblazoned on it. I don't know her well enough yet to determine if it suits her. Her independence would seem to support the bold colors. Her fierce protection of her brother would as well. I push that thought away for now as I climb onto her bed and set my mouse and phone on the night table.

"Rest, gorgeous," I murmur before kissing her forehead and tackling my work inbox. Two hours later, I clear my inbox and message Sam, requesting a call or meeting next week. I need to talk to him about my plan. He's levelheaded and will see holes even I may not see. I handle similar tasks daily for my clients, but this is about me and my future. Another pair of eyes I trust will add a level of comfort before I start searching for the right opportunity for me. He'll set me straight if I'm missing any key elements. Closing the lid, I set my laptop beside my phone and tug Noelle against me. She mumbles something, but I can only make out my name as she snuggles deeper in my embrace.

My plans for our date tomorrow will not work anymore. I planned a hike in the Santa Monica Mountains and then out to dinner. We'll figure out something else. For now, I inhale the soft scent of lavender and relish how her luscious curves mold into my arms. Never once have I felt the pull toward a woman that I feel for her. I was going crazy with worry when she didn't respond. Some might say I overreacted, but arguably she only has Kate here. It just didn't sit right that she missed not only our evening video call but our morning texts too. Listening to my gut paid off. She wasn't okay.

As I lie here holding her without falling asleep, I take my time memorizing her: the single freckle on the back of her right earlobe, the slope of her neck, the dip of her waist, the flare of her hips, and her perfectly polished toenails, which are now peeking out of the duvet. I know the moment she wakes up from her nap. Her breathing hitches, and she tenses slightly before snuggling deeper into my arms.

"How are you feeling?" I press my lips to the back of her exposed shoulder.

"Better. I'm not cold anymore; although I think that is because of you." She turns slightly to look at me.

"Do you want me to move?"

"No, not at all. Being in your arms is—"

I lean forward, interrupting her with a kiss on her jaw. Turning in my arms, she places her hand on my cheek before deepening our kiss. It's as hot as I remember. As much as I want to feast on her mouth and the rest of her gorgeous body, I rein myself in. Less than a day ago, she was violently ill.

"You should probably focus on gaining some strength before we continue this."

She draws her lower lip between her teeth. Holy hell! "*Tesoro*, stop."

She releases her lip, and her hazel eyes widen. "What does that mean?"

"It means 'treasure' in Italian." I may have rendered her speechless. "I'm not going anywhere. There is no rush. Kissing you could become an addiction for me." I lean forward, lightly brushing my lips across hers. "Let's see what you have to cook or what local places deliver that you think you can handle."

"You can cook too?"

"I'm not bad."

"You might need to prove that, babe." She throws down a challenge. I'm man enough to face a cooking challenge. I'll tackle any challenge she hurls my way.

"You're on! Let's wait until you can eat anything though, okay?"

"Deal."

After standing, I walk around the bed, offering her my hand. Her delicate fingers slide into my palm. She doesn't wobble, yet I slide my hand around her waist anyway. Her breasts press against me, her chest rising and falling in anticipation of what I might do next. As much as I want to kiss her repeatedly, I press my lips to her forehead and take a step back. Threading my fingers into hers, I lead her back to the dining table and pull out her chair.

"What do you think you can handle? You have pasta, chicken, eggs, and some veggies," I list after perusing her cabinets and fridge.

"Something boring. If you want to order food, I'll have more toast and the ginger ale."

"I'll make you some toast and make an omelet for myself. I love breakfast for dinner." I pull some ingredients for my meal out, setting them on the granite countertop.

"So do I. I'm a breakfast fanatic; all day everyday would work for me."

I hear faint music coming from her bedroom. Noelle rises from the chair but sits right back down. Taking two large steps, I drop to my knees by her side.

"Are you okay?" I take her hands in mine.

"Just dizzy."

"I'll get you some juice, and then I'll find your phone."

"Thanks. It's either on the dresser or in my tote."

I set the juice next to her before going in search of her phone. I come up empty on the dresser, so I carry her tote out to her.

"You could have gotten it out."

I shrug and return to cooking. I purposefully make a larger omelet than I would eat on my own. Noelle eats half of it. I'm glad she's able to eat and keep it down. After cleaning the kitchen, we snuggle up on the chaise to watch a movie. She opts for *A Few Good Men*. I've spent numerous Friday evenings at home watching movies, but this one rates at the top of the list. Despite the brevity of our relationship, I feel oddly comfortable here right now, like she and I have been together for years.

As the credits roll, I ask her, "Are you going to be okay by yourself?"

"You're leaving?"

"I only stayed last night because I was worried. So much so that I slept with you instead of on the couch."

"Please stay. I know how off the wall this will sound, but I feel like I've known you much longer than I have."

I nod and pull her even closer.

NOELLE

It took some convincing, but Cash stayed with me last night. I appreciate the chivalry, both for staying with me when I was sick but also knowing he should leave. Waking up with Cash is... so many things. He looks peaceful when he sleeps. The only other time he looks peaceful is when he's looking at... me. Aside from his strong jaw with a cleft chin, his dimples ratchet up his features one-thousand-fold. Kate's right. He's hot! He clearly works out, but I think his workouts aren't the typical cardio and weights. It's something else like rock climbing or spinning. His body is strong and hard with muscle.

Honestly, I'm surprised he isn't awake. On the East Coast, it's near eight. Cash is sound asleep on his belly. The ridges of his back are mesmerizing. Easing out from under his corded right arm, I pad to the bathroom. I'm not dizzy anymore, which is a plus, but I'm starving. Eating half of Cash's omelet last night wasn't my intention. It was delicious; plus he didn't stop me from stealing food from his plate.

As I pass my bed toward the kitchen, I steal another glimpse of him. He's utter perfection. While I understand what he meant about zip codes, it was a chest-tightening gesture to fly here early simply to check on me. After I start the coffee, my phone chimes.

Kate: How are you feeling? You seriously failed to mention how hot he is.

Me: Making progress. I feel a bit weak. I'm going to make some breakfast. Did I?

Kate: Yes, you did. Eat up. TTYL.

Me: Bye.

After filling my cup, I start to make a second one when strong arms wrap around me. Too bad he put a shirt on.

"Morning, gorgeous. How are you feeling?" He presses his mouth to the nape of my neck.

I fail to hold in a soft moan. "Right at this moment, pretty amazing." I turn in his arms. Fresh out of bed Cash with mussed hair and stubble is… holy hockey! I can't resist. I slide one hand up to his jaw. He palms the back of my head, angling it before sealing his mouth over mine. Arguably, this is the third time we've kissed, and it just keeps getting hotter. I open for him, and he explores my mouth with his tongue. I arch forward to feel him pressed against me. Fire truck, that feels good! Pulling his lower lip between my teeth elicits a low growl. I slide my fingers beneath the hem of his shirt. Hard ridges and curves meet my fingertips.

My skin tingles as he moves the strap from my tank top down my arm, kissing the exposed skin with his hot mouth. I release a breath slowly. His hands slide down my sides, coasting over my curves. His large palms grip my ass just before he lifts me effortlessly into his arms.

In a few long strides, Cash lowers me onto the chaise, climbing to hover over me. Gripping the hem of his shirt, I tug it off.

"Noelle," he murmurs while I explore his chest with my mouth. Each time my mouth touches his skin, he releases a shallow breath.

"*Tesoro*," he whispers.

When I look up at him, he seizes the moment to retake my mouth with a searing kiss. I melt into him. Moving slowly, Cash kisses a trail down my neck, passed the bend of my elbow, to the center of my hand. Hitting different spots on his return path, Cash pauses just enough for me to notice before blazing a trail down the valley between my breasts. He mumbles something unintelligible against my skin before lowering himself on top of me slowly. Dragging my fingernails up from his waist, I slide them around his shoulders to cup his face. The look in his eyes is unmistakable. I feel it too.

"Please tell me," he whispers near my ear.

"You're tempting, very tempting." A large part of me wants to throw my morals out the window to find out how he feels filling me. I'm struggling because I see potential for us despite our home addresses.

"As are you," he replies, rolling us onto our sides. He brushes a few stray strands away from my face, sending warmth over me.

"What did you say before?"

Inhaling sharply, I reply, "I said—"

"You don't have to tell me."

"Yes, I do. Honesty is the only way to go. I said this is intense. Kissing you is intense."

Blunt honesty is rare. I appreciate it. Most people sugarcoat things. In my opinion, it isn't worth it. Say what you mean; own it and the consequences.

"Yes, it is. More intense than I've ever felt before."

"Me too."

He presses his lips to my forehead, the tip of my nose, and lightly to my lips. "Let's go make some fresh coffee." I kiss him quickly one more time before heading to the kitchen.

Coffee in hand, we snuggle up on the terrace. I could get used to having a shirtless, sexy man in my home in the morning.

"How are you feeling?" he asks.

"Pretty good. I'm not dizzy or feverish, just a little hungry." This is our first time enjoying a quiet morning together. I feel like we have been doing it for years. "Does this feel surreal to you too?"

"Like you and I have been sharing our morning coffee for years? Yes, it does."

"What do we do about it?" I ask, unsure if there's an answer that will make sense.

"Here are a few things I know: I like you a lot. I want to learn everything about you, and I want to spend time with you. The rest we can figure out together. Does that work for you?"

"Definitely."

"We should get started on that breakfast for you." Cash rises from the couch.

I follow him into the kitchen. The muscles of his back are taut as he walks. He sets our cups near the coffee maker and starts making more.

"Does blueberry pancakes and bacon work?" I ask, surveying the fridge. "Cash?" When I turn around, he's staring at the ceiling. "Did you hear me?"

"Yes, but first I watched you rummage in your fridge. The pattern on your ceiling is perfect for your décor choices."

I feel my cheeks redden. "I'm sorry," I murmur, feeling a tad self-conscious.

"Don't be. Pancakes and bacon are fine. Can I help?"

"Sure."

Cash finishes brewing fresh coffee. "How do you take this?"

I reply and finish gathering all the ingredients we need. After setting a cup near me, he starts adding items into the bowl. We add to the batter and fry the bacon. We move around each other seamlessly. I love having him here. The weekdays are going to be less fun than they were before I met Cassius Morgan.

After devouring our delicious breakfast, we decide to walk to the beach. It's not very sunny today, but I need to get out of my house. Walking hand in hand with Cash on the beach sounds perfect. Just like our first date, we walk fingers intertwined to the shore.

Due to the weather, very few people are at the beach today. As we stroll along in the shallows, Cash explains his day job in more detail. It's fascinating. It makes sense that he was able to work here yesterday. He spends much of his time reviewing documentation, reports, or on the phone. We also talk more in depth about M and the center.

"He needs individualized support. I may not love where I work, but I'm professionally qualified to help him. Sheila knows that. I can't figure out why she won't allow me to help him."

"What do you mean 'qualified'?" Cash shifts his arm around my waist, pulling me against him.

"My teaching degree is in education. My master's degree is in special education with a focus on developmental disorders."

"That's amazing. Is it worth standing up to Sheila?"

"M is worth it; every student is. Losing my job isn't. He won't get any of the support he needs if I don't work there anymore. Plus, she is angling for a way to fire me. I have applications pending in a few other places. The interview on Wednesday went well. Although, that job would require me to take a pay cut and work more hours."

"I understand. How are you? Do we need to go back?"

"I'm fine. I will need some more food though. What did you plan for our date today?" The cool water swirls around our feet as he lowers his arms around me, resting his hands on the curve of my ass.

"It doesn't matter. This is perfect." Leaning forward, he wets my lips with his tongue before dipping it into my mouth. I moan softly while pressing my body against his. One of his hands slides up my side to my jaw. He breaks our kiss, reminding me where we are.

"Yes, it is. Not going to share?"

"Nope, a guy needs to protect his dating secrets. We'll go on that date someday, don't worry."

"Fine, I give." I kiss him softly.

Cash curls his arm around my waist before leading me back toward my condo. We order takeout, pour some white wine, and spend the evening talking.

CASSIUS

We may not have spent our time on the date I planned, but I don't mind. I was scared seeing her curled up on the cold floor on Thursday night. The level I worry for her this soon should frighten me. Perhaps the fact that I'm ready to find my one and only lessens that fear.

Up until a few years ago, I spent most of my evenings out, whether with clients or looking for a woman with wife potential. I don't mean looking as in I stood in a bar surveying the options. The women I dated ranged from boarding-school-educated debutantes, to my brother Sam's assistant—that didn't go well—and a maid at an upscale hotel. I didn't narrow the field like Margaux would have. She would have stopped with educated debutantes.

As I sit here once again in the cockpit to return to New York with Mrs. Waller, my chest tightens. It tightens with worry that she's alone, the realization that my huge penthouse will seem even more lonely, and I don't want to wake up alone. Those thoughts refocus me on my plan to change my profession.

After completing the postflight checklist, I text Noelle to let her know I'll call her later. As I move to my car, my phone chimes with a few new messages. One from Sam and one from Mina.

Sam: I can talk tomorrow or stop by with dinner on Wednesday.

Me: Let's do dinner.

Sam: I'll be there by six.

I focus on Mina's next.

Mina: How are you?

Me: Just landed. I'm doing well. You?

Mina: I'm great. I have a few appointments in New York in the next few months, including a wedding. I'm staying with Sam, but I want to make sure we get together.

Me: You let me know when and where. I'll be there. Love you bunches.

Mina: Love you bunches more.

After chatting with Noelle briefly, I fall into my bed. The workday will arrive before I know it. Thankfully, my boss is flexible when it comes to my second job. He doesn't know the main reason I left on Thursday evening was Noelle.

My work inbox is manageable when I arrive on Monday. My assistant, Myles, informs me there is a staff meeting at ten. Right now, I wish I picked today as a work-from-home day. I sift through the email and sort as necessary. I narrow them down to three that require attention today. After the staff meeting, which was simply so the higher-ups could have some face time, I handle two of my tasks rather quickly. I buzz Myles and ask him to set an appointment with Stacy for later this week.

Stacy might be able to provide me with some leads for my future. I'm also sure he will keep my confidence when I share my plans.

After work two days later, I meet up with Evan and let him beat me up in the ring. Luckily, I keep my focus at least enough to avoid another stinging uppercut. I'm sure Noelle was serious about her no-more-injuries-on-her-account edict. She is on my mind consistently. I look forward to our daily texts and our nightly video calls.

When I arrive home from the gym, I shower quickly, and dress comfortably. I set out two place settings for dinner just as the elevator announces Sam's arrival.

"Thanks for coming." I free the food from his hands.

"You clearly have something big to discuss." After shucking his jacket and tie, Sam grabs the plates and follows me to the terrace. "I'm still bummed this wasn't available when I was looking for a home. I'm envious of your terrace."

"You're welcome here anytime. You know that."

"I do. What's up?"

I take a long sip of my wine before sharing with Sam. "First, as of right now, only one other person knows I'm considering this, so please keep it to yourself until I figure all this out. I want to leave investing and fly full-time."

"Wow! Okay, what brought this on?"

"I was talking with someone, and she asked me why I only fly on weekends if I prefer it over investing. She's the only person I have ever admitted that to until now."

"Who is she?"

"Her name is Noelle. I met her through an airline client. She makes me see life differently. Her outlook is refreshing. Have you ever felt like you've known someone forever even during your first or second meeting?"

"Yes, I felt that once."

Genuine surprise takes residence on my face. I wonder who the mystery woman is. Sam is tight-lipped about his relationship history. Like me, he has been single for several years but for distinct reasons that don't include not being able to find the one.

"I've been around her three times, and I feel like she's been my best friend my entire life. Plus, she's crazy smart, kind, and sexy as sin."

"I'm not going to pry into your reasoning, but does she know who you are?"

"She knows enough." Noelle knows about my profession, my dysfunctional parents, and the fact that I earn a lot of money. Does she realize how well known my family is? Probably not.

"What are you thinking?"

I hand him the outline and plan I created after I talked with Noelle. I take a few bites of my meal and a heavy sip of my wine. Feeling surprisingly lighter, I glance skyward, wondering if Noelle is home yet.

Between bites, Sam flips through the plan, nodding and making approving gestures as he reads. I polish off my wine and dinner. Leaving Sam on the terrace, I place my plate in the sink and refill my glass.

"This is insanely detailed. You've covered the timeline and a buyout. What do you want? Do you want to simply fly more or jump into ownership which would allow you to fly if you chose to?"

"I'm leaning towards ownership and flying a little more than I do now."

"This plan is solid. Who are you going to add to the circle to help you find the right investment?"

"Stacy Sanders, he was one of my college roommates and is a partner at my firm."

"Makes sense. What about your trust?"

"Aside from a knowledgeable set of eyes, that's the part I need you for. Does any of this go against the requirements of our family trust?" Overall, I'm not overly concerned if I can't draw on my trust anymore. However, I would prefer not to run afoul of our parents' rules. If I don't have to divulge that I changed professions, then they won't have any ammunition to decrease my inheritance.

"I don't believe so. I'll verify, but I believe the only requirement is that you're gainfully employed or seeking employment if you're laid off or fired. No restrictions as to what type of employment that I recall. I think there is a provision that states a gap of gainful employment longer than six months triggers stop payment measures." I nod and glance at my phone when it chimes. My heart starts to beat faster, but I know it's still too early for Noelle to be home.

"Thanks, Sam. I appreciate your keen eye. Anything going on with you?"

"Nothing. Work is great! For now, that's enough. When the time is right, I'll find someone." He left off the *again* this time. We never mention her name unless Sam says it first. Meghan was his first love. Honestly, I'm not sure he has fully recovered, despite the amount of time that has passed.

I know better than to press about Meghan. "Glad to hear it."

"I should get going. I have an early call in the morning."

He doesn't, but Sam prefers solitude like I do. Like I used to. Now I want to share all my time with her. After bringing the remaining dishes to the sink, I thank my brother again and he heads home. My attempts to set him up in the past with potential mates have been met with cancellation or gruff behavior. It isn't purposeful, but I have refrained after the last set of complaints from my friends who have been interested in Sam.

After a few hours video chatting with Noelle, I fall into my bed, hoping to rush through tomorrow so I can see her again, even if it's through my phone.

NOELLE

Since I was ill last Friday, I consider forgoing my previously scheduled day off tomorrow. Not only am I keeping it, but I'm contemplating hopping on a plane to New York. Only one person will talk me off the ledge if I'm truly out of my mind.

After catching Kate up to the thoughts in my head, I ask her straight out. "Am I out of my mind?"

"As your bestie, generally, I would say it's too soon. However, he flew across the country to check on you for your second date. As many times as you have spoken to him, he's listening. Not only did he recall where you live, but he remembered me, Kiely's Tavern, and Keyton. He's clearly interested. Plus, a trip to New York City in the late spring sounds amazing."

"You always know what to say. I'm going to text him to see if he's flying this weekend. You're the best, Kate."

"I know. Don't do anything I wouldn't do."

"What does that eliminate?"

"A few things if he has a red room. Otherwise, not much."

"Oh my God! Love you." Before losing my gumption, I text Cash.

Me: Morning. Are you flying this weekend?

I can't pull it back now. Deep down, I don't want to. He strikes me as someone who knows what he wants out of life. The time I've spent with him so far has been amazing. It's a tad impulsive to fly to him to visit. However, so was our first kiss. The memory of that moment flashes through my mind. I was so excited that he could get me to the wedding. Each kiss after that one has been increasingly hotter. I can't imagine how more will feel. *Am I ready for that? Is visiting sending the wrong message? No, get a grip.*

I finish getting ready for my workday and hustle out the door. Not only do I have to work with my students today, but I need to fill in two spots for career day next Friday. Maybe Cash is available? That's nuts. He has a full-time job in the city.

When I arrive at the center, M's mother is struggling with one of his episodes near the cubbies. He's thrashing, refusing to take off his jacket, sort his lunch box, and turn in his work.

"May I?"

"You think you're better than me, don't you?"

I channel my inner calm. She's frustrated and upset. Clearly last night and this morning have been rough. "Not at all, Mrs. Sanfilippo. I just have a little more training."

She throws her hands up in the air as I bend down to M's level.

Whispering, I say, "Mason, can you take a deep breath with me?"

He nods and follows my lead.

"Again." Inhale. Exhale. "Again." Inhale. Exhale. "Can you show me what upset you?"

He takes my hand and leads me to the front door of the center, pointing at the parking lot. "The car," he mumbles.

"What happened in the car?"

"Someone almost hit us here this morning. Mommy mad. I upset, and Mommy yelling." Some of his words are hard to understand, but that's the basic gist.

"Do you need more time to calm yourself?"

Mason shakes his head.

"Please go follow our morning routine."

He nods, squeezes my finger, and slowly walks back into the classroom. Mason attempts to empty his bag. Flustered by the zipper, he throws the bag to the floor. His mother yells at him. In response, he curls into a ball and starts rocking back and forth.

"See, look what you've done. You have no clue what you're doing." His mother points her finger at me.

Sheila finally intervenes. "Mrs. Sanfilippo, Noelle's response was perfect under the circumstances. Removing your son from the structure he has here will be detrimental to his development."

Holy hockey! She just defended me. The world must be turning inside out.

"I want a plan for my son showing how this center can help by the end of the day. If I'm not confident you can accomplish the goals, I'll be removing him from your care. Have a good day." Mrs. Sanfilippo storms off.

I take a seat on the floor near Mason until he settles down. When he's ready, we follow the morning routine, and I set him up with his first task of the day.

I settle into the office about thirty minutes later, put my lunch away and start sorting my email when Sheila appears at my door.

"Please complete the plan Mrs. Sanfilippo wants for her son by three today. Your job depends on her acceptance of the plan."

I nod curtly, simply to keep my harsh words to myself. Mrs. Sanfilippo is the only parent who has issues with how I handle the students here. Ugh! A faint chirp sounds in my purse. Even though I should start on this plan right away, I check my messages first.

Cash: No, I'm not flying this weekend.

Me: Would you like some company?

As I typed my response, my heart rate ticked up considerably. I toss my phone back into my purse before pulling up the plan I started to create for him a few weeks ago. Thankfully, I saved it. It'll seem like I'm working on it all day today though. After a quick peek out at Mason, I get back to work on his plan. I'll put in the effort for him. In the end, if I lose my job, I'll be able to say I did everything I could for him and for me.

Cash: At the risk of sounding eager, hell yes!

Me: Perfect! I'll let you know my travel details when I have them.

Near lunch, I take a short break to book a flight to New York, gobble up my food, and push away thoughts of Cash. I need to focus on the plan. Focusing on Cash is a distraction, even if it's a wanted one. I spend the rest of my day tweaking a developmentally accurate plan for my student. Just after three, Sheila reviews it, giving her stamp of approval. Unfortunately, that's only half the battle. It doesn't matter if Sheila approves. My job lies in the hands of M's mother. Sheila suggests that I leave before Mrs. Sanfilippo returns to pick up her son. Without a second thought, I rush home to pack, then talk to Cash.

After chatting for a little while, I go to bed to hurry up time. Bright and early, I head to the airport. After settling into my seat, I promptly go back to sleep. The faster this flight passes, the sooner I'll be in his arms. After deplaning, I text Cash.

Me: What's your address? I can meet you there instead of you picking me up.

Cash: Turn around, tesoro.

Butterflies take flight in my stomach. I thought I had more time to prepare for this moment. Slowly I turn to my right. Cash is leaning up against one of the pillars holding a huge bouquet of yellow roses with red tips. I've never seen roses that color before. I resist the urge to run to him just barely. My feet carry me as fast as possible without seeming like it's been ages rather than a week.

He wraps his arms around me. "I missed you," he whispers in my ear.

"I missed you too. Thank you. These are amazing." I take the flowers from him before kissing his lips lightly. He threads his fingers into mine, pulling my rolling carry-on behind us.

In the back of my mind, I know Cash lives in the same atmosphere as Nicholas. Like my brother, he doesn't flaunt it. As we move through the parking lot, Cash opens the passenger door of a luxurious BMW. I can't even fathom how much it cost.

"I'm so happy you're here." He starts the car and drives to his home.

CASSIUS

Every time I know I'm going to see her, my nervous energy ratchets up. Yet the instant she touches me, my nerves fade away. Driving toward my home, I intertwine my fingers with hers before kissing the top of her hand.

"Have you been to New York City before?"

"I've been here once, maybe twice for one of Nicholas's premieres. Usually I attend the premiere, his afterparty, and then go straight home."

"Is there one thing you want to do while you're here?" I can see the wheels turning in her gorgeous mind. I decide to wait her out rather than press her for an answer. I pull into the parking structure of my building and into my designated parking spot. My SUV occupies the next spot. Although I prefer to walk, more practical than this car, especially in the city for daily driving. After I park, she still hasn't answered my question. In fact she has been silent for the last five minutes. "Noelle, why are you spooked?"

"You can see that?" She doesn't look at me.

"I can feel it." I lift her eyes to mine with my other hand. Heat runs up my arm when I touch her. This is a true test of my restraint. I want to kiss her senseless right now. She smells amazing even after flying across the country. Her breathing is a tad shallow for my liking. "I can get you a room if you don't want to stay with me."

"It's not you. Well, it's you, but not in the way you think. Hopping on a plane for a weekend trip to spend time with a man is so far outside the norm for me. I think it just caught up with me."

"How can I help?" I slowly drop my hand. Her gaze follows.

"I just need a minute." She inhales and exhales while slowly lifting her eyes back to mine.

"Take all the time you need. I meant what I said; I'm not going anywhere, *tesoro*."

"Cassius." She leans forward, her forehead against mine. The moment her lips touch mine, I want to let go, to kiss her with everything I have—just not here in a parking garage. Either she senses my hesitation or she realizes where we are. "I'm ready when you are."

I take that to mean, she's ready to go inside. Deep down, I think she may mean something more.

"Stay there. I'll get your door." I hurry around the car and pull out her luggage and flowers before opening her door. She takes my offered hand and stands. Her mouth is a breath away from mine. I kiss her softly before closing her door behind her.

After a short elevator ride, we exit in the lobby. Arthur greets us.

"Good evening, Mr. Morgan."

"Good evening, Arthur. Did Ella have her daughter yet?"

"Still waiting. This one is stubborn."

"Your newest granddaughter will be here soon. This is Noelle Barnett."

She extends her hand.

"It's a pleasure to meet you," Arthur says before kissing her hand.

"You as well. Such a gentleman. You might learn something from him." She winks at me.

I smile. Arthur laughs softly.

"If you need something and I'm not available, Arthur is your best bet. I'll give you his information when we get upstairs," I inform her.

"Here are the items you requested, Mr. Morgan. Have a wonderful evening."

"Thank you, Arthur. You as well." I slide the envelope into my pocket and guide Noelle to the elevator.

As the door closes us in, she mumbles something under her breath.

"What?"

"Nothing," she replies immediately. The tone and sharpness of her reply indicates she didn't want me to hear her. Stepping into the alcove, I open the door to my home. If she weren't Ellis Barnett's sister, I would be worried about bringing her here. In fact, I would have rented a hotel room for the weekend instead of sharing my personal space with her.

"What do you say to authentic New York style pizza for dinner?"

"Sounds perfect."

"Anything you don't want on your pizza?"

"I'm game for anything except anchovies. Yuck!"

I laugh. "One pizza with extra anchovies coming right up."

"Bathroom?"

"The bathroom is the first door on the left."

"Thanks."

I order our dinner and pour two glasses of white wine. When I hear the water turn off, I hustle down the hall to grab a hoodie for her just in case she didn't pack one. When I return, she's gazing out the French doors.

"Cash, this is amazing!" she gushes when I stand next to her.

"It's why I bought this place. The outdoor space is spectacular. Come on." I reach for her hand. Every time, I marvel at the feel of it twined with mine. How perfect it is, her hand in mine. I hand her a glass before leading her outside.

Settling into the corner of one couch, I open my arms for her. She curls into me like at her condo. I kiss the top of her head as she wraps her arms around me.

"I'm so glad you're here. I missed you more than I should admit." I drag my thumb up and down her upper arm.

"I'm glad I came too. I apologize for before. Not only is coming here a big deal but work yesterday was awful. The fate of my job is in someone else's hands."

"Please tell me, sweetheart."

"I will, just not now. I want to enjoy being here with you. I don't want to worry about my job, M, or anything else that's going on outside of your four walls, at least tonight. Is that okay?"

"Of course." I pull her even closer to me. All too soon, our food arrives. Too soon for me to let her go, but not for my hunger pangs. She joins me in the kitchen.

"Where are the plates?"

"To the left of the stove."

"Do you need silverware?" To most, this is an innocuous question.

"You can't eat New York style pizza properly with silverware. Please tell me you don't use silverware."

"Is that a deal breaker?"

"Maybe," I reply with a grin on my face.

"Crisis averted. It's sacrilege to use silverware for pizza. What is a deal breaker?"

Plates, napkins, and a bottle of wine in hand, she follows me back onto the terrace. I place one slice on each plate and refill our glasses before taking a seat next to her with one leg bent on the cushion facing her.

"Oh my God! This is so much better than pizza in California," Noelle states before taking another huge bite.

After inhaling an entire slice, I pull another out of the box.

"Most of my deal breakers wouldn't apply to you."

"Why?" she asks as she grabs a second slice of pepperoni for herself. I appreciate that she actually eats food—hers and mine.

"I have a checklist, which sounds callous, but as you already know, my parents' marriage was a business deal. I don't want that. I want the fairy tale. Nothing short of blissful happiness for myself and my wife. I realize how that sounds coming from a man whose parents' marriage is basically loveless. The vows didn't mean what they should, at least to my parents. As far as I can tell in the time I've known you, none of my deal breakers apply to you. You believe in monogamy, you don't want my money, you love your career and children. It scares me and makes me hopeful at the same time."

"It might sound callous to someone who doesn't know the truth about your parents' marriage or who has never seen a truly love-filled marriage. I want the fairy tale too. Even though I only had them for a painfully limited time, my parents were happy. It's what I want for myself." After a gulp of her wine, she continues barely above a whisper. "How well we fit scares me too."

Taking the glass from her hand, I set it on the table. Cupping her flawless face in my hands, I draw my thumb across her lips. Her gorgeous eyes flutter closed. She pulls in a breath before setting her hands flat on my chest. I can feel her through my shirt. Each time I kiss her, the anticipation of how it will feel is intense. So far, each kiss is incrementally better than the last. I press my lips to the tip of her nose, forcing her to open her eyes. Her eyes tell me everything I want to know.

She wants me as much as I want her, but like me, she's scared out of her mind it won't work.

Sealing my lips over hers, I kiss her like I wanted to when we were in the parking garage. She tastes like wine and hope. Hope for the possibility of happily ever after. The possibility of forever. As I withdraw, her tongue surges forward, exploring the depths of my mouth. I slide her thin cardi down her arms to her elbows. Her skin is soft under my fingertips. I kiss along the curve of her elegant neck and across her shoulder. Her fingers move quickly down the column of buttons on my shirt. Before pushing the shirt off, she draws her hands over my chest, sending sparks straight southward. After discarding my shirt, I pull her into my lap while guiding the cardi to the deck. The heat of her core against me teases my arousal. Her chest rises and falls in an increased rhythm. We pause for a slight moment before her mouth returns to mine.

After exploring her mouth again, I move over her chin, down her neck, to the sweet-smelling valley between her breasts. I draw my tongue back upward before gripping the hem of her tank top. Lifting it over her head reveals a black lace bra with split cups.

"Holy f… you're—" If I lean forward an inch, I could take her nipple into my mouth. She interrupts me by pressing her lips to mine. I tear my mouth away before moving down to her breasts. I nip, kiss, and mark the swells of her chest while rolling one of her nipples between my fingers.

"Cash."

I tease her nipple with my tongue. Latching on with my teeth, I gently pull forward, so it's fully exposed through the cup. I suck it to a taut peak as her head falls backward. Arching forward, she grinds against me. Her heated core rocking against my hardened cock feels spectacular. The fireworks are real and continue to increase in intensity.

I glide my hands around her back, unclasping her bra. Flattening my hands against her heated skin elicits a soft moan. As I draw my hands down her back, I feel her shiver.

"Your hands and mouth feel incredible on my skin," she whispers near the shell of my ear before nuzzling my neck.

"Your skin is so soft."

She slides the straps of her bra down her arms, allowing it to fall to the deck. It's as if time stops for a moment. This stunning woman is in my arms, and the rest of the world falls away. It's just us. There is no work drama, no family drama, just me and her. Exactly how it should be.

Breaking her gaze, I palm her breasts while kissing a path down between them. A heavy sigh slips from her lips. Shifting to the left, I lower her to the cushions. I return to my quest of marking her with my mouth, starting at the underside of her breast, over her rib cage, and down to her waist. I freeze watching her hand slide from view into her jeans.

Popping the button, I shimmy her jeans off her creamy, toned legs. The scrap of lace covering her matches the sexy bra on the floor. I see a flash of uncertainty in her eyes.

"I want to watch you make yourself come apart."

She nods before moving her hand deeper into her sexy panties. I draw my tongue around her nipple before biting it. Her fingers plunge in and out of her folds as she gets closer to her release. Pulling back, I roll her nipples between my fingers. Her breathing reduces to hard pants. Increasing the pressure, I pinch her harder. Her skin is flush, and her hips arch off the couch as she convulses under me, her hips rubbing against my arousal.

Watching her come apart is exquisite. I look forward to giving her the same pleasure in the future. I've never seen a woman take control like that. It's alluring and captivating.

NOELLE

With the pace of a snail, I regulate my breathing. I haven't come that hard... ever, and Cash didn't even touch me. He'll ruin me if his hands and mouth are any indication of how well he uses his hard, sculpted body.

"That was breathtaking, *tesoro*," Cash murmurs against my neck. His weight on top of me makes me want to forgo all notions of decency and decorum for waiting.

"The pressure was too much. I needed to let go."

"How long?" he asks, lifting his head to look into my eyes.

"Depends on what you're asking. If you mean with someone else, it's been years."

"How is that even possible?" Surprise crosses his eyes.

"It was my choice. I didn't set out to limit my sexual experiences, but it turned out that way."

Cash pulls me against him while turning us on the couch so we're on our sides facing each other. I tuck my left arm under my head, resting my right hand in the middle of his rippled chest. His left hand moves up and down my back from the curve of my ass to my shoulder blades, chilling my skin with each pass.

"When most people were experimenting in high school and college, I was grieving. It took me just over a year to accept that we were orphans. When I went to college, I started feeling abandoned again because I felt like Nicholas left me too. I know it isn't true, but it's how I felt at the time. I didn't go on a date until I was a junior in college." I'm surprised that I can lie here with him basically naked and talk about this.

"It makes sense. At the risk of sounding like a guy, the men you did go out with were fools for failing to treat you well. I'm glad they messed up."

"I am too." I slide my hand up to his cheek before brushing my lips lightly across his.

"Have you given any more thought to what you want to do tomorrow?" he asks.

"Not at all. I came to see you. I don't care what we do."

Cash nods before slowly getting up from the couch. After locating my tank top, I pull it on. While Cash gathers the clothes, I make a trip inside with the dishes. When I return, he's staring at the sky. I look up and note it's overcast; he couldn't possibly see any stars tonight. Then I recall the last time I found him staring upward. I grab his shirt and throw it on over my tank top, fastening some of the buttons. It hits high on my thighs.

"Better?" I draw his attention back to me.

"Somewhat. You look hot in my shirt and little else."

I feel my cheeks redden at his comment. I grab the pizza box and the glasses for another trip inside. I wash the dishes before setting them to dry.

"Where are the plastic wrap or bags?" I ask the empty kitchen. I start searching in the drawers but fail.

"What do you need, sweetheart?"

"Plastic wrap or plastic bags."

"I probably don't have either. Generally, there aren't leftovers when I eat pizza." I nod before wrapping the pizza in paper towel and setting it in the fridge. "Ready?"

I follow Cash to what I presume is the master bedroom.

The room is huge with at least two closets. The furniture is more comfortable than I expected. The large wooden bed boasts gray and navy linens. There's a small sitting area with a fireplace. French doors lead onto the terrace.

"The bathroom is through there. There is room in the closet on the left if you need to hang anything." I set my bag on the dressing bench and pull out a dress I brought with me. After hanging it in the closet, I grab my necessities and head into the bathroom. Feeling Cash against me clothed did not prepare me for seeing him naked.

"Holy hockey!"

Cash looks up as he's pulling on a pair of boxer briefs.

"I'm sorry. I'll come back." He's... sweet mercy. Carved abs, coveted V, thick, round....

"*Tesoro.*" As I turn to leave, he wraps his arms around me from behind. "I should be sorry. I should've closed the door. Very few people know where I live for a host of reasons. I have never had an overnight guest. Even Arthur was surprised when I added your name and requested a card for you."

"It's fine. I wasn't thinking."

He turns me in his arms, and I see concern written on his face.

"Truly, I'm fine."

He nods. I'm not entirely sure he believes me. I don't believe me. Heat rushes to my core at imagining how he'll feel buried inside me.

"I just need to plug in my phone. Does yours need to be charged?" Cash asks.

"Probably. It's on the bench next to my luggage. Thanks."

After kissing me softly, he steps aside. Closing the door, he leaves me alone in the bathroom. Pulling myself together, I strip off his shirt, my tank, and panties. I brush my teeth and hair after redressing. When I step back into his room, Cash is removing pillows from his bed.

"Which side do you want?" he asks.

"You choose. I don't really have a preference."

He chooses and slides into his bed. Replacing my items in my bag, I slide under the sheets with Cash. Even though this isn't the first time, it feels different. Perhaps because this is his home, not mine, or perhaps because of his admission that no other woman has slept here before. Maybe just maybe this could work out between us. It'll be hard considering our zip codes, but we want the same things out of life. Taking a risk with him could be everything I ever wanted. He wraps his arm around my waist, drawing me against him.

"Good night, *tesoro*," he murmurs with his lips against my shoulder blade.

"Good night, Cash." I burrow deeper into his arms and fall asleep.

Sleepiness falls away slowly for me, especially when I don't have an alarm. I imagine it's later here than I normally rise given the time difference. Rolling over, I glance at the clock. It's near nine in the morning and Cash isn't in bed anymore, but the pillow smells like him, peppery and fresh.

Grabbing his sweatshirt on the bench, I zip it up in search of coffee. I fumble through making a cup with his fancy coffee maker, but I still haven't seen Cash. I follow the noise down the hall to his office.

"Did I wake you?" he asks as I approach.

"No, not at all. I'll let you finish." I turn back toward the kitchen.

"Sweetheart, stop." I do as he asks. "You aren't intruding. I was just passing time. I don't have anything specific to do. I don't work at home, especially on weekends, and even more so when I have a gorgeous woman to spend time with. Come here, please. I didn't want to wake you. You looked peaceful and sexy asleep in my bed."

I round the desk, stopping in front of him. Placing his hands on my hips, he guides me into his lap. "My sweatshirt looks better on you too," he says before kissing me tenderly. "Are you ready to tell me about work? Maybe over breakfast?"

"Sounds good to me. I could use more coffee too."

"Is that your vice? Coffee."

"Caffeine, not necessarily coffee, but it's readily available."

After selecting what to eat, we move around the kitchen, making breakfast and talking about the issue with M and how his mother holds my job in her hands. Between bites of an amazing omelet that Cash made for me this time, not his I'm stealing from, I explain about career day.

"I can do it." He sets down his cup.

"I can't ask you to take time off to come talk to the students at my school."

"You didn't ask. I offered. Plus, it's a long weekend. I assume you don't have to work on Monday either."

"No, I don't. Wait, you're going to be in California for four days?"

"Would you like some company?"

As if I would say no. I want as much time as he's willing to give me. "Absolutely!" I lean across the table and kiss him hard. I'll only have to sleep alone for three nights this week. Having him to kiss good night and more for four days in a row. Fish sticks!

"Care to share what just went through your mind? Was it hot?"

"How do you do that?" I ask, staring straight into his chocolate eyes.

"I pay attention, and staring at you is rising quickly on my list of favorite things to do, second only to kissing you."

"I agree with your list. My thoughts may have been on the sexier side, but that's all I'm sharing."

"What if I were to tickle you? Would you share then?"

"Nope, not even then, but I don't recommend tickling me. Someone always gets hurt, just ask Nicholas. It was usually him."

He lifts his hands in mock surrender.

After finishing breakfast, we spend the afternoon traipsing through Central Park. I've never been here before. We walk hand in hand. It's gorgeous. Green expanses with people milling about. Some are walking, others running, biking, playing frisbee, or reading in a shady area. Cash does most of the talking, pointing out the landmarks like Belvedere Castle, the Gapstow Bridge, and the Conservatory Garden. Cash shows me the statue of Balto and Hans Christian Anderson. We walk through the zoo like my students would, oohing and aahing at the animals.

"I saved the best for last," Cash said, stepping into the penguin exhibit.

"How did you know?" I kiss him.

"I told you, *tesoro*. I pay attention."

I try to recall telling him penguins are my favorite but fail. Maybe he saw something when we looked at the zoo map. I watch the penguins swim in their habitat in Cash's arms until they kick us out.

"Thank you. I had a wonderful time with you today."

"You're welcome. I did too. Dinner in or dinner out?"

"Would you mind going out?"

"Not at all.

CASSIUS

Suppressing the thought that she goes home tomorrow, I focus on our date tonight. I call to secure a reservation. Hopefully, they can meet my request of privacy. If not, fine, but I prefer to have our first date in New York City as private as possible. Seeing other people and introducing her to whomever we may come across doesn't concern me from the standpoint that I'm not single anymore. She and I should probably talk about that. Not that I think she's seeing anyone else, and neither am I. Do we need to talk about it? I'm not sure. Avoiding press coverage as long as possible is my main goal.

My family is well-known among the New York elite. By association, so are my siblings and me. I'm in an awkward spot; I want to shout to anyone who'll listen that I found an amazing woman. On the other hand, I want to keep us in a private bubble as long as possible.

I left my bedroom about fifteen minutes ago. As I was leaving, I heard the shower turn off. I'm intrigued how long it takes her to get ready. At least this time, she only has one outfit to choose from, unlike our first date. I've seen her sick and pale, fresh out of bed in the morning, and even impatient and angry. She's beautiful always.

"Cash, could you come here?"

As I approach my bedroom, she's pulling on a pair of low heels. Her dress is a simple sheath dress in a deep eggplant color. Her hair is up, exposing her elegant neck. "You look gorgeous."

"Thank you. You look pretty dashing yourself. Could you zip this and put this necklace on for me?" She turns, offering me her back and a view of the exposed creamy skin from the curve of her low back up to the nape of her neck covered only by a red lace bra. My thoughts plummet into dangerous territory. I've seen her panties. Imagining what matches this bra is intoxicating. "Cash."

"Yes, *tesoro*." I step closer to her. I should simply grip the zipper and pull it up, but that isn't my style. Not with this flawless expanse of skin at my fingertips. I crouch and lean forward, pressing my mouth to the small of her back. I rise inch by inch, dragging the zipper upward. A soft moan escapes her lips, and her head falls forward. "I love finding the spots that make you inhale sharply," I murmur near the shell of her ear. She simply nods before lifting her hand with a necklace in it. Crossing my hands in front of her, I clasp the necklace, wrap my arms around her, and press my lips to the curve of her neck. "Ready to go?"

"Yes." A simple word, that in this case says so much more than she intended.

As we step off the elevator, Arthur greets us.

"Good evening, Mr. Morgan. Miss Barnett."

"Hi, Arthur. Are you a grandfather again?" Noelle asks.

Arthur smiles. It's endearing that she recalled our conversation, especially considering her feelings were a mess just before that. "Yes, thank you. Valentina was born late yesterday. She and Ella are doing great! Have a great evening."

After the short car ride and a brief walk hand in hand, we arrive at the Tavern on the Green.

"Good evening, Mr. Morgan. Miss Barnett. Your table is right this way." The host leads us to a corner booth in the horseshoe area of the bar room. "Your server will be over shortly."

"Why do I have the feeling you asked to be tucked away?"

"I did. Does it bother you?" Covering her hand with mine, I move my chair closer.

"No," she sighs. "Given who my brother is, I understand why you value your privacy. I do too. Generally, the press doesn't bother me anymore. There were a few inquiries after his engagement, but the regulars know I would never violate Nicholas's privacy for any amount of money. You're concerned that I'm putting myself back out in the spotlight again."

"At least here in the city, yes. The moment the public learns about you, the press and my parents, especially my mother, will seek you out. She doesn't have access to my home, but I don't want you to feel trapped there either. I don't want to share you with anyone just yet."

"Oh."

"I want it to be just us as long as possible. You know as well as I do, the press is awful. Maybe we'll get lucky and some aristobrat will get into trouble the same day our first photo makes a splash on Page Six. If you don't want me to limit our exposure, I won't do it again."

"I understand, and it makes complete sense. It's sweet actually."

I lift her hand to my lips and kiss it. There is no limit to what I would do for her. It scares the hell out of me and makes me happy at the same time. Our server joins us, listing the specials and takes our drink order.

After placing our order, we chat over drinks. Our server brings our appetizer. We opt to share the chopped salad. As we dig in, the host approaches our table, indicating that someone would like to stop by our table. I nod. Before I'm able to warn Noelle, he's standing by our table.

"Nice to see you again so soon. Evan, this is Noelle." I greet him with a bro hug.

"You're the one with the stinging uppercut," Noelle says. Evan extends his hand to her and she takes it.

"Guilty."

Noelle retakes her seat, replacing her napkin in her lap.

"I just wanted to say hello since you skipped out on your workout this morning. Enjoy your meal. It was a pleasure meeting you, Noelle."

"You as well, Evan," Noelle replies as he walks away. "College roommate and trainer, right?" I nod. "You didn't have to skip your workout for me."

"I know. I wanted to. I want as much time with you as I can have. Skipping one workout isn't a big deal. Are you afraid my carved abs will go away?"

Her laugh warms my soul. "No, not at all, but they are spectacular. You even have the coveted V." She winks.

I love how honest she is. To most men, it would be unsettling. To me, it's enchanting. Our entrees arrive, and we feast on sirloin and lobster risotto. We spend our meal talking about everything and nothing. It's easy and pleasant. I could listen to her talk for hours and never tire of hearing the sweet tones of her voice. Even the way she tucks a loose strand of hair behind her ear makes me twitch with desire. She's stunning, and it's effortless.

We opt to bring a crème brûlèe back to eat on my terrace. After sharing the decadent dessert, we curl up under the stars and promptly fall asleep. Near two, I carry her to my bed until morning. As much as I would like to avoid the sunrise, it will come regardless of my desire to keep her with me indefinitely. At least this time, it's only three sleeps before I can kiss her again.

After a difficult goodbye at the airport, I check to see if Evan has an opening today. After a quick stop home, and I'm in the ring with him burning off some calories and some angst from letting her leave. Letting her leave isn't true; she needed to go home, but damn if I didn't want to let her go. After a grueling boxing session, I chat with Evan during my cooldown.

"You left out that Noelle is drop-dead gorgeous." He takes a deep swig of his water.

"I didn't think it was a detail you needed to know. Would you have shared with me if the situation were reversed?"

"Hell no! I wouldn't have let me stop by your table last night either."

I laugh. "She's amazing, Ev. The only problem is her address, and it's way too soon to deal with that elephant-sized problem."

"You care about her," he says before pointedly draining his water bottle.

"I do."

"I'm happy for you, man. Just don't screw it up."

"I don't plan to."

I scurry to the locker room, grab my bag, and hustle home to be available when my woman calls. I love the sound of that. My woman. After a short call, I collapse into my huge bed, wishing I weren't alone.

NOELLE

After a wonderful weekend in New York with Cash, I'm exhausted but looking forward to seeing him again in a few days. Frankly, I don't like waking up alone. That is a monstrous problem given where we lay our heads at night.

I need to pin down all the details for Friday. I hustle into my office and send confirmation emails to the participants for career day. Thankfully, with Cash's offer to speak, I'm back up to six presenters with the barista I added just before I left for the weekend.

When I arrived this morning and Mason was already here, I felt relief. Unfortunately, the trend will continue until Mrs. Sanfilippo makes her decision about my plan and keeping Mason at the center. It's a unique type of torture that I wouldn't wish on anyone.

My head and my heart are still in the clouds. I care about Cash, and I hate that he's so far away. It's too soon to feel as deeply as I do and to bring up the huge geographical problem we have between us. Should I look for a job in New York? Talking to him about that might make the most sense, but it's so soon. *Isn't it?* All those quotes about love happening on its own timeline are absurdly on point right now. Am I in love with Cash? Not yet, but I'm well on my way. I can imagine myself waking up with him years into the future and little boys who look like him running around in a fenced backyard and at least one little girl who has her daddy wrapped around her tiny finger. Pulling myself out of my head, I focus on the responses I've already received from my confirmation emails. Thankfully, each one is positive. I might just be able to pull this off after all.

The rest of my workday passes without incident. I message Nicholas to catch up as I walk to my car.

Me: How are you? How is married life?

Surprisingly, he answers promptly.

Nicholas: I'm well. Married life is fantastic! How are you?

Me: Work is so-so. I've been looking for a new position for the last six months or so. I had an interview that went well. Hopefully, something will pan out.

Nicholas: Sorry about your job. Sheila again?

Me: Yup.

Nicholas: How is Kate?

Me: She's well. I met someone. I'm not ready to share too many details because it's new but...

Nicholas: I'm happy for you. If you need Blaine to check him out, let me know. Love you lots.

That is precisely why I don't want to share. We should probably consider telling Nicholas.

Me: I will. Love you lots more.

After starting some wash when I arrive home, I pull out my yoga mat and stretch on my patio. Midway through my workout, a pair of Keds appear near my face as I hold a downward dog pose. They could only belong to one person.

"Hi, Kate. Give me a minute." Finishing the position, I shift into the warrior one and inhale deeply a few times. "How was work?"

"Hi to you too! Work was fine. Why didn't you call me when you got home last night? I was worried." Kate has worry and anger written on her face, but I don't think it's for my well-being.

"If you were worried, why didn't you text me instead of stewing all day long? If Cash worries you, why would you let him stay here with me alone for our second date?" She attempts to answer but fails to find a suitable response. "What's really going on?"

"Have you checked him out? Have you googled him?" I know she means well, but she should worry about her own relationships or lack thereof as the case may be.

"No. I have no reason to google him. I trust him, and he won't lie to me. Also, he works for Nicholas, at least tangentially. I'm sure Nicholas required a background check."

"I googled him and found pictures of him with a different woman on his arm in every photo."

Cash was genuine when he told me about his past dates. I have no reason to question his responses.

"Did you happen to check the dates of those photos?" I know if she checks, it will bear out the truth.

"Why would I bother to do that?"

"If you bothered to do that, you would see the photos are old." I wait as Kate pulls out her phone and digs deeper into the images, shaking her head. "He was honest about that. Here's a new one of you walking in Central Park."

I take her phone and glance at the image. Cash and I are strolling over the Gapstow Bridge hand in hand. We look happy and normal. It felt that way too. Regardless of his tax bracket, Cash is a wonderful, smoking-hot guy with a stellar kissing ability.

Kate points out, "It's only a matter of time before they figure out Ellis Barnett's sister is dating one of New York's most eligible uber-rich bachelors."

"I'm acutely aware of what it means to date Cassius Morgan." Despite the distance between us, I want more. So much more. "We talked about it at dinner on Saturday. My brother is a well-known celebrity. For the most part, the press leaves me alone because they have tried and failed to get information about Nicholas from me. The same will hold true for my relationship with Cash."

"You slept with him, didn't you?" she accuses.

"Why would you even ask me that? You've known me for seven years. When is the last time I slept with anyone? What is the real problem, Kate?"

She takes a deep breath and exhales harshly. "You're going to leave me. Even in the brief time you've been dating him, you're different."

"Kate." She's right. Cash makes me happy.

"You glow when you say his name. You care about him already. I don't want to be here alone. We have a pact. Neither of us can fall in love, and you're going to break it." Her tone shifted. She's happy for me, but sad for herself at the same time.

"Kate, I love you like a sister. It was an impossible pact from the moment we curled our pinkies together. One of us was going to break it wide open. I care about Cash very much. So much so that I'm scared. I've never been scared before in a relationship because I haven't made it this far."

"He's right there with you. No man gets on a plane to check on a woman after just one date unless he's in deep. He cares about you too. I may not be able to find the guy for me, but I can see love. Cassius Morgan is well on the path to falling for you." Kate throws her arms around my neck. "I'm sorry I was a bitch. How was your trip?" After asking, she walks into the kitchen, whips open the fridge and starts pulling out a massive amount of ingredients. Kate cooks when she's unsettled. Far be it for me to stop her, if she needs to cook, I'll eat. While Kate busies herself making dinner. I clean up my mat and check my messages.

Cash: Hi gorgeous. I'll call you when I get home from the gym.

I smile. "Did you call Keyton?" I ask her as I wash the cooking dishes she has already dirtied. She turns from the stove and glares at me. "Why not? He looks like a surfer with pale blue eyes. He's your type, hands down. He's persistent and genuinely likes you."

"What if he falls flat too? What if the problem is me?" Kate has had a string of bad luck with men like me—until Cash.

"You don't honestly believe that, do you?"

Kate plates the food and carries two dishes to the terrace. "No, not really. I just don't want to be alone for the rest of my life."

"Keyton has been courting you for the last few years. Say yes. Go out on a date with him. We'll always have half-price apps and exemplary service even if it doesn't work out. If it does, then both of us will be happy in love."

I dig my fork into the pile of food that Kate served. How she made this with the stuff in my fridge is beyond me, but either way it's delish.

"I'll consider it. That's my final offer."

"Good. What's on tap for this weekend? Any parties planned? Cash will be here on Thursday for the long weekend. He agreed to talk to my students about one of his jobs."

"That's nice of him. Is he coming to Kiely's?"

"I don't know when he will get here yet. Would that be an issue?"

"No, just wondering. Keyton said something about a bonfire on Saturday night."

"That sounds fun." Any amount of time I can snuggle up with Cash sounds amazing to me. He seems to have a need to touch me all the time. I love when his hands are on me.

"I'm sorry for barging in here. I always thought it would be me breaking our pact. I'm glad you found each other. I'll miss you when you leave."

"I understand. Thanks, babe."

After washing her plate, Kate hugs me tightly and leaves. I hurry through the shower before talking with Cash.

I answer his video call near eight.

"Hi, *tesoro*. How was your day?"

"Hi. It was great. I confirmed the guests for Friday and prepared the program. What about you?"

"What are you wearing?"

"I ordered a few sets of pajamas a few months ago, but they were backordered." I lift my phone further away so he can see more. There were three sets: red, teal, and black that include a silky camisole top and shorts for sleeping. I chose the black tonight.

"Holy hell. You look sexy in the clothes you have been sleeping in. What am I going to do with those?"

"Same as you do with the other ones: look, touch, and take off."

He groans before a sly smile overtakes his face. I feel a tad guilty for torturing him from a distance, but it's what we have right now.

"Images of you in that is going to keep me up tonight."

"I would apologize, but I'm not sorry." We chat more about his day and our potential plans for the long weekend before hanging up. Soon I'll be able to fall asleep wrapped in his strong arms.

CASSIUS

As I predicted, I sleep horribly. Noelle covered in lace and silk is impossible to put out of my mind, especially when our call is just before I'm supposed to sleep. After two cups of French press coffee, I trudge out onto the sidewalk toward my office.

"Good morning, Mr. Morgan. How was your evening?" Myles asks as I approach my office.

"Fine and you?"

"Same. Your meeting with Mr. Sanders is set for eleven. Otherwise, your schedule is clear for the day. Also, quarterly reports are due in three weeks."

"Thanks, Myles." I step into my office and review my plan before meeting with Stacy. In the back of my mind, I consider how this will affect Noelle and me. Finding an investment for my future couldn't possibly make it worse; we already live on opposite sides of the country.

After letting out a deep breath, I knock on his office door, divulging my innermost thoughts to someone other than Noelle and Sam is just moments away.

"Come in, Cash."

"Stacy, thanks for seeing me."

"Anytime. What can I do for you?"

"After some recent soul searching and a push from someone I care about, I need to make a change. I would do this myself, but I want everything to be carefully reviewed and vetted before I take this huge step." After that intro, I explain to Stacy what I want to do, why, and how soon.

"I'll need a detailed plan and a letter of intent as if you were my client."

I hand him a copy of my plan and a letter of intent executed by me for the holding company I created for this purpose.

"Thorough as always. Are there any restrictions on location?"

"I would prefer to stay in the continental United States, ideally in the tri-state area. If that isn't available, the Northeastern U.S. and then Colorado."

"I can work with that."

"Stacy, I would like to keep this private as long as possible. The circle is exceedingly small, just three people other than me."

"Understood. On one hand, I'm surprised that you're willing to take this risk, but on the other, I'm proud of you choosing to live your life fully."

I rise from the chair, extending my hand to him. "Thanks, man. I'll see you in the ring after work. Please say hello to Jocelyn for me." Stacy and his wife have been together since college. They have had some issues having a family and recently decided to adopt. The process is long, especially considering they are seeking a newborn. Hopefully, soon they will have a family. It has been hard on their marriage.

"See you then. I'll let her know."

Leaving his office, I feel lighter and know who I want to call. I know she isn't available for a few more hours during her lunch. I don't want to tell her this news over the phone even though her sound advice pushed me to take this chance. My gut is telling me it will work out, but my head and my heart aren't fully on board. I'm talking about the deal, not her. I know she and I will find a way to make our relationship work. It'll likely require change or sacrifice for one or both of us, but for the first time in my life, I'm willing to do whatever it takes. I have never met someone like her, and I doubt I ever will again.

Me: I'm counting the hours until I can see you again. Call me at lunch if you can. xoxo

Placing my lunch order with Myles, I sink back into my office chair, considering the gravity of what I just put into motion. I'm not having second thoughts. I already ran through the comprehensive list almost daily for the last two weeks. Cautious optimism is a more apt description. I contemplate letting Mina in on my plans, but decide to wait and just check in.

Me: How are you?

Mina: I'm well. You?

Me: Same. I'll be gone for the long weekend, but Sam will be available.

Mina: I'm fine. I have Peter. Love you bunches.

Me: I'm still getting used to that.

Mina: I know.

Me: Love you bunches more.

After wolfing down my lunch, I research a few more opportunities for my latest client. He's looking for a storefront in a beach community as close to the water as possible. This store will hopefully be the first of at least five locations. Personally, I think he is out of his mind, and due to my long history with him, I told him as much. He's adamant about moving forward with this investment. I even had him sign an acknowledgement that I warned him his strategy wasn't sound. Surprisingly, he signed it without a second thought. At least I know I covered myself and the firm when this deal goes sideways. My gut says it will. My gut is rarely wrong.

Evan and Stacy took turns throwing punches at me last night in the ring, and Stacy pounded me mercilessly tonight. My focus wasn't solely in the ring. Even with her admonishment in my head, my mind still wanders to her in every unfilled moment and even some when I should focus on boxing gloves flying toward my face. I'm exhausted, but I know that less than a day from now, I'll be able to spend time with Noelle. I'm excited to see her at work and speak to her students. She sent possible questions from her students for Friday afternoon. They range from: Is it hard to fly a plane? to can I try on your hat? Grabbing my bag from my locker, I head home to pack for a long weekend in sunny California, but first, I want to hear how her day was.

"Hi, *tesoro*," I answer while lowering myself into the chair in my sitting area.

"Hi. How was your day?"

"Pretty great actually. I found a potential investor for a client and started the process for another client. The best part is I get to hold you tomorrow."

"That's fantastic! I love that last part quite a bit myself."

"What about you? How was your day?"

"I planned for every potential hiccup for Friday. Hopefully, I didn't miss any. Each presenter has a ten minute window to talk and ten minutes for questions. That puts the overall program at two hours. It's long for some of the students, but most will be engaged for the entire presentation."

"I know you prepared from the questions you sent, but damn, that's down to the minute. I'm proud of you."

"Thanks. We'll see if I pull it off."

"Of course you will. I have no doubt."

I smile. "You believe that because you want to snuggle with me."

"That's only partially true. I believe that because you will pull this off with precision, and it will be amazing. Not only do I want to hold you in my arms, but I want to kiss you until you can't breathe." I want to explore her luscious curves in depth. Thinking about her in my arms wearing next to nothing and the taste of her on my lips tents my shorts.

"Holy hockey! Yes, please." She fans herself. Good to know that I affect her with the same tenor as she affects me. "What time will you be here tomorrow?"

"I should be able to meet you at Kiely's if you and Kate are still going after work."

"I can go home instead, if you want."

"No, not at all. Private air travel is less structured than commercial. We could leave later or earlier depending on the clients or available runways. In this case, it'll be the runway because my client is always on time to visit her grandson. I'll text you when I land and see where you are. Does that work?"

"Yes, that works. Get some sleep. I can't wait to see you tomorrow."

"I can't wait to kiss you until you can't breathe."

"So much for sleeping tonight. Good night, Cassius."

My reaction to her using my full name is visceral. She's the only woman who makes my name sound decadent. I will never let another woman use my full name for the rest of my life.

"Good night, *tesoro*." As I take a deep breath before ending our call, she drops her phone to the floor. She doesn't realize she hasn't ended the call yet. When she leans down to pick it up, I have a clear view of her ample breasts. Now I'm more aroused than I was before.

"*Tesoro*, you didn't hang up."

"I'm sorry. I'm clumsy when I get anxious."

Concern rushes through my veins. I worry about her enough being basically alone. What is she anxious about?

"Do I make you anxious?"

"Yes. No. Not exactly." She sighs.

"Please explain." In this moment, her West Coast address is screwing with my head. I want to be there to soothe her more than I want my next breath.

"You're just...."

I wait patiently for her to continue like I did in my car after picking her up at the airport.

"You're everything. The idea of us scares the hell out of me. How I feel when we talk, and especially when you're with me, it scares me." She exhales, holding the bridge of her nose between her thumb and index finger. "Thinking about you or when I'm with you, I feel like I'm losing control. Then you touch me and I'm instantly calm. Am I imagining all of this? We just seem to fit too perfectly, at least this soon. Does that make sense?" Hearing her feelings out loud makes my chest tighten.

"No, you aren't imagining any of it. Our chemistry and connection are off the charts. I feel it too. Being with you is effortless and comfortable, like we've been best friends since childhood. However, kissing you... touching you, rocks my world."

Even though the screen is small, her eyes turn stormy with lust. Hermione's time turner would be useful right now.

"Thank you for listening. All of this is new to me."

"You're welcome. Me too."

"You should get some sleep before you need to fly tomorrow. We can talk about this more while you're here."

I nod despite my desire to keep her talking. "I would have preferred to have that conversation in person."

"Me too. We'll finish it in person."

"Good night, *tesoro*."

"Good night, Cassius." This time I wait until she ends the call.

NOELLE

I don't regret spilling my feelings to Cash last night, but they made for a restless night and a long day at work. Mason was at the center today. As each day passes, my hope of keeping my job increases.

"You look terrible," Kate says as I drop onto the stool next to her at Kiely's after work.

"Thanks." Always great to hear a dose of reality from your bestie.

"Shouldn't you be all blissed out and excited?"

"I didn't sleep well last night, and the kids were crazy today. Plus, Cash and I talked about a few topics that should have been done in person."

Kate's eyes move to the bar. Keyton is chatting up a blonde sitting alone. Her show of jealousy happens every so often, even though she hasn't said yes to his invitation.

"Would you just say yes, already? Put both of you out of your misery."

Keyton delivers the blonde's drink before approaching our table with our standing order.

"Hi, Keyton."

"Hi, Noelle. You look like you had a crappy day."

"I did."

He sets our drinks on the table.

"Yes!" Kate blurts out.

"What?" Keyton and I ask in unison.

"If your offer still stands, I would like to go out with you. Does it?"

Keyton sets the tray on our table and walks around to Kate's side. Offering her his hand, he helps her stand. Keyton towers over Kate.

Looking down at her, he says, "Yes, my offer still stands. It's about time you accepted. I'm going to kiss you." Keyton cups her face, bringing his lips to hers. Cheers from his coworkers erupt from behind the bar. After pulling back from her lips, Keyton whispers something to Kate before grabbing his tray and walking back behind the bar.

"Oh my God! That was fantastic! I'm so happy for you!"

"I can't believe I just did that!" Her skin is flushed.

"What did he say?" I ask, wondering if I were in her situation would I share. I probably wouldn't.

"He said he would kiss me properly without an audience."

"Wow! *Wow!* Well, cheers to you and Keyton!" Kate and I clink our glasses together and take a celebratory sip.

"What are we celebrating?" His voice sends shivers over my entire body. I turn to see Cash just inches away. Before I can answer, Cash slides his hand around my jaw, dragging his thumb across my lips before kissing me.

I take a moment after he pulls away to gather my senses before replying, "Kate finally accepted Keyton's invitation for a date."

"Kate."

"Cash."

Not even Cash's presence can make the stupid smile on Kate's face dim. Maybe, just maybe, my bestie will be lucky in love this time around. I certainly am.

"How was your flight?"

Cash sidles up next to my stool, pushing his bag beneath the table. I should have just gone home so he wouldn't have his bag here. "Nice and smooth."

"I'm sorry, I didn't think about your luggage."

"It's no problem. How was work?"

"The kids were off the wall today because of the long weekend, and I didn't sleep well last night."

Leaning forward so only I can hear him, he says, "I'm sorry, *tesoro*. I didn't sleep well either. Maybe we should have kept talking."

Holy hockey! When he calls me that, I seriously feel gooey inside and lose my ability to think straight. That isn't true; Cassius Morgan makes me feel like that every second of every day.

"We can talk more later. Do you want a drink?"

"I'll get it. Do you want another?"

"No, I'm fine."

"Kate?" Apparently, she's still lost in Keyton's mouth on hers.

"Huh?"

"Do you want a refill?" Cash asks again.

"No, thanks," Kate replies, her eyes locked on Keyton talking to the blonde again. He's just talking to her, but she is flirting like he's the last man on earth.

"He's just doing his job, K."

"I know."

I glance over at Cash waiting patiently for his drink. Wearing jeans and a dress shirt, I realize he must have changed after his flight here. If he didn't sleep well either, he must be exhausted. After he returns, we chat a bit with Kate and leave as soon as he finishes his drink. Kate moves over to the corner of the bar to wait for Keyton's shift to end.

As soon as my front door clicks closed, Cash pulls me into his arms. His mouth claims mine like we've been apart for a year, not a few days. He strokes my tongue with his. The intent feels more like staking a claim. Kissing Cash is always intense, but this is different. Travelling over to my ear, his lips send bolts of need between my legs. Lifting my chin, Cash exposes my neck to his tongue. As he kisses downward, I fumble with the buttons on his shirt. After successfully dropping his shirt to the floor, Cash tugs my shirt over my head, adding it to the growing pile on the floor. His dark eyes widen. My workday lingerie is generally boring, and this isn't one of my sexier sets, but apparently, it's fine for Cash. It's just a simple unlined, black lace bra and matching thong.

"You're gorgeous."

We move further into my condo, tongues tangling, surging back and forth against the wall in the hallway. The muscles of his back are taut under my fingers. Cash drops to his knees, removing my shoes. I drag my fingers into his dark hair. Inch by inch, he kisses his way up my legs to the hem of my pencil skirt. Sliding his hands beneath the hem, he pushes it up to my hips. Gripping my ass, he continues kissing upward along my inner thigh. My core clenches as his breath ghosts over me. Teasing the edge of my thong with his tongue, Cash inhales sharply in response to my tightening grip on his locks.

Looking up, I can see the questions in his eyes. Are you okay? Do you want me to stop? After receiving a slight nod, he continues to rise, pressing his mouth up my rib cage to the swell of my breasts. Once he stands, he cages me against the wall. He's pressed against me, and it feels delicious and luxurious at the same time. Dropping my hands, I unbutton his jeans and push them to the floor. My heart is pounding in my chest, my breathing is shallow, and I want so much more. Momentarily, fear grips me. There is no going back once we do this. I feel like I'm standing at a point where my whole life is about to change.

"*Tesoro.*"

I lift my eyes to meet his. His hands grip my hips while mine rest on his chest. His heart rate is fast against my palms. The feel of his fingers digging into my flesh is intoxicating. "What are you afraid of?"

"Making us real. Believing how I feel is real."

"We are real. Real. Scary. Amazing."

"How do you know?" I whisper.

"You make me feel things I've only dreamed possible. You make me think about my life and how I want to live it with you."

I slide my hands up around his strong jaw, tugging his mouth to mine. Wrapping his arm around my waist, Cash turns toward my bedroom. A few long steps later, my calves come up against the dressing bench at the foot of my bed. I'm dizzy from our kisses. His large hands coast over my curves before he unzips my skirt, pushing it to the floor. I step out of the pooled fabric while Cash licks a path over my breasts, teasing my nipple through my bra before unclasping it. He guides me down to the dressing bench at the foot of my bed. Pushing my thighs apart, he settles between them on his knees. Latching onto my nipple, Cash nips and licks it into a tight pink peak. He draws his hand down my side, over the flare of my hip, to my toes. Everywhere he touches makes my skin tingle, making me wetter than I have ever been before. Sweet mercy! He makes me feel sexy and desired.

Moving outward, he licks down my rib cage and in toward my navel. When he drags his tongue up over my core through the satin, it sends a small shudder through me. It's been so long. Taking control of my thoughts, I focus on now, not worrying about past experiences or what happens next. I lift my hips so he can shimmy my thong over my hips.

The first stroke of his velvet tongue hits me like a lightning bolt. I grip his shoulders as he licks my folds. As he surges in and out, my core tightens with his rhythm. Circling the nub with his tongue, Cash slides his fingers from top to bottom, teasing my rear entrance before plunging his fingers into my heat. Twisting, turning, forward, and back, I arch off the bench to absorb all the sensations spiraling through me from his fingers and tongue. His mouth was dangerous and should come with a warning. Cassius himself needs a warning label. My stomach tightens as my orgasm moves closer and closer. My thighs quake as my orgasm rushes through me. Releasing my hands from his shoulders, I slowly relax.

Rising to his feet, Cash guides me up onto my bed, kissing his way upward before turning us onto our sides. I slide my hand to palm him through his boxer briefs.

"We can wait, *tesoro*."

I hear the sincerity and genuine concern for me in his voice.

"I want you now."

Leaning forward, he kisses me. The tender kiss makes me consider waiting. I want him, and it isn't going to lessen if we wait. Slipping beneath the waistband, I surround him with my hand and stroke him over and over. Feeling him against me, seeing a glimpse of him naked, and touching him are hugely different things. Not only is his chest sculpted and his abs carved, but he's well-endowed. He growls deeply.

"I need you to stop if you don't want me to come from your hand like an overeager teenager. Condom?"

"In the bathroom. Middle drawer in the back."

Cash jumps off my bed. When he comes out of the bathroom, he's naked. He drops an extra packet or two on the bench before climbing back onto my bed. Crawling up from the bench, he settles between my thighs. After sheathing himself, Cash leans forward, kissing me softly. The tip lightly grazes my heat at the same time. The anticipation of how we will feel makes my pulse race. Slowly, he pushes forward. I turn my head to the side to process how full I feel.

"Are you okay?"

"Yes, I just need you to go slow."

Nodding, Cash moves slowly forward until he's fully seated. The discomfort gives way to the pleasure of him deep inside me. As if he knows, he starts to move, thrusting forward and pulling almost fully out. The fervor of this moment isn't lost on me. I have never felt this connected to a man ever before. Each thrust sends spikes of sinful pleasure through me. As I get closer to my release, Cash moves faster.

"Baby."

The tightness that comes just before an explosive orgasm is rapidly taking hold of me. I shudder as my walls tighten around him. The muscles of his arms are taut as he throbs inside me. Rippling sensations move through me as he empties in a few deep thrusts.

"Holy hell!"

Cash lowers himself on top of me. My mouth near the hollow of his collarbone, his lips curved into a smile against my temple. "Does that qualify as a curse?"

"Yes, hell yes."

"Hearing you curse is hot!"

I laugh softly, taking in his weight on top of me and the depth of my feelings for this insanely perfect man. I'm falling for Cassius Morgan, and everything surrounding him is terrifying.

CASSIUS

"Don't go. Stay with me," I plead as she wiggles out from under my arm. Making love to Noelle last night was life altering. We put one more packet to appropriate use before falling asleep naked and sated. It felt different than ever before. More passionate and raw. She's the only woman I have ever shared a bed with overnight. The distinction is telling.

"I can't. We have a big day today. I need to get to work."

Watching her move around naked first thing in the morning is sublime. "Can you tell me the schedule while you shower?"

"Sure, but you'll have to get up."

"Slave driver, sexy though you may be."

Grabbing her robe, she disappears into her bathroom. Pulling myself up, I follow her to the bathroom, leaning against the sink. I would give anything to have enough time to step under the hot spray with her right now. Pushing away my sensual thoughts, I focus on her words instead of her shape through the glass. Noelle fills me in on the schedule. I'll take an Uber to the center, and we'll come home together. Watching her towel off, I resist every urge to take her against this counter. Once she ties her silky robe, I kiss her softly and pad to the kitchen to make coffee.

"Do you eat breakfast before work?" I ask from the kitchen.

"Normally, yes, but I'm running late today and you're to blame."

I walk to her room with coffee in hand. In the time it takes me to brew two cups, she's almost ready to leave. Dressed in a navy shirt and a sweater with white capris. Her damp hair falls down her back as she sprays her perfume and puts on a watch.

"That's impressive. You smell amazing. Where is the lavender from?" I ask, handing her a cup of coffee.

She takes a soothing first sip. "Thanks. The lavender is in my bodywash." She loops her arm through her tote and walks to the kitchen. After pouring her coffee into a travel mug, she turns toward me. "I'm so happy you're here. There's a key in the far right-hand drawer if you want to go out. I'll see you later at the center."

"*Tesoro*, I'm happy to be here." I pull her against me, pressing my lips to hers softly. "I want to talk more about our call from the other night after career day and a few other things."

She nods before kissing me more deeply and grabbing the doorknob and walking away.

After finishing another cup of coffee, I change into workout clothes and head out for a run. Noelle is highly organized. The key is exactly where she said it was. I push myself through a long run on the sand before checking my work inbox. I have the day off, but I have some time before I need to leave.

The ride to the center is shorter than I anticipated. I'm about forty minutes early. I consider going in but decide against it. Taking a seat on the grassy area, I watch the kids play on the playground, hoping to catch of glimpse of Noelle. She's probably obsessing about the details for this event. A streak of red hair dances in my line of sight. She's helping a little girl down from the slide. Later when a woman dressed in scrubs and one dressed from a coffee shop enter the center, I decide to go in as well.

Noelle greets the women and directs them to a small room to wait. The presentations will be outside because it's a warm, sunny day and the kids will have more space. She extends her hand to me as I approach her. I take her hand and pull her closer to me so only she can hear me.

"I would prefer to kiss you." I refuse to let go of her hand.

"As would I, but it isn't appropriate."

As I walk away to join the other presenters, my client Mrs. Waller breezes through the front door of the center. Her grandson must attend this childcare center. I wonder which one he is.

Noelle escorts Mrs. Waller into the waiting room with the career day presenters. Early guests and the presenters are waiting for the set up to finish. Before leaving, Noelle looks directly at me. I can read her fairly well already. She's grateful I'm here but is thinking about not being able to kiss me hello.

"Cash, what a pleasant surprise." Mrs. Waller shakes my hand.

"You as well. I assume your grandson attends this center."

"Yes. Mason is a wonderful boy. What brings you here?"

Mason can't be M, could he? That is a crazy coincidence. Noelle has issues with his mom, not his grandmother.

"I offered to help when Noelle indicated that two presenters backed out."

"Are you a couple?"

I hesitate to answer her.

"Sorry, I didn't mean to pry."

"It's fine. We met recently. I don't know how to label our relationship right yet."

"Understood. She's wonderful with the children and beautiful as well," Mrs. Waller replies.

"She is." I watch her through the window as she sets up a table and a few chairs along the edge of the blacktop area. Just before two, the teachers at the center escort the students outside in an orderly procession. A dark-haired woman, who is likely Sheila, Noelle's boss, guides the presenters and guests outside. There are six presenters, and I'm slated to speak fifth. The first speaker starts her presentation, but Noelle is nowhere to be found. She hasn't come outside yet. Sheila instructs one of the teachers to handle the questions while she moves to speak to Mrs. Waller, standing near the back of the room.

"Mrs. Waller, would you come with me?" Sheila asks before leading her inside. The assistant teachers are handling the students and assisting them with sitting in their seats and listening to the accountant who is speaking now. Just two more presenters before I speak. My concerns increase the longer Noelle and Mrs. Waller are inside.

After introducing myself, I explain my job to the students. Their questions are cute and interesting. Is it hard to fly a plane? Do you have to go to college first? Do you have flight attendants? Is the plane heavy?

As I answer their questions, I see Noelle near the door leading into the center. She looks distraught. Seeing her upset concerns me. Her job is already unstable as it is. I glance her way again and catch her eye this time. She smiles softly before looking away. Whatever happened with Mason, it wasn't good.

After the final presenter, there's a reception with cookies and punch. A few of the parents compliment me on my answers to their children. One of the moms asks a few questions that border on too personal before her daughter pulls her away for cookies. I was polite with my nonanswers.

"Mr. Cash," a quiet little voice calls from behind me.

"Hi, Annaliese. Nice to see you again." I crouch down to her level. Today she's wearing a floral dress and white shoes with huge bows on them. She's adorable.

"Is Miss Noelle your girlfriend yet?"

"No, but I would like her to be my girlfriend."

"You should ask her."

I nod as her mother approaches.

"Annaliese, leave him alone."

"Mom, I wanted to see how it was going with Miss Noelle."

"I'm so sorry," her mother replies.

"It's no problem."

"Mr. Cash, Miss Noelle is happier. You should talk to her."

"I will soon."

Annaliese throws her arms around my neck, squeezing tightly. I hug her back before her mom ushers her away. As the crowd thins, Noelle is no longer outside. Stepping inside, I hear talking from an office. I recognize Noelle and Mrs. Waller's voice, but not the third one. There's a young boy curled up in the fetal position on the floor with a woman who I assume is his mother. I continue walking out the door to wait for Noelle. I was hoping this would go well for her, but it appears that wasn't in the cards. Well, the career day part was delightful.

Thirty minutes later, Mrs. Waller, a woman who I assume is her daughter or daughter-in-law, and a young boy leave the center. The boy is frustrated and not leaving willingly. The mother needs to wrestle the boy into his car seat. Mrs. Waller gives me a polite nod before sitting in the car. Soon thereafter, Noelle leaves the center. Despite what I know was a horrible day, she takes my breath away. Her hair is in a pile on top of her head with a few strands falling around her face.

"I'm sorry you had to wait for me. This afternoon didn't go as planned."

"There's nothing to be sorry for. All your planning helped the staff pull off a great event. You should be proud of that. As far as your student, I'm sure you did everything you could. Watching you with them is mesmerizing."

"Let's get out of here. Do you mind if we stay in tonight?"

"No. Do you have food I can cook, or do we need to order in?"

"I don't have enough food for you. I planned to go shopping with you after work, but I just want to go home."

"*Tesoro*, relax. I just want to spend time with you. I don't care where we are or what we eat."

She rounds her car to the passenger door. As I open the door, she hands me her keys before sitting. I resist the urge to kiss her—just barely.

NOELLE

Our first order of business is Chinese takeout for dinner. In the time it takes for us to change, our food arrives. Cash pours two glasses of white wine while I grab the plates and utensils. We dine al fresco. Apparently, I'm starving. I haven't said a word since we came out here. I eat most of my dinner and start picking at Cash's too. I love that he doesn't mind sharing his food.

"You really don't mind me eating off your plate?"

"No, why would I? I kiss you thoroughly as often as I can; why would I care about your fork in my food?"

After that answer, I lean forward, brushing my lips across his. He tastes sweet like honey and wine.

"Are you ready to talk?"

"Work or our call?"

"Either, both, or neither."

"I fully expect to lose my job next week. Honestly, I'm surprised she didn't fire me today. I owe that to Mrs. Waller, but I think she only pushed off the inevitable."

"Remember I told you my client flies here to see her grandson every two weeks."

"Yes." I take a heavy gulp of my wine.

"Mrs. Waller is my client and apparently M's grandmother."

"Wow, that must have been surprising for both of you today."

"It was. Do you want to talk about Mason? What happened that you missed the event you so painstakingly planned?"

My heart squeezes a bit. I appreciate that he knows this event was a big deal for me.

I sigh deeply. "When Mrs. Sanfilippo arrived, Mason was engaged in an activity. Rather than wait for him to come to her, she interrupted, throwing him off. When she tried to get him to hurry, he had a meltdown. When I approached Mason, his mom had a tantrum herself, claiming I had no business taking care of her son. Mason started rocking in his seat. When his mother touched him, he started shouting. I attempted to suggest a way to diffuse the situation, but the insults got worse. Sheila left at this point."

"She came outside and brought Mrs. Waller over to you. I was standing beside her when she asked."

"I tried a few times to get Mason to look at me. When he did, I asked him to breathe with me. It worked the last time he threw a fit with his mother."

"That was the day she asked for the plan for Mason?"

This man is truly a gift. He listens when I share things about my work. No man has ever done that before. It's insanely endearing. Just another reason why he's a unicorn among men.

"Yes. It worked. When they returned, Sheila sent me outside to the presentations. I'm sorry I missed most of yours."

"I know you did the best you could. There'll be others." He presses his lips to my forehead. "What was the meeting about?"

I take a deep breath and let it out slowly. "Mrs. Sanfilippo asked for withdrawal papers for Mason. Mrs. Waller tried to talk her out of it. She stood up for me. Apparently, she witnessed my attempt to soothe Mason. Mrs. Sanfilippo conditioned Mason's return to the center on my termination. When Sheila acquiesced, Mrs. Waller asked for the weekend to discuss the matter with her daughter. Sheila agreed to wait until next week for her final decision."

"That's awful. How long have you been working there?"

"Since I graduated from college." I hang my head. I suppose it could be worse; I could be alone right now.

Cash lifts my eyes to his.

"You did everything you could for Mason and to save your job. Mrs. Waller is great, but it seems her daughter is difficult or at least is in denial that her son has developmental delays. Everything is going to be fine."

I lean into him, resting my head on his arm. After a few minutes, I rise, taking the dishes into the kitchen. "Do you want more wine?" I ask from the kitchen.

"Sure."

He moves to the couch. I hand him his refilled glass and cuddle next to him when I return.

"Our little matchmaker asked me a question today."

I look over at him. "Did she ask you when the wedding is?" I giggle.

"Sort of. She asked me if you were my girlfriend yet. She said you must be because you're happier."

Annaliese isn't wrong. I am happy, anxious sometimes, but happier.

"What did you say to her?"

"That I want you to be, but I haven't asked yet. It seems silly to ask given our ages. It also seems obvious to me because I care about you. Noelle, will you do me the honor of being my girlfriend?"

I laugh softly. "Yes, Cassius, it'll be my honor to be your girlfriend."

He takes my glass and sets it on the table next to his. Before pulling me closer, he tucks one of the loose strands behind my ear. Goose bumps skitter on my skin from his touch. Cupping my jaw, he seals his mouth over mine. I savor every second. His kisses feel decadent and possessive.

Pulling back, he says, "Perfect. That should resolve most of your anxiety about us."

"It does. What else did you want to talk about?" Our ability to talk about everything leads me down a road I've never been near before, a road with open, honest communication and no fear of judgement for my thoughts. The road to the fairy tale. Except for one issue—a huge geographical issue—I feel as if we could make this work.

"Two things: my job and your brother. Which do you want to handle first?"

"My brother. I told him I met someone but didn't share any details. He asked me if I wanted Blaine to check said guy out."

"Who's Blaine?"

"Blaine is a friend of Jacob's, Nicholas's head of security. He's a private investigator and white-hat hacker. I didn't say this to him, but I assume he already ran a background check on you, or he wouldn't let Kelly near you. He's overly protective of his wife, rightfully so."

"Are you concerned about me?" he asks in a serious tone. I almost miss the slight crack of levity.

"I wouldn't have invited you in after our first date if I was." I'm only concerned that I'm in too deep too fast.

"That would have been problematic."

"Why?"

"We wouldn't have been able to find out if our chemistry truly is white-hot if I never kissed you a second time."

"It's definitely white-hot." I kiss Cash so hard it makes me dizzy. A tad might be the wine, but the rest is him—all him.

"They ran a deep check when I applied for my job at the firm, considering the financial information I have access to, and a second one when I applied to fly, considering the clientele of the airline."

I appreciate the information, but I didn't need it. "I'll tell my brother the next time I talk to him. It should probably be sooner rather than later since our photo was online."

"You googled me?" Genuine surprise laces his tone.

I laugh. "Kate did because she was upset about me breaking our pact."

"What pact?"

"We pinky promised neither of us would fall in love—a pact doomed from the start. She freaked out because you make me happy. Happier than I've ever been before. To prove you're not good enough, she googled you. A photo of us walking in Central Park is among the rest. The photo tags you, not me."

"You make me happy too, *tesoro*. We should talk to your brother soon considering the photo. The paparazzi might not know it's you yet, but Ellis will."

I'm not concerned about talking to Nicholas. He doesn't meddle in my love life. I'm only sharing because Cash works for him and he's a celebrity, if you will. I hope to tell him before he sees photos of us together. If there are photos from our stroll, there are likely more from dinner or even at the airport. Entertainment photographers like to catch celebrities or, in my case, rich bachelors in a state of normal. Obviously, a photo of a female celeb not at her best would sell more, but either way, they need to get paid.

"We can call him tomorrow. Does my brother know flying is your second job?"

"Yes, but I don't know for how long."

I wrinkle my brow, wrapping my head around his words. "You didn't!" I'm ready to jump up and down.

CASSIUS

"I did."

"Really? I'm so happy for you!" She throws her arms around me and kisses me. Slow, sensual kisses follow my announcement until I pull back to look at her. Never has anyone been genuinely happy for me when they wouldn't benefit in any way. Nothing about this deal will help Noelle. While I'm confident she and I will grow old and gray together even at this early stage, it'll get harder before we get there. Plus, the fact she's about to lose her job doesn't help matters. It's easier to make life decisions when nothing is forcing your hand. No one approaches the heart, mind, and soul of Noelle Barnett. No woman I've ever met even comes close.

Resettling on the couch, Noelle turns to face me, her legs bent over my thighs.

"When you went to the beach with Kate, I spent the rest of the afternoon thinking about what you said about my jobs. Well, that isn't true; I've been thinking about it since we talked, but that day I acted. I wondered what I was waiting for. Honestly, I was waiting for you. No one has ever been able to read me like you do. To see that flying is my passion, and I invest to make other people more money. I sat down and drafted a plan to resign from investing to make flying my job."

"I was just being honest. Tell me more."

"I know you were. That's why it hit me hard. You ask tough, real questions, and I love that about you." While I've fallen for Noelle, telling her so soon isn't a great plan. "Right now, only you, Sam, and Stacy know about my plan. I might share with my other siblings soon. I shared with Sam about a week after I created the plan. Stacy is another roommate from college who works at my firm. I need him to handle any deal I decide to make for myself. Having someone with the same knowledge look over any deal is a good business decision; plus, he's my friend and partner. He won't steer me wrong. Basically, Stacy is doing for me what I do for others every day. He's seeking an investment for me, specifically one where I can buy an ownership stake in a private airline. I would prefer to be the sole owner, but I don't know what is available or where at this time. It'll allow me to fly a little more and run the company. My plan sets a deadline for the end of this year."

"That's amazing! Are you going to leave New York?"

"It's a strong possibility."

"What about your siblings?"

"I fly planes, sweetheart. I can go wherever I want, whenever I want, especially if I own the airline. Plus, Billie moved to Maine. I don't see Auggie being able to stay in the city to build his restaurant without buying a boatload of prime real estate and paying for rezoning and other things. Sam—he's tough. I know he dislikes many things about living in the city, but so far he hasn't had a reason to leave." I have a reason—she's brilliant, beautiful, and kind—but I don't want to scare her away.

"Did you just say Billie? I thought your sister's name was Mina."

"It's both. My sister's name is Wilhelmina. When we were young, her nickname was Mina. After her accident, she wanted a fresh start and now goes by Billie. I'm still working on calling her Billie. Why?"

"I met your sister at Nicholas's wedding. She's beautiful, gracious, and Kelly's business partner. Her fiancé, Peter, is Kelly's brother."

"I didn't know they were the same person. Small world." I yawn deeply, resting my head on her shoulder. Changing time zones usually catches up with me when I'm already on my way back home. I wonder where home will be by the end of the year. I'm excited to find out.

"You must be exhausted. Let's go to bed," she suggests. We bring the remaining dishes into the kitchen before turning in for the night.

"Morning, gorgeous." I lean against the doorframe to her patio. She's curled up, her long, creamy legs tucked under her, wearing a silky robe with coffee in hand. Her hair is in a topknot and glistens in the morning sun.

As I move closer to her, she replies, "Me? Please, I'm a mess in the morning. You, on the other hand, with your mussed hair, no shirt, and low-slung shorts are absurdly hot."

"You think I'm hot?" I sit on the arm of her chair.

She rolls her eyes. "You know I do." She peers over the top of her glasses. Holy hell, her with glasses is sexy-librarian hot. Leaning down, I kiss her softly.

"Do you want another cup?"

"Sure do. You want help?"

"I can handle it, and then we can figure out our plan for the day."

When I return with two cups of steamy caffeinated goodness, Noelle has moved onto the couch. I hand her a cup and take a seat next to her. We discuss our plan.

After dressing, we grab carryout breakfast at a coffee shop around the corner from her condo and walk the beach. It may be a holiday weekend, but the beach is still empty this early.

After turning back toward her condo, I decide to make us more official. "Are you free on the first Saturday of September?"

"Probably, why?"

"I would like you to accompany me to the benefit for the arts gala in New York." When she opens her mouth to answer me, I stop in my tracks, pull her roughly against me, and press my finger to her plump pink lips. "Before you answer, I can't protect your privacy at the gala. There will be photographers and paparazzi. If we make it that far without a splash on Page Six, attending that event as a couple will do it. Also, my parents will be in attendance. I'm not suggesting I don't want you to meet them. You're impressive, and they will love you. I don't want *them* to meet you. As much as I limit my time with my parents, I want the same for you." I lower my finger slowly, replacing it with my lips. After I pull back, I see her expression is somewhat serious.

"I appreciate your concerns, but we can't hide forever. Honestly, I'm surprised we made it this long. I would love to attend with you. Black tie?"

"Yes, black tie."

"You in a tux, I can't wait to see that."

"There you go again saying you think I'm hot."

"You're hot in everyday clothes. A suit, ticks that up even more. You in a tux will be a whole different level of absurdly hot."

I lean over and kiss her quickly. As we turn the corner for her street, she stops, pushing me back against the building.

"What the . . .?" Damn, that hurt. She's stronger than she looks.

Now she puts her finger against my lips, but I don't think it's for a great reason.

"Jimmy, the local paparazzo, is standing on the sidewalk outside my building."

"Oh. Well, let's go chat with him."

"No. I'm going to talk with him alone. He's innocuous. Always polite. Just doing his job."

Intertwining her fingers with mine, she leads me back toward the beach. At the next corner, she gives me directions to the back entrance onto her patio.

"I don't like this, *tesoro*. Let me come with you," I plead, hoping my strong, persistent woman will relent.

"I'll be fine. I'm sure it's about Nicholas and Kelly."

"I'm going on record that I'm against this plan. I care about you. Let me come with you."

"I care about you too, which is why I need to talk to Jimmy alone. I'll meet you inside."

After kissing her possessively, I reluctantly release her hand. I watch frozen in my spot as she disappears around the corner. I'm warring with myself whether to follow her or go inside like she requested. I want to shield her from the drawbacks of being my girlfriend. *Get it together!* She's Ellis Barnett's sister. She isn't a stranger to the paparazzi. She can handle herself. All those things are true, except this time, it could be about us, not Nicholas and Kelly.

NOELLE

"Good morning, Jimmy. How are you?"

Jimmy is tall and lanky with a baseball cap and long shorts. He's alone today. Generally, there are two or three other photogs here at once.

"I'm well. How are you?"

"Good."

"Do you have a comment on your brother's wedding?"

"No comment." I take a step or two up the concrete staircase.

"Any comment on your relationship with New York's most eligible bachelor, Cassius Morgan?"

"No comment. Have a good day, Jimmy."

"There are photos of the two of you together. Care to address them?"

"No comment, Jimmy." I continue up.

"Care to comment on the report that Brittany Templeton is pregnant with Mr. Morgan's child?" My heart plummets to my feet. I knew he was too good to be true.

"No comment. Have a great holiday, Jimmy." I try to keep my voice at the same pitch answering each question. The last one is exceptionally difficult. I shove my key into the outer foyer and close it behind me. After taking a few deep breaths before I open my door, I slip inside. I stalk over to the French doors and let Cash inside.

"*Tesoro*, talk to me. What did he want to know?"

"I need a few minutes. I don't want to say something I might regret."

Cash pulls his fingers through his hair. Holy hockey, he's tempting.

"Can I hold you at least?" he asks, opening his arms to me. My chest tightens thinking about his strong arms around me and how much I need him to do just that.

"No." I stalk away to my bedroom. The urge to bawl is rapidly increasing. *I will not cry*, I repeat in my head over and over. Yet I can't stop the stream down my cheeks. I know the correct response is to talk to Cash, but I'm angry at myself for letting him in so quickly. *It may not be true*. Either way, it hurts. Maybe I'm not cut out for a high-profile relationship. I pace around my bedroom, frantically trying to sort my thoughts and feelings. Awhile later, I'm not even sure how long, Cash knocks on the door softly.

"Can I come in?"

"I would rather you not see me like this." Catching a glimpse of my blotchy, swollen, red face, it's better for him to stay outside, at least for now.

"*Tesoro*, please talk to me. I'll stay here if that's what you want, but please talk to me."

I move to the door and sit with my knees pulled up to my chest on the floor facing it.

"He asked about Nicholas and Kelly's wedding. Then he asked about my relationship with you and the photos. Apparently, there are more."

"Okay, that can't be the issue. What else?"

Damn him for knowing me so well.

"I have no right to be jealous, upset, or anything because it's so early, but who is Brittany? Did you lie to me?"

"I will never lie to you. I care about you. Please open the door."

The strangled, pleading tone of his voice tugs at my heart. Leaning forward, I turn the knob, opening the door slightly.

"Can I come in?"

At my nod, Cash sits on the floor facing me after closing the door, his legs bent on either side of me. He reaches his hand to my cheek, wiping a single tear away. "Don't cry, *tesoro*. I've never lied to you."

"Who is Brittany?"

"My mother set me up on a date with Brittany. I'm sure Margaux thought we had a lot in common because she went to a prestigious boarding school and business school. We had dinner, that's all."

"When?"

"A week after Nicholas's wedding."

"Did you sleep with her?"

"No."

I have no reason not to believe him, and I'm acutely aware of how the tabloids twist stories and headlines.

"Jimmy asked me if I wanted to comment on her pregnancy. Apparently, you're the father."

"*Tesoro*, I have only been with you. There's no chance I'm the father."

I let out a breath I didn't know I was holding. I lift my legs over his and scoot forward. He wraps his arms around me, pulling me in close. "We need to talk to Nicholas."

"We will after you relax. I care about you. I haven't nor will I ever lie to you. I promised you complete, blunt honesty. I honor every promise I make."

I nod against his neck before gazing up at him. Hurt, fear, and care stare back at me.

"I care about you too. I was fine until he threw the baby question at me. I'm sorry I doubted you."

"Going public with me isn't going to be easy."

I hear the unspoken questions. Are we done? Can you handle this? Do you still want me?

"I don't want to break up."

"Neither do I."

While in his arms, I memorize him more thoroughly. His dimples get me every time he smiles.

"We should order some groceries and call Nicholas. Do you still want to go out tonight?" Part of me wants to show him off at the bonfire, but the other part wants to keep him to myself as much as possible.

"Let's see how the afternoon goes."

After placing a grocery order, I call Nicholas, who surprisingly answers right away.

"Hi. How are you and Kelly?"

Cash is sitting beside me on the chaise dragging his fingers up and down my forearm. Who knew that feels amazing?

"We're well. How are you?"

"I'm fine. I need to tell you more about the guy I've been seeing. It's Cash."

"I know."

"What do you mean you know?" I ask, surprised and slightly angered.

"Blaine alerts me when your photo is posted on any entertainment sites. I saw photos of you in Central Park, at Tavern on the Green, and a beach somewhere."

"You're having me watched?"

"No. I'm just making sure you're treated fairly by the press. Why are you telling me now?"

"This morning there was a local photog on my doorstep when we came back from a walk. He asked about photos. I only knew about the one from the park. Cash and I decided to tell you last night, but it was too late to call."

"Is he with you now?"

"Yes."

"Do you want me to send Maia or Connor for a little while?"

Both work for Jacob and rotate on Kelly's security team. I haven't had personal security since I graduated from college. One of my floor mates realized that Nicholas was Ellis Barnett and made a few threats against me. Once I graduated and had my own place, the need evaporated.

"No. Jimmy has always been appropriate when he questions me. I just wasn't prepared for one of the questions he lobbed at me today."

"The pregnancy rumor?"

"Seriously, have I been living under a rock? Yes, the pregnancy rumor."

"No, ignoring the headlines is a promising idea. Hashing out every false rumor or accusation will take a toll on your relationship. As odd as this may sound, just be honest with each other and never believe a headline or story until you have talked to him. If you change your mind, let me know."

"I will."

"Thank you for telling me."

"You're welcome. Have a great holiday."

"You too. Love you lots."

"Love you lots more." I set my phone on the end table and curl into Cash's arms. I'm still unsettled about the whole Brittany thing. I'm sure Cash is telling the truth. Perhaps I will need to take Nicholas's advice to heart and use it.

"Do you always say 'love you lots'?" Cash asks before kissing the top of my head.

"Yes, why?"

"My siblings and I say 'love you bunches.' It's interesting that we both have that with our siblings."

"It is."

An hour later, our grocery delivery arrives. After emptying the bags, we set up an antipasto plate, add some wine, and sit on the patio talking about various topics, mostly his plan for his future.

"Tell me more about your day job and how a deal works. I know you aren't staying, but it will help me learn more about you."

I listen to Cash explain a basic deal and how each aspect would work from start to finish. Not once do I feel dumb for asking a question or a clarification of something I don't understand. Cash is genuine. It's an impressive quality. He's extraordinary all around. It's rare to find someone who is the total package and doesn't know it.

CASSIUS

Newspapers and websites have slung rumors and other untrue headlines since I became an adult with a huge trust fund, not to mention my lucrative position as a partner in a venture capital firm. Never have they affected me like earlier today. It crushed me seeing how Noelle looked asking about Brittany. When she refused to let me in to talk, I scanned the entertainment sites. When I found a few headlines regarding the pregnancy, I contacted my attorney to see if I have any recourse as the stories are patently false. I probably don't, but it's worth a try. I will do everything in my power to make her happy.

"*Tesoro*, do you still want to go to the bonfire?"

"Yes, why?"

"We dozed off. It's near seven. We should get moving." Luckily, the bonfire is at the beach near her condo.

"Do you need to check outside first? Does Jimmy normally hang around for lengthy periods of time when you blow him off?"

She smirks. "No. Typically, he leaves after he asks his questions." I stick my head out my front door and see a few people near the entryway, but I can't determine who they are. "We can just leave out the back."

"That's fine when I'm here, but I don't think that's safe for you alone."

"Not you too. Ugh!"

"What does that mean?"

"Nicholas asked if I wanted him to send Maia or Connor for a while."

"It's not a horrible idea."

"I'll consider it if it gets worse."

I pull her into my arms. Her body against mine makes it difficult to think. Even clothed, I have issues containing my desire for her. Every time we kiss is better than the last. Learning her is fast becoming my favorite pastime. I pull her lower lip between my teeth, nipping gently before dipping my tongue into her mouth. When I draw back, her tongue follows to explore the depths of my mouth. After kissing until we're both searching for air, we gather a blanket and some hoodies for our evening out. Following her out her patio door to the parallel street, we walk back to the beach.

"You made it," Kate says as we approach the raging fire, throwing her arms around Noelle.

"Hi, Kate," Noelle says.

"Kate."

"Cash."

"Seriously, I need you two to get along. Today has been enough," Noelle mutters.

"Truce." I extend my hand to Kate. Noelle hasn't had time to share what happened today, and she likely won't.

"Truce. Just don't hurt her and everything will be fine."

"I won't."

Noelle and I spread our blanket next to Kate and Keyton. I've never been to a bonfire on the beach before. It's fun and relaxing. We sit absorbing the heat from the fire, talking amongst ourselves or simply enjoying the calm. There are four other people, but they're just friends. Kate and Keyton take off for a walk about thirty minutes after we arrive.

"Thank you for inviting me. I've never been to a bonfire before. It's fun." I share with Noelle.

"You're welcome. Really? What else haven't you done before?"

"I'll let you know when you suggest something."

Feeling my phone vibrate in my pocket, I glance at the number.

"Sorry, this is work. I'll be right back." I walk away to take the call. After a brief exchange, I return to the blanket. I sit behind Noelle and pull her against me like on our first date. I don't miss the soft sigh falling from her lips. I have a deep desire to learn what makes her moan every single day.

"Everything okay?" she asks, settling against me. Lavender teases my nose.

"I guess. Mrs. Waller cancelled her return flight."

"Okay. Does that impact you in any way?"

"No. The only change is Mrs. Waller won't be on the plane back to New York on Monday morning." As we finish talking, Kate and Keyton return from their walk. Kate looks flushed. Kate and Noelle jump into a conversation that only the two of them can understand. I thank Keyton again for his help when Noelle was sick and continue to enjoy her warm body in my arms. As the fire dwindles, so does the group. Noelle and I are the second couple to leave.

"Thank you for coming. I know Kate isn't your biggest fan." Noelle shares.

"I think Kate would dislike any man who divides your attention from her."

"Ouch!"

"That wasn't meant as arrogant as it sounded. You're happy and you aren't available for Kate on a whim. At first that's hard on a friendship. Deep down, Kate is happy for you."

Rather than take the risk that Jimmy or someone else is at the front, we enter through her patio. I feel as if we're sneaking around like teenagers breaking curfew.

The next morning, the sun peeks into her bedroom, warming my arm. Noelle is still sleeping, facing me with one arm under her pillow and the other draped over her waist. Her silky red camisole and matching shorts cover almost nothing, especially with the lace accents in appropriate—exposing her breasts—places. Resisting the urge to pull her nipple into my mouth is getting increasingly more difficult. Instead, I place a kiss on the top of her hand, the middle of her forearm, her upper arm, and the cap of her shoulder.

"I love waking up with you," she murmurs, her eyes still closed.

"I love waking up with you." Moving inward, I kiss along the lace edge of her camisole. Goose bumps erupt along her chest, and a soft moan falls from her lips. Her fingertips graze my chest in intoxicating lines. As I drag the thin silk strap down her arm, I latch onto her nipple.

"Cash," she whispers, digging her polished fingernails into my skin.

I draw a circle around her nipple with my tongue while pinching the other one. In a quick movement, Noelle pushes me to my back and straddles my hips. She's deceptively strong. Crossing her arms in front of her, she lifts the camisole over her head.

"Better?" She leans forward, offering herself to my mouth, her auburn tresses framing her flawless face.

Instead of answering her with words, I bite down on her nipple, making her shout my name. I feel her heat through her shorts and mine. Pressing her breasts together, I nip her other pink peak as she rocks against me. When I release her, Noelle moves slowly down my chest, marking every few inches with her hot mouth. Licking my nipple with her tongue, she sends tingles down my spine. She travels down my rib cage to the point of my hip.

The closer she gets to my cock, the higher it jumps. Dipping her hands under the waistband of my shorts, she pulls them down over my feet. Climbing back up, she kisses a path along my leg and inner thigh. The warmth of her tongue touching my shaft has me arching off the bed. She licks upward toward the tip, circling it with her tongue. Holy fuck! As she teases the tip more, I focus on the blue of the sky to prolong these moments of pleasure. After taking me in her mouth, Noelle sucks me deep. I can feel the back of her throat. I lean up onto my forearms to watch her beautiful mouth surrounding me. Each moment brings me closer to my release. Gripping under her arms, I pull her up.

"I wasn't done."

"I know." I'm not a patient man; when I want something I go after it. Pushing her shorts and panties aside, I swipe my fingers up her folds.

"You make me so wet," she murmurs as I bury myself in her core. With wide eyes, she meets me thrust for thrust. Gripping her hips, I lift as she bears down. No one has ever taken me so deep before. Her walls are tightening around my throbbing cock.

"*Tesoro*, come with me." Her hands fist the duvet around my rib cage. As I get closer, so does she. Her rhythm increases to match mine. As I explode inside her in short bursts, her body shudders with pleasure and she plummets over the edge.

She lowers herself, plastering her perfect breasts against my chest, her mouth near the crook of my neck, her soft hair fanned over my arm. I've never felt this way before. There is only one explanation—her. Slowly regulating my breathing, I realize I'm so raptured with her, I didn't use a condom.

"*Tesoro*, I'm sorry."

"What's wrong?"

"I didn't use a condom."

"We. I'm just as much to blame as you are, but I have an IUD." I nod. "Do you need me to move?"

"Not yet."

She nods against my neck, and I draw my hands up and down her back.

After a second round, we make a hearty breakfast and lounge around during the rainy Sunday. Never have I wanted to stay put with a woman. Trapped inside with Noelle makes for a perfect day. Being anywhere with Noelle is unmatched. Unfortunately, tomorrow I need to go back to New York. Near ten we climb into her bed.

Waking to Noelle's mouth on my body the following morning is a fantastic wakeup call despite the fact I need to leave here today. Even though I assure her it isn't necessary, she drives me to the airport for my flight home. A few too many sensual kisses have me rushing through the terminal. I miss her already and it has been less than thirty minutes since her lips caressed mine.

NOELLE

The remainder of the holiday creeps by. I'm out of sorts, and my home feels empty without him. I miss him desperately, and it's only been a few hours. To clear my head, I lace up my shoes and walk around my neighborhood, ending near the pier. I sit on our bench—it's not technically ours, but it is to me. Unfortunately, the beach is bustling with people on this warm, sun-filled day. I'm not able to relax as much as I would like. Returning home, I flow through a long yoga practice to clear my mind. Feeling a bit more zen, I check my messages. I was actually zoned in during my yoga. I didn't hear any of these messages come through.

Kate: Are you free? I want to talk about Keyton.

Me: Yes, I'm free. Are you visiting or calling?

Kate: Visiting. I'll be there in twenty.

Me: Okay.

There is a text from Noah too.

Noah: How are you?

Me: I'm well. You?

Noah: Relaxing today, but work is busy right now.

Me: Good for you. Love you lots.

Noah: Love you lots more.

Finally, there are a few from Cash.

Cash: I miss you already.

Cash: My huge bed will be lonely without you.

Cash: I'll call you later tonight. xoxo

Me: I miss you. My bed will be lonely too. Talk to you later. xoxo

As I finish a bottle of water, Kate comes in through the front door. She looks happy but also has concern on her face as well.

"Hey." Kate says closing the door behind her.

"Hey, yourself."

"Thanks again for coming on Saturday. I know you prefer to stay home in general."

"We had a wonderful time. That was the first bonfire Cash has ever been to."

"That's surprising."

"Maybe a little. What's up?"

Kate bends my ear for the next thirty minutes about how well things are going with Keyton and apologizes for not listening sooner while gushing over his bedroom skills. I tune out most of the details. I won't share any details about me and Cash. She can fill in as she wishes. The best thing about inviting Kate over is that she cooks when she's chatty. A little over an hour after she arrives, she's plating a beef stir-fry for the two of us.

After dinner, Kate scurries home to call Keyton and get ready for her work week. She's a chemist who works in a secure lab. I would be bored to tears with her job, just like she would be pulling her hair out with mine.

I attempt to keep myself busy to ignore the fact I could be unemployed by the end of the day tomorrow. After a short video call with Cash, I snuggle under my sheets to sleep. My pillow smells like Cash, and it helps me slip into dreamland with him as the star.

The moment I arrive at the center the next morning, Sheila asks me to join her in the meeting room. "These papers arrived over the weekend." She hands me the withdrawal papers for Mason from the center signed my Mrs. Sanfilippo. "I'm sorry, Noelle. Your employment here will end at the close of business tomorrow. Please take today and tomorrow to complete reports for the students and complete the termination packet. I'll send you information pertaining to your vacation buyout, sick-time payment, and accrued bonuses by the end of the day."

"Thank you, Sheila."

As she leaves the room, I sink deeper into the office chair. I knew this was coming. All my preparation for this moment doesn't even come close to being enough. I think twice about pulling out my phone, but then realize I don't work here anymore. So what if she sends me packing today instead of tomorrow?

Me: Can you talk?

I barely press send and my phone is ringing.

"Morning, *tesoro*. You didn't even get to check your email, did you?"

"Nope. Mrs. Sanfilippo signed and sent the paperwork on Saturday morning."

"I'm sorry. Even though you knew it could happen, it still feels pretty crappy."

"It does." This center was my first job in my field. It's devastating to lose it due to a mother's failure to see a teacher hell-bent on helping her son.

"What is the plan?"

"I have today and tomorrow to finish my evaluations and reports for the students. Beyond that, I have no idea right now. I'm sorry to lay all of this on you."

"No, I care about you. I always want to be your first and only call whether something is fantastic or awful."

"Thank you. Will you call me tonight after training with Evan?"

"Of course. Talk to you later."

"Bye." I end the call, shoot off a quick text to Kate, and stare at my phone. Taking a deep breath, I pull myself up and leave the meeting room. After a peek in at the classrooms, I clear my inbox, forwarding all the messages to Sheila. I didn't answer any of them, just forwarded them to her. She can deal with all of it now. Gluing myself to my chair, I plow through the reports as efficiently as I can. Near two, I stumble on Mason's and bite the inside of my cheek to stop the tears from falling. The rest of my day is a blur of reports. Arriving home, I polish off some leftovers and fall into my bed.

After a long pep talk with Cash last night, I finish the remaining reports near one on Wednesday. Luckily, I was able to send letters to my students with sweet goodbye messages before Sheila cut off my access to the client list. As I move my personal items to my car, I see Sheila leading a woman into her office. I catch her before she steps inside.

"Who is she?"

"I'm interviewing her to replace you."

"How long have you been interviewing?" I knew she was ruthless, but damn my chair isn't even cold.

"A few weeks. I was going to fire you on Friday regardless of Mason's meltdown. Good luck to you."

I pause only to consider the ramifications of giving her a piece of my mind in front of the candidate for my job and decide there aren't any. "I have held my tongue for the last eight months working for you. Your desire to have only elite clientele in this center has detrimentally impacted the level of education your staff can provide at this center. Your sole focus should be your students, not the bank balances or the political affiliations of their parents and grandparents. You failed Mason Sanfilippo, not me. Good luck finding someone to replace me who will put up with your meddling and inaction." I turn on my heel and stride out the front door of the center. Thankfully, I make it to my car before bawling my eyes out. I pull out of the parking lot and park at the fast-food chain across the street. After a decent, cleansing cry, I drive home.

When I arrive home, I receive a text from Kate indicating she'll be over after work to drink with me. I unload my boxes, setting them on the island. I have a few hours before Kate arrives, so I stroll to the beach. Before Cash, I would just walk around my block a few times rather than trek to the shore. The memories of our time here make him seem closer. In my head, I know that's silly, but my heart feels differently.

That evening, Kate and I drink too much wine. During those few hours, I make a personal plan for the near future. I book a flight and pack my bags while laughing with Kate. My work future, that's a different story. For now, I'm taking a break.

When Cash video calls, I answer on the first ring.

"Hi, sweetheart. How are you?"

I may be tipsy, but my man is hot even through my phone. It feels fantastic to say that—my man.

"I'm so-so. Kate is here, and we had way too much wine. I stopped before she did."

"Is she staying there?"

"Yup, she passed out on the couch. I took her keys away when she got here."

"How are you doing?"

"Even though I knew it was coming, it still hurts."

"I know. What is your plan? I'm sorry I can't see you again this weekend. I'm scheduled to fly."

"I understand. I'm going to visit Nicholas and Kelly in Maine. I want to stop into the store and design a dress with Kelly for the gala. Plus, she raves about the ice cream from a local place. I'm going to leave early tomorrow morning. I'll stay until Sunday at least. Beyond that, I'm not sure."

Maybe I should talk to Cash about where to apply for a new job. There isn't anything keeping me in California except Kate. I love her like a sister, but I can't stay here for her. I need to make choices for my future—ones that ideally include waking up with Cash every morning.

"I'll call you after I get settled in Maine tomorrow."

"I'm sorry I can't be with you right now."

I see resignation on his face about the distance between us. I don't blame him. I feel it too. Maybe I can fix that address problem by searching for a new job closer to Cash. But what happens if his deal is in Texas? Then what? We need to talk about it in depth and soon. Just not today.

"Good night, *tesoro*."

"Good night, Cash."

CASSIUS

I may not be able to be with Noelle until Friday night, but I'm going to make sure she knows I care about her. I didn't share that I'm flying to Maine this weekend. Now, I can surprise her. I'll call Mina first thing in the morning. I also plan to get an update from Stacy as well.

After a restless night's sleep, I drop into my office chair bright and early. Noelle has been on my mind even more so now that I know I will see her tomorrow. I need to set up a few surprises first. I send a quick email to Stacy and clear my inbox. I have an easy day today. Near nine, I text Mina.

Me: When you have a few minutes this morning, could you call me? Nothing's wrong, but I need a favor or two. Maybe a bunch.

I take a trip to the break room for a fresh cup of coffee. As I turn to leave, Kip asks about a photo he saw of me over the weekend.

"Who is the redhead?" he asks, pointing to our photo on the screen. There are a few in the gallery. Thankfully, only I'm tagged.

"My girlfriend. You don't need any details other than she's taken."

"Easy, Cash. We're friends. I'm not looking for her number. Unlike you, I'm not ready to hang up my party shoes. Plus, she's not my type."

"She's brilliant and gorgeous. How is that not your type?"

"Curvy blondes are it for me. I can readily admit, your girlfriend is hot, but she isn't for me. All I mean is you haven't been out with anyone more than once in years. You're also extremely private. It must be serious."

My possessive and protective instinct just came out in full force on Kip. He's aware of my family name and what it means in this city.

"Sorry, she's going through some stuff with her job. We are serious. I tried to avoid the photos, but that's virtually impossible in the city. I wanted to give her a little more time, but that wasn't in the cards."

"I hope it works out for you. You've been happier in the last month or so. I assume it's because of her." I nod. "Good for you. I'll see you in the ring tonight." Kip leaves the break room. While a fourth cup is lot for one morning, I need it today. Myles pops his head into the break room.

"Sir, your sister is on hold for you."

"Thanks, Myles." I hustle back to my office to talk with Mina.

"Hi, sis. How are you?" Since the accident and her leaving New York, my sister is much happier. Peter, her fiancé, pushes her into a state of sheer bliss.

"I'm well. How was your long weekend in the sun?"

"Good. That's partly why I'm calling. First, I made a huge decision. I plan to leave investing and move into flying full-time."

"That's wonderful! Who knows about this?"

"Right now, Sam, Stacy at my firm, and Noelle."

"Who is Noelle?" Mina asks with a hint of glee in her voice.

"Where are you?"

"I'm just outside the Perk."

Luckily, I remember where that is from my visit last year. "Give yourself some room away from other people, please." I give her a second and then admit, "Noelle is my girlfriend."

Squeals come through my phone so loud, I need to pull it away from my ear.

"Are you done?"

"Not yet." She continues her joy in between a myriad of questions about how we met to if I love her. I can't see myself without her, but I'm afraid I'll scare her away if I tell her this soon.

"If you want answers, you need to calm down." Since Mina met Peter, she wants everyone around her to be as deeply in love as she is. It's sweet. Until I met Noelle, it was annoying as hell.

"I'm ready." Mina listens intently as I explain who Noelle is, how we met, and a basic outline up to today. Then she asks, "What can I do for you?"

I explain what I need and give her my credit card number to pull off my requests. I have no idea how Noelle will react, but I don't care. I want to cheer her up a bit.

"Thank you, Mina."

"I'm so happy for you. I can't wait to get to know her better. She and I only talked a short time at the wedding. She's smart, beautiful, kind, and down to earth."

"She's all of those things and more. Are you and Peter free for breakfast on Sunday?"

"I'll clear our schedule if we aren't."

I would too if the situation were reversed. "I'm looking forward to it. I'll see you in a few days. Thanks for your help. I love you bunches."

"See you soon. I love you bunches more."

I end the call with my sister, hoping Noelle doesn't hate surprises or being taken care of. I'm less worried about the surprise than the taken care of part of this plan. I want to give her everything, but she wants to handle it herself. It's endearing and frustrating at the same time. I realize it's counterintuitive to not wanting a corporate wife, but there it is. Can't I desire to take care of her even if she wants to work and take care of herself at the same time?

Me: Good morning, beautiful. Have a safe flight. xoxo

Noelle: Morning. Thanks. I'll call you tonight. xoxo

As my day winds down, I review an email from Stacy. He has two potential deals in the works. He plans to provide me with more details early next week. With that bit of good news, or the potential for good news, I trudge to the gym hoping to get rid of some of this angst.

In the locker room, Kip and Danny are dressing for tonight's session.

"Kip, sorry about earlier."

"No worries. I'm glad you found someone. You've been waiting for the right woman long enough."

"Thanks."

Kip may not be ready to hang up his dancing shoes, but he will one day. We step into the ring, and Kip and I slug it out for almost the full hour. Exhausted, we sit on the bench before heading home. Well, I head home. Kip showers and heads to a bar for an evening out. Good for him. That isn't for me anymore.

You may not know it yet, but I'm coming for you sweetheart.

NOELLE

The flight to Portsmouth is smooth, so smooth I sleep through it. Late nights on the phone with Cash are great, but apparently it is catching up with me. After collecting my luggage, I take an Uber to Kelly's store, So Elegant. As I step into the store, I notice the decor. It's gorgeous. There's a seating area off to one side with white couches and a tufted ottoman near two tablets. The other walls are lined with gorgeous couture dresses in all styles and colors. I've seen Kelly's work, not only on screen, but her wedding gowns. She is a master of design and fabric.

"Good afternoon, welcome to So Elegant. How may I help you?"

"I'm here to see Kelly. Is she available?"

"Kelly isn't available. I'm Billie. Maybe I can help you."

I knew she looked familiar. We spoke at the wedding. Billie is tiny with blonde hair and light eyes. She's Cash's polar opposite.

"Hi, Billie. You may not remember me, but we met at Ellis and Kelly's wedding. I'm Noelle."

"Hi, Noelle. It's good to see you again. Kelly and Ellis left for Paris early this morning for fabric Kelly needs for an upcoming film she's working on."

"Oh, that's unfortunate." While I formulate what to do next and where to stay, I ask, "Are all these designs Kelly's?"

"The designs here are half mine, half Kelly's, depending on the day. Do you need a dress?"

"Yes, your brother invited me to a gala in September. I need a dress."

"That's wonderful. It's an amazing event. I met my fiancé at that event. I can help you design one if you would like. Also, I have a message for you from my brother."

"You do?" Oh, Cash, what have you done? Billie hands me an ivory envelope with my name on the front. How did he pull this off? I shouldn't be surprised. Nicholas pulls off insane feats for Kelly, like getting her favorite ice cream from Maine delivered to their rehearsal dinner in Colorado. This looks like it's handwritten by Cash.

Tesoro,

I'm sorry I can't be there with you right now. With a lot of help from Mina (Billie), I set up a few things for you. Please go and relax, and I'll see you tomorrow night. xoxo

Cash

I do my best not to swoon in front of Billie. He'll be here tomorrow night. I thought he was flying. I was so wrapped up in my own drama, I never asked where. I just know it wasn't to California. I'm an awful girlfriend. I hang my head a bit.

"Whatever you're thinking, forget it."

"Is that a Morgan trait?" I'm shocked she sees I'm chastising myself.

"What?"

"Being able to read people well." I just inadvertently told Billie her brother can read me well.

"No, not even a little. My big brother has a huge heart that he has kept under lock and key waiting for the right woman. After talking with him, I realize he gave it to you. He may not have come out and said it yet, but he will. Whatever you think you missed, forget it. Cash didn't even notice. If he did, he won't mention it. The entire time he and I were planning and talking about you, I could hear his happiness through the phone. Thank you, Noelle."

"I don't know what to say."

"You don't have to say anything. Just take care of him."

"I will." As long as he will have me.

"What type of dress style works for you?"

Billie and I discuss the design for a dress for the gala before I leave the shop. I give her my contact info so she can send me proposed designs in the next week or so. Apparently, part of Cash's plan includes me staying at Billie's condo near the beach. After giving me directions not only to a coffee shop called the Perk but to her condo, Billie hugs me tight.

"I'm thankful you missed your brother's rehearsal and were waiting with Cash."

"I am too."

Billie hands me a set of keys, her business card with her cell phone number, and a bag with two more envelopes and a gift box.

"This bag came with the first note. I'll see you on Sunday for breakfast." Apparently, I have a breakfast date with Billie and presumably her fiancé.

"Thank you, Billie. For everything."

"You're welcome. Have a wonderful time."

I make a quick stop into the Perk, which Billie recommended. It's cute and decorated like Central Perk from the show *Friends*. A bubbly young woman named Becca waits on me.

With a maple walnut scone and a latte in hand, I pull my luggage behind me to Billie's condo. As I walk, I absorb the smell of the ocean off to my left. Around the corner there's a quaint village with shops and restaurants. It's wonderful here. The pace is much slower than home. A decent amount of people mill around past dinnertime this evening.

As I step into Billie's condo, the scent of flowers hits my nose. There are yellow roses with red tips as well as red roses. The red outnumbers the yellow. The arrangements have the yellow near the top increasing down to the red. I have a suspicion I need to research the meaning of the colors. After circling the room and smelling the flowers, I open the gift bag Billie gave me.

There are two more envelopes and a box. I open the envelope marked number two. Inside is an appointment card for a day spa for a massage, manicure, and pedicure for tomorrow at ten in the morning.

Me: Can you talk?

Almost instantly, my phone rings.

"Hi, *tesoro*." His deep velvety voice is amazing, especially when he calls me that.

"Hi."

"I'm sorry I didn't ask where you were flying."

"Don't be. You have other things on your mind. Plus, it made my surprises possible. Did you cheat?"

"No. The third envelope and the box are still sealed." Now, even more, I'm contemplating what could be in that box. The wrapping is nondescript.

"Thank you. You can open it tomorrow afternoon. How was designing with Billie?"

"Your sister is amazing. You weren't kidding when you said she was opposite of you. Her design style is a little trendier than I usually prefer, but we'll see what she comes up with."

"Billie will design something that works for you. She designed Della's wedding gown outside of her normal style. Just be honest with her, and you'll love what she creates."

"I don't need all of this, Cash." No one has ever been this thoughtful before.

"Need, maybe not. Deserve, absolutely. Please go and relax, and I'll be there as soon as I can after my flight."

"I'm not very good at this."

"Neither am I. I never wanted to be until you."

Holy hockey! "I'll see you tomorrow. Good night, Cash."

"Good night, *tesoro*. Sweet dreams."

I sigh as I push the end button. My heart feels like it may explode. I've fallen for Cassius Morgan completely and unapologetically.

After smelling the roses, literally, a little longer, I change into comfy clothes and curl up on the couch on Billie's balcony. She has an amazing view of the ocean, which is directly across the street. It's so peaceful here, even with the vacationers walking on the street below. I can only imagine the calm during the winter. Even though I slept on the plane, I turn in early for the night.

The smell of the ocean wafts in through the doors of the master bedroom. I understand why Billie chose this condo. Taking my morning coffee to the balcony, I inhale deeply. My phone chimes with a text message.

Cash: Good morning, gorgeous. I can't wait to kiss you. xoxo

Me: Morning. Me either. xoxo

I smile and dress for my trip to the spa. Cash truly outdid himself with this surprise. This day spa is tranquil, quiet, and exactly what I needed. I need to thank Billie for helping Cash too. Almost four hours later, I'm relaxed, my fingernails and toenails polished to perfection, and pampered just enough.

Now, what to do with myself until Cash arrives. After stopping in for an iced coffee, I round the building to see if Billie is in. This coffee shop would make a serious dent in my wallet and be problematic for my waistline if I lived here.

"Welcome to So Elegant. I'm Poppy. How can I help you?"

"Hi is Billie here?"

"Yes, may I ask your name?"

"Noelle."

Poppy is a tiny woman with a dark, pixie haircut and colorful clothes. She must be another one of Kelly's designers. I wonder what her design style is. Kelly's is a modern twist on classic designs. Billie is a bit trendier with sharper lines.

"Hi, Noelle," Billie says, pulling me into a tight hug.

"I came to thank you in person. Your condo is delightful. That terrace is a slice of heaven at any time of the day."

"You're welcome. It is. It's why I bought it. I'll do anything for my brothers. To date, planning your surprises has been the most fun favor I've ever done. I'm glad you went. You look relaxed and pampered, which is exactly what Cash wanted for you."

"I am. I'm not used to being treated well." Again, I spill a bit of truth about Cash and me.

"I remember that feeling. Thinking 'He's too good to be true. It won't last.'" I nod. "Peter completely blew every other man I dated out of the water. I don't mean he went overboard every time, but he pays attention. I'm trying to say Cash cares about you, and you clearly feel the same. Did you open the box yet?"

"No, he asked me to wait until later today. Do you know what's in the box, Billie?"

"I don't. I'm curious though."

"That's too bad. I'm dying to know."

The phone on the counter rings and Poppy answers it, indicating the call is for Billie.

"I'll see you on Sunday. Thank you so much." I hug her quickly and slip out the door. Rounding the building again, I walk along the shore in the shallow water. It's slightly overcast, so the beach isn't overly crowded. Only diehards come to the beach with overcast skies. After a few trips to the end of the sand and back, I return to Billie's deck.

Cash didn't miss anything in his planning. Along with the flowers, spa treatments, and gift I have yet to open, Cash made sure I had everything I needed. The fridge is full, and so is the wine rack. There are some advantages to having obscene wealth. The key is when to use it and when to hold back. Near six, I can't take it anymore. I waited longer than he asked. Pulling the wrapped boxed out of the bag, I shake it once. No sound. Hmmm.

Tesoro,

I want to look, touch, strip off, and taste when I get there.

Cash

Holy hell! Heat rushes to my core just thinking about him doing those things to me. I tear open the wrapping to find a box with a large LP on the lid. I have no clue where this box is from. Pushing back the tissue reveals a gorgeous set of laced-trimmed, gray silk pajamas, a chemise, panties, bra, and a matching robe. The label says La Perla. He went all out. I immediately send Cash a text.

Me: I opened the box. Where are you?

CASSIUS

The moment I get to my rental car, my phone chimes with a text from Noelle.

Me: I'm on my way.

I drive as fast as I can without getting pulled over. Not only am I excited to see her, but I'm equally interested in seeing my gift on her. Parking in Billie's assigned spot, I hurry upstairs. Blood rushes through my veins, and my heart is racing.

After unlocking the door, I set my bag near the side table and search for Noelle. She's a vision standing on the terrace looking at the ocean.

Approaching the threshold, I say, "*Tesoro*, turn around." As if time is standing still, she slowly turns to look at me.

"I missed you so much." She steps forward into the living room. My sexy bombshell slides her hands up my chest before cupping my cheeks.

"I missed you." I take my first taste of her today. Sealing my mouth over hers, I tease her with my tongue. I savor her in my arms. The silk skimming over her curves is luxuriously soft. Lowering her hands, she tugs my shirt out of my waistband. Her fingertips dip below the hem, heating my skin with her touch. I drag my palms up her outer thigh, gathering the robe at the same time. As my hands climb higher, I fail to feel anything other than her creamy soft skin. She pushes lightly on my chest, taking a step backward.

Everything around me just falls away. I can only hear my heart pounding in my ears as she unties the silken sash nipping her waist. I move forward, cutting the space between us in half. Her robe splits open only enough to give me a peek of the curve of her breasts down to the apex of her thighs until she drops the robe to the bend of her elbows. I tear my shirt over my head before caressing her skin down from the center of her breasts to her clit.

Her head falls back as my fingertips travel lower. Gripping her hip, I turn her away from me. A noticeable moan escapes her lips. I toe off my shoes, kicking them to the side without releasing my possessive grip on the flesh at her hip. I ease off my pants and boxer briefs, pushing them aside. Noelle lowers her arms, letting the robe pool around her feet. Drawing her against me, I press my arousal against her heart-shaped ass. Teasing her nipple with my fingers, I move my other hand inward from her hip. I skim my fingers over her sex.

Widening her stance Noelle invites me to touch her, her arm over her head gripping the back of my neck. Slick heat meets my fingers as I delve deep into her core. Plunging in and out, I curve my digits to hit the perfect spot to push her to the edge of pleasure. Her hips move against me as she gets closer and closer to her first release of the day. As her muscles tighten around my fingers, I trail a path across her back with my mouth. A whimper echoes around us as she shakes in my arms.

When the shudders subside, I take a large step forward, guiding her over the arm of a chair. Lowering to my knees, I flatten my tongue against her folds. Her hand fists the throw blanket draped over the chair the moment my tongue touches her core. I lift her leg onto the ottoman to open her more to me. Nipping her nub, I draw my fingers up and down her folds. With each pass, she rocks deeper against me. As her hips push harder, I lick, suck, and nip faster.

"Holy fuck, Cash!"

Curse words fall from her pouty lips as she convulses above me in the throes of a second orgasm. As she relaxes, I sit back on my heels and stand. When she turns to face me, I scoop her into my arms and carry her to the bedroom. I lower her to the bed with her legs dangling off the side. Settling between her thighs, I press the tip of my cock against her hot center.

"Open your eyes. I want to watch them change as I bury myself inside you."

Her eyes widen, staring deep into mine. I push forward into her with one hard, deep thrust. A look of heat and something else stares back at me. Noelle hooks her ankles around my hips, drawing me even deeper. I've never felt carnal pleasure like this with anyone but her. Only her. I start to move, and she meets me each time with equal pressure. Her walls tighten around me as I throb inside her.

"Let go with me," I say before emptying inside her with hot bursts. Her thighs quake as she trembles with pleasure around me as I lower myself on top of her. I grip her waist and climb onto the bed with her. Rolling us to our sides, I brush my lips against hers.

"Hearing you curse is sexy as fuck. I want to make you come every single day just to hear you swear."

She buries her face into the crook of my neck. "I'm game if you are," she replies, her face blushing as she looks up at me.

"Oh, I am. I don't like being away from you," I confess. I don't know where I will end up, but I know I want her with me.

"I don't like being away from you either. Thank you for today. You really didn't need to do all of this for me. Although, the lingerie is exceptional. Over the top and crazy expensive, I'm sure, but perfect. How did you get the right size?"

"You mean aside from painstakingly memorizing your curves every time I touch you or taste you?"

She smirks. "Your hands and mouth are skillful."

"That's all?" I raise an eyebrow.

"No, that's not all. Do you really need your ego stroked right now? We're naked and still catching our breath."

Laughing, I confess, "I asked Kate. I wanted it to be right."

"Wow, she didn't tattle. I'm shocked. Glad but shocked. How was your flight?"

"Too long."

"How is that possible? You only came from New York."

"I wanted to skip it to be with you."

She leans up, pressing her lips to mine before settling on my chest, her arm draped over me. "Have you heard from Stacy yet?"

"He sent me an update yesterday. I'm meeting with him early next week. He has two potential options for me to review."

"That's great! I'm so proud of you for taking the leap toward what you love."

"A brilliant, gorgeous, kind woman who I care about very much made me realize that I should chase my happiness and never settle because we never know how much time we have left."

"She sounds amazing," she replies with a grin on her face.

"She is." I lean forward, kissing the top of her head. "How are you doing?"

She sighs deeply before answering. "I did everything I could to help Mason and keep my job. I'm sad, but there was nothing more to be done."

"I know you did. What are you thinking going forward?"

"Honestly, I can go anywhere, do anything."

"What does your dream job look like?" I wonder if the center was what she wanted or if she had other aspirations.

"It doesn't matter. I can't afford to make my dream happen."

"Humor me. What does your dream job look like?" I might be able to help her if she is willing to do some work. The issue is going to be where I end up.

"I would open a center for kids like Mason, a specialized center focused on students with developmental delays who need individual plans and care with a focus of providing early intervention and support once they are school age."

"Impressive. Why do you think you couldn't afford to open a center like that? You've clearly thought through what you want to do, who your clients would be, and there is a need for a center that caters to those students."

"It was never something I thought could be done without some real-world experience and some business know-how that I don't possess."

"I do." I'm treading lightly here. I didn't know her answer would fall right into a spot that I have exceptional aptitude.

"What are you saying?"

I'm unsure if she is upset or genuinely intrigued. "If you want to look at all of your options, including your dream job of opening or buying a center, I can help you with the aspects you need assistance with, like financing and business know-how."

"I won't take your money, Cash."

"I know, which is why I didn't offer it. I love your fierce independence. It's attractive." It's also another reason I care about her. She isn't a gold digger like other women who would want to date me. In fact, she pushed me to follow my own dream, which will require a hit to my portfolio and a pay cut, at least in the short-term. "Will you at least consider it as an option?"

"I didn't think it was even a possibility. I'll consider it."

"Thank you. That's all I ask."

"Did you eat?" She looks up at me.

"No. I needed to get here. I wanted to be here sooner. I loathe the fact that you live across the country from me."

After my response, she pushes up, sealing her mouth on mine. Rolling, I hover over her, kissing her without reservation. When I break away, my chest tightens at the realization that I will never tire of kissing this spectacular woman. I'm head over heels for her.

"I'm not a fan of how far away I live from you either. You should eat. I'm sure the groceries you had delivered include something we can eat or cook. Plus, I'm hungry."

"I won't wither away. I don't want to let you go just yet."

"I'm not asking you to let me go. I don't want you to, but I want to take care of you too."

I can't argue with her logic. For me taking care of her today includes ordering groceries, a spa day, and sultry lingerie. For her it means making sure I eat something. I press my lips to hers again before relenting.

NOELLE

Sliding out of under Cash's arm, I pull on my robe before padding to the kitchen for some coffee. With a fresh cup in hand, I curl up on the terrace. I feel his presence before he says anything.

"Morning, *tesoro*. Do you need more?" Cash leans down to kiss me, the scruff on his chin pricking my skin.

"Yes, but I can make it."

"Stay there. I'll bring you a fresh cup when I join you."

I hand him my empty cup. This area is calm perfection with the ocean breeze, the cute little shops, and the lack of photographers. It's peaceful.

"What going on in your beautiful mind?" Cash asks, handing me a refilled cup.

"I have been here for roughly two days, but the people, the pace, and the calm are unsettling, in a good way. The slower pace is a welcome change." Sidling up next to me, Cash takes a big sip of his coffee before answering.

"I felt that the moment I visited Mina for the first time. We ate our lunch in peace. No one stopped to ask how my parents were, no one asked for business advice, and no photographers skulked in the corners hoping to learn who my lunch date is."

"Do you have a preference where your new home is?" I ask, knowing it's on my mind as well.

"Honestly?"

"Always. I expect nothing less."

"I realize it's soon, but I want to be where you are. When I have more information from Stacy about the options, I would like your opinion."

"I want to be with you too. In fact, would you be opposed to sharing your bed for a while?"

"Again?" His face falls slightly as he shakes his head.

"What do you mean? Oh, our second date. Sorry. Wait, you were going to ask me to come to New York?"

"Noelle, will you come to New York with me on Sunday?"

"You and your traditional norms. Yes, I'll come stay with you in New York while I search for a job."

He sets his cup on the side table and kisses me boneless. How am I going to function each day when he kisses me like that? *Isn't that exactly what you want? Yes, absolutely, yes!*

"While I appreciate your exceptional kissing abilities and welcome more and often, I was asking something a bit more in depth. Do you want to live in a big city, would you prefer somewhere like here, the middle of nowhere, or somewhere in between?" I turn to face him, placing my legs over his thighs.

Absently, he drags his fingers up and down my legs while he considers his answer. "As long as—"

"I'll ask in smaller parts. Do you want kids?"

"Yes."

"How many? One or five?"

"At least a boy and a girl. If that takes five, five it is. My only caveat is she must be as gorgeous as her mother."

My heart and my ovaries just exploded at the same time. It's as if he can hear my innermost thoughts. Word for word, that would be my answer to the same question. I attempt to speak but fail.

"Did I lose you with five?" Concern laces his tone. "*Tesoro*, please tell me. You've never been unable to talk to me. Please don't start now, especially with this discussion."

I inhale and slowly exhale while formulating my answer and decide to stick with my complete honesty policy. "If you asked me that exact question, my answer would mirror yours."

Cash leans forward and kisses me, his kiss laced with every ounce of his desire for our future. He may not have come out and said the three tiny, all-powerful words, but he's telling me with his mouth. No image of my future doesn't include Cash every day.

"Ask me something difficult. I can handle anything with you beside me." He resumes brushing my legs with his fingertips. Each pass creeps higher.

"Do you want to raise your family in a big city?"

"No, but where this deal is will play a role in how far outside a major city we can live." He just said *we*. "What about you?"

"Growing up in Colorado with a yard and a dog was amazing. We were close enough to major city amenities like shopping, dining, and an airport. However, the proximity I have to the shore in California is wonderful. Just like here."

"Does it need to be an ocean or just water? Do you want waterfront or simply easy access to walk the shore? Will a lake work?"

"I haven't really thought about it in depth. If I needed to rank the type of water—ocean then lake."

Content with my answer, Cash moves to get up for more coffee. "Another?" He lifts his cup. I nod. "What do you want to do today?"

"I've never been here before. I would like to find Dunne's Ice Cream. Kelly raves about it. Otherwise, I'm open to explore wherever."

"I can share the places Mina took me to when I visited her."

When Cash steps away to get another cup of coffee, I move to the railing. People dot the beach for a morning walk or jog. Am I out of my mind going to New York? Normally, I would ask Kate, but it's still early at home and she'll tell me I'm crazy. I've never felt like I do with him, and it keeps getting stronger.

After a second cup, Cash and I opt to walk the beach. Absorbing the sunlight, cool water, and the sand between my toes hand in hand with my gorgeous man is helpful for my mental health. Losing my job is hard to wrap my head around. Even though I did everything in my power, I still lost. Next, we visit the Nubble Lighthouse and Dunne's. The views at the lighthouse are breathtaking and serene. As we walk up the steep driveway, the majestic lighthouse is straight ahead. It's a stunning sight. The rock outcroppings diffuse the ocean water battering against it. Cash stands behind me, his arms around me, hands clasped at my waist.

"How are you doing?" His ability to know when I need support is uncanny.

"It hurts. It's only been a few days. I have to figure out where to look and consider your suggestion more in depth."

He nods against my shoulder. "I'm here to help you when you want to talk more or ask questions."

"Thank you."

Cash guides me to the bench. We listen to the water hit the rocks before making our way back to the car.

The menu at Dunne's is extensive. Choosing our ice cream flavor for lunch may prove difficult. According to Kelly, the mocha chip and Maine blueberry are to die for. Billie recommends the chocolate extreme.

"What can I get for you?" the perky blonde asks as I step to the window. I notice her gaze shift off to my left where Cash is standing. Sometimes I catch a glimpse of him and wonder how on earth I landed a guy that hot.

"I'll take a scoop of Maine blueberry and one maple walnut."

"And for you, sir?" she stumbles over her question as Cash moves closer to the window.

Stare all you want honey, he's mine. Every tall, dark, and absurdly sculpted inch of him.

"I'll have a cookies and cream and chocolate extreme." After Cash pays for our lunch, we move to the end of the counter to wait for our order. With our dishes in hand, we grab a table. Cash sits next to me, straddling the bench facing me.

"Wow, Kelly was right. This is amazing!" I savor the ice cream on my spoon. So much so that I lick the spoon clean. I immediately take a second spoonful and lick the spoon clean again. Cash sets his hand on my hip, forcing me to look at him.

"You can't eat like that in public. It makes me want to do things to you that aren't appropriate," he whispers.

I lean even closer to him. "Like what?" I drag my tongue along the shell of his ear.

"*Tesoro*." Hearing him call me that is one thing, but hearing it laced with sexual desire is so much more. "I'll show you tonight. Please behave."

"I'll do my best, but I make no promises that I won't turn you on in public."

"You will fail miserably if that is your benchmark. I'm turned on whenever I'm close enough to hold your hand."

Sweet mercy! I would give anything to talk to my mom right now. To ask her how she knew my dad was the one for her. I only have one person who comes close—Mabel. I'll call her soon.

CASSIUS

Showing Noelle the area like I live here is fun. I'm thankful Mina took me around when I visited her last year. After our trip to the lighthouse and for ice cream, we wander around the quaint village before eating dinner at the inn.

"Have you been here before?" Noelle asks over her menu.

"Yes. Mina brought me here when I visited her." An older woman, thin and well dressed, and an older man dressed in a suit approach our table. Clearly, they are on a date.

"Noelle, what are you doing here?" the woman asks.

"Mabel?" Noelle jumps out of her chair, throwing her arms around the woman. "I came to visit Nicholas, but he's travelling with Kelly. What are you doing here?"

"Since Nicholas spends much of his time here now, so do I. Although, now that he's married, he doesn't really need me to make sure he eats well. Plus, Samuel and I have been seeing each other for a while."

"Happy looks gorgeous on you," Mabel says, releasing Noelle.

"Noelle Barnett. It's a pleasure to meet you." Noelle extends her hand to him.

"Samuel Cavallaro," the man introduces himself.

Cavallaro. That sounds familiar.

"Cavallaro? Are you related to Kelly, Norah, and Joseph?" Noelle asks.

"They are my children," Samuel replies.

"Nice to meet you. Mabel and Samuel, please meet my boyfriend, Cash Morgan."

It feels fantastic to be introduced like that. Standing from my chair, I shake Samuel's hand just before Mabel pulls me into a huge hug.

When Mabel releases me, Samuel inquires, "Any relation to Billie?"

"She's my younger sister."

"It's a pleasure to meet you. I've heard wonderful things about you and your brothers." I don't miss his failure to mention my parents. I nod to acknowledge his statement and lack of statement at the same time.

"Would you like to join us?" Noelle asks.

"No, thank you, dear. We just finished our meal. It was lovely to meet you, Cash." Mabel hugs me again.

"Take care of her," she whispers while hugging me. I nod as she releases me. I will as long as she will have me.

After they leave, our server approaches with our drinks and takes our dinner order.

"What did she say to you?"

"She asked me to take care of you."

"That's interesting."

"Why is that interesting?" I imitate her voice.

"Are you sure you want to mock me? Do you recall the last time that happened?"

"Yes, I do. The last time I mocked you, we shared our first mind-blowing kiss."

Her face changes before my eyes. *I'm right there with you, tesoro.* I just hope one of us doesn't have to compromise too much to make it happen. I understand compromise will be necessary, but can each of us chase our bliss and end up together?

"Cash."

I lean forward, brushing my lips across hers. "Why is it interesting, sweetheart?" I bring us back to the topic at hand.

"Your sister asked me the same thing."

"It's nice to know others can see us too."

"Yes, it is."

Our server arrives with our dinners, and we enjoy our meal while discussing our ideal place to live in more detail. Honestly, all of it could be moot depending on what Stacy finds for me. The hard question is whether I could pass up on an ideal situation because it won't work for the woman who urged me to seek out the same opportunity. The woman who speaks to my heart on a level far beyond words.

A more pressing reality is Noelle is coming to stay with me tomorrow. I've been wracking my brain, wondering how or if I should approach the idea of having security for her when she goes out. Predicting the behavior of photographers and paparazzi is one thing I've never been able to do. I hope it isn't necessary, but at the very least, Ellis has already approached the idea of security with Noelle. If I urge her to follow through, she may not push back so harshly.

"Cash." Hearing Noelle call me pulls me out of my thoughts. "Do you want dessert?"

"Not from here."

The instant she processed my words, her face turns from flawless to pink in a flash. I hand our server my card. Her return seems to be taking much longer than necessary. I'm sure Noelle's fingertips running up the inside of my thigh under the table might have increased my urgency to leave. I scribble my name on the receipt and rise from my chair, threading my fingers with hers.

"I had no idea I was that irresistible," I murmur in her ear as we step onto the sidewalk for the short walk to my sister's.

"Are you sure about that?" she asks, raising her eyebrow. She is untucking my shirt the moment the door snicks closed. As we dance toward the bedroom, articles of clothing line the floor. As much as I would like to savor her, an entire day of her touching me and being near me has frayed my resolve. The heat from her fingers gliding up my thigh at dinner snapped the grip I had on my desire for her. I need to feel her writhe in my arms. Now.

"Cash, I want you now."

"As you wish, *tesoro*." I thrust deep into her hot, wet center to the root, only to pull out and bury myself deep until we both fall over the edge of pleasure in unison.

The sheer amount of need that I have for her rocks me to the core. Never have I felt this way about a woman before, and I refuse to let her go. Not only does she have a body made for sin, one I fully intend to study in excruciating detail for the rest of my life, but her mind is equally as impressive. After a second round, we collapse into bed until our breakfast with my sister and Peter.

After following Mina's directions, we arrive at Rick's. The restaurant is located on the ground floor not too far from the condo. Mina leaps into my arms as we approach the table.

"I'm so happy to see you here." She releases me and hugs Noelle. Peter and I exchange a handshake before taking our seats.

"Thank you so much for letting us use your condo. The location is wonderful," Noelle says.

"Anytime," Billie replies with a smile.

After a long perusal of the menu, we place our orders. I chat with Peter about his work and their new home. When he proposed to Mina, he not only did it with a ring but with the ocean view home of her dreams. Noelle and Mina are chatting on their side of the table, giggling like high school besties. Whatever they're talking about made Noelle blush. I'm glad they get along well. Both deserve another solid friend in their lives.

After breakfast, Noelle and I hurry back to the condo and pack to fly to New York. Fortunately, there was space on my flight, so Noelle didn't have to travel alone. However, she's mostly on her own for the actual flight because no one can enter the cockpit. After the other passengers deplane, I escort Noelle to the tarmac and complete a final check of the plane before turning it over to the crew.

Near six, I pull into my parking spot. This time, Noelle isn't nervous. She's happy. I pull our luggage out of the truck before opening her door.

When we enter the lobby, Arthur addresses her first. "Good evening, Miss Barnett. Mr. Morgan."

"Hi, Arthur. How are you and Eloise? Ella and Valentina?"

"We're well. Thank you for asking."

"You're welcome. Good night."

"Good night."

We empty our luggage and change out of our travel clothes. Noelle tucks herself into my side on the couch on my terrace. This is what I want. She is what I need. Every. Single. Day.

"What is your plan for tomorrow?"

"I need to update my resume again, and I'll need to shop for some clothes. I only packed for a few days."

"The keys are in the far left-hand drawer of the island. Make sure you bring your card with you too."

"Do you have food, or do I need to grocery shop too?" I love that she wants to do that, but she doesn't have to.

"My groceries get delivered every Monday. You don't need to wait for them."

She nods and snuggles deeper into my side. A few hours later, after the sun falls beneath the horizon leaving behind a dark sky with twinkling stars, we cuddle in my bed until morning.

NOELLE

My reality creeps back in slowly. I'm unemployed with no prospects on the horizon given I don't even know where I should look, but I'm snuggled deep into Cash's luxurious bed. Moving my arm, I realize he's no longer in bed. It's a workday after all. He needs to go to work. When I open my eyes, I find him staring as he leans against the door.

"Morning, gorgeous." He moves to sit on the edge of his bed.

"Morning."

He's already showered. Either his bodywash or cologne smells fresh first thing the morning. I want to open each button of his perfectly pressed shirt and drag him back down to his bed with me.

"I love having you in my bed looking like sin first thing in the morning. Your hair cascading over my pillow, the small of your back exposed, and one of your cute feet peeking out from the bottom."

"Too bad you need to leave; you look pretty hot yourself right now."

"The suit does it for you?"

"I don't need the suit, but it does tick your hot level up a bit. I may need to skip panties for the gala to handle seeing you in a tux."

"Holy hell! You can't tempt me like that, or I'll never get to the office on time."

We won't make it to the gala either. I consider behaving, but that isn't me. I reach up, sliding my hand around his neck and pulling him down to my mouth. I kiss him deeply before reluctantly releasing him. I want this every morning. I need him.

He stares at me for a moment before speaking. "I'll call you later, near lunch. Have a great day."

"You too." I reel in my desire to keep him here with me. Realizing more sleep isn't in the cards, I pull on my robe and pad to the kitchen for coffee.

I find him already in the kitchen. Apparently, he had the same idea as me.

"You didn't have to get up this early. Want a cup?"

"Yes, please. I can't go back to sleep now. I'll work out and then shop." After setting a cup beside me, Cash fills his and pulls me against him.

"I'm going to have to get up earlier," he murmurs against my mouth before kissing me again.

I pull his lower lip between my teeth.

He groans before pulling away. "So much earlier," he mutters softly as he grabs his coffee and walks with purpose to the door. I restrain myself long enough for him to step outside. It would be in poor form for him to be late the first day we wake up together.

After a long yoga practice, I dress for shopping. I search for the closest shopping mall and realize that I have to use his car. Staring at the keys in the drawer, I remind myself it's just a car. Yes, he has as much money as Nicholas, but it's just a car. It likely costs insanely more than mine, but it's still just a car. I grab the keys to the BMW and my purse. I verify that my card is inside before stepping into the elevator. I wave to Arthur as I round the corner to the garage elevator.

Pushing my nerves aside, I familiarize myself with the car and input the address for the mall. Giving myself a pep talk, I put the car in reverse and head out. I hit a few department stores and grab an iced coffee. I consider downing it instead of taking the risk of spilling it in his car but decide to savor it. My phone rings while I'm driving back to Cash's. I let it go to voice mail.

"Good afternoon, Miss Barnett. Do you need some assistance with those?" Arthur greets me upon my return.

"Hi, Arthur. No, thanks. I'm fine. Have a good day."

"You too," he replies with a smile.

After setting the bags on the island, I put the keys away and check my phone. There are some texts and a voice mail. I respond to the texts first.

Nicholas: How are you? Billie told Kelly you came to Maine. I'm sorry we weren't there.

Me: I should've called first. I was upset about my job and needed to leave. I'm hanging in there. I'm in New York with Cash for now.

Nicholas: Let me know if you need anything. Love you lots.

Me: Love you lots too.

I shove my phone in my pocket and grab the bags. After putting away my purchases, I pull out my computer before answering Kate.

Me: As far as Cash, things are amazing. Work, finding a job – not so much.

Kate: Do you have a plan yet? When are you coming home?

Me: I'm in New York for a little while. I want to see Nicholas.

Kate: Didn't you just go to Maine?

Me: He's in Paris with Kelly.

Kate: Oh. You won't be back by Thursday.

Me: Probably not. How is Keyton?

Kate: I should have given in so long ago. The things he does with his tongue. He's gifted.

Me: TMI, Kate. TMI.

Kate: LOL. Nothing to share about Cash?

Me: Nope.

Even though Kate is my bestie, I'm not sharing anything about how amazing Cash is, especially in bed.

Kate: Gotta get into the lab. TTYS.

With a water in hand, I set up my laptop on the outdoor dining table. As it boots up, I listen to the voice mail.

"Good morning. This is Georgia Waller, Mason Sanfilippo's grandmother. I contacted Sheila at the center, and she indicated she let you go. I would like to speak with you about a job opportunity. Please call me back at your earliest convenience."

I jot down her number and stare at my phone as if an explanation is somehow hidden within its depths. A myriad of options and questions float through my head. How on earth did she get her daughter to change her mind about me? Why is she calling me from New York? The list continues into a deep hole of what-ifs. As my mind spirals, my phone rings in my hand.

"Hi, *tesoro*. How was your morning?"

"Successful on the shopping front. You?"

"Just a normal Monday. I'm meeting with Stacy in a little bit to see his progress. We can talk about it over dinner. Could you take out some chicken or pork?"

"Sure. Mrs. Waller just left me a voice mail. Did you have anything to do with it?"

"No, I didn't."

There is a slight edge to his response. He wouldn't lie, so it's something else. Perhaps apprehension that I don't want to stay. I thought I was clear on my feelings about that. Maybe not. It wouldn't bother me if he did reach out to Mrs. Waller on my behalf. I don't want to go home. I want to be here with him. Who cares how I get a new job?

"Did I ask something wrong?" I inquire, knowing that talking is the only way to move forward.

"No, why?"

"I hear something off in your voice. I don't care if you did call Mrs. Waller. I was just asking."

"I didn't. I was concerned because I asked about owning a center of your own. I don't want to push you, but I also don't want you to leave either."

"I don't want to leave, Cash. Other than you, everything else in my life feels off balance. I haven't decided against my own center yet. There are so many issues with that. We can talk more in depth when you get home."

"Okay, sweetheart. It's time to meet with Stacy. I'll see you later."

I end the call and reach out to Mrs. Waller, leaving her a voice mail. When I hang up, I hear ringing like a phone, but don't know where it's coming from. I realize too late; it's the intercom for Arthur. I push the button to recontact.

"Good afternoon, Miss Barnett."

"Hi. I didn't know how to answer. I think I hung up on you. I apologize."

"No problem. The grocery delivery is here. Would you like me to send it up?"

"Yes, thank you."

After accepting and putting away the groceries, I head back outside to work on my resume. As I make the updates, I consider my options for opening my own center. It would be a dream come true. *How much compromise will it take to have him and my career? Is it even possible?* The sound of my ringtone pulls me out of my head.

"Hello."

"Miss Barnett, this is Georgia Waller. Thank you for returning my call."

"You're welcome."

"I'm reaching out for a few reasons. I want to apologize for my daughter's behavior. She was never able to handle Mason's disability well. I read your proposal to assist Mason with his developmental delays. I'm impressed. I would like to meet with you to discuss implementing your ideas."

"Mrs. Waller, thank you for the call. An apology isn't necessary. Did you say 'was'?"

"Yes, my daughter died of an aneurysm about a week ago."

Holy fuck! She must have sent the withdrawal papers just before she died. I wasn't a fan of Mrs. Sanfilippo's handling of her son's disability or her temperament, but I never wished her ill will.

"I'm sorry for your loss."

"Thank you. I would like to set up a teleconference with you to discuss how I can help Mason."

"Do you live in New York?"

"Yes, why?"

"It's a long story, but I'm in New York right now as well. Would you prefer to meet in person?"

"That would be lovely. Does tomorrow at ten in the morning work for you?"

"Yes, that's fine."

Mrs. Waller gives me her address, and we end the call. I have no idea what this opportunity entails, but I'm intrigued. I finish the edits to my resume and change into my bathing suit to catch some rays while waiting for Cash to get home.

CASSIUS

I'm not a clock watcher, never had reason to be, yet I'm mentally ticking off the seconds until it's a reasonable time to rush home to her. My day wasn't overly taxing. Stacy presented me with two options. One is absolutely not a sound deal; the second might be a maybe. Noelle and I need to talk more in depth.

After a brief chat with Arthur, I ride up to my home. As the doors open, I notice it's eerily quiet, as if she isn't home. I love thinking of this as her home. For me, she is my home. Tugging off my tie, I scan the kitchen and find pork in a water-filled bowl in the sink. I step into the bedroom finding jeans and a blouse on the bed. My pulse starts to race imagining water running over her lush breasts, down her smooth belly to…. The shower is off.

Setting my tie and jacket on the bed with her clothes, I glance outside. Holy mother of… Noelle is lying on the chaise in a teeny red bikini. The curve of her breasts is barely contained by the triangles of fabric that should be secured at her neck—they aren't. My gaze follows her taut abdomen to another scrap of fabric, which—in my opinion—also fails to cover enough of her. Never once have I been this protective and possessive of a woman. My woman. Even as I slide the door open, she doesn't stir.

"You will not wear that anywhere else," I order, stepping beside the chair,

effectively blocking the sunlight.

"You aren't the boss of me." She opens her hazel eyes wide.

"Try harder. One of your students could create a better retort than that."

A flicker of sadness creeps into her eyes, but just as quickly it's gone. "Are you just going to gawk or kiss me?"

Straddling the chair, I lift her legs, setting them on the deck. Lowering myself to the chair, I lean forward and press my mouth to her hip and travel upward to her lips, pausing to properly savor her nipples.

"Can we do this every day?" she murmurs against my lips.

"Yes, I want to come home to you every day. But my earlier statement stands; you will not wear this bikini anywhere but here."

"A tad possessive, don't you think?" There is a slight hitch in her voice.

"It's not possessive when you're already mine. It's protective."

"Yours, huh?"

"Yes, mine." I explore her mouth to bolster my statement with necessary evidence before savoring her from head to toe on my terrace. After an orgasm or two, I follow her naked curves to my bed and lose myself in her. I would happily stay here tangled with her between my sheets except for the fact I'm starving. Almost two hours after I arrive home, we start cooking dinner.

"I got a call from the flight manager today. Mrs. Waller cancelled her flights to California going forward. I wonder what happened?" I chop veggies for our stir-fry.

"Her daughter died last weekend." I pause to look at Noelle's expression to verify I heard her correctly.

"Yet you still lost your job."

Noelle nods. "She must have sent the paperwork before she died. Mrs. Waller said she died of an aneurysm. She didn't pinpoint when though, and I didn't press. Either way, Sheila said she was going to let me go. Mrs. Waller just bought me a few days."

"What did she want?"

"She wants to talk about how she can help Mason. Mason lives here now. Apparently, Mrs. Sanfilippo was a single mother. Mrs. Waller reviewed the plan I created for Mason, and she was impressed. She wants to discuss ways she can implement it."

"That's fantastic! When are you meeting her?" I lean forward, kissing her before throwing the meat into the pan.

"Tomorrow at ten. Do you always walk to work?"

"Always is a strong word, but often. Why?"

"I just don't want to take your car if you need it."

"Take whichever one you want, or I can buy you something that suits you better."

"What do you mean whichever one?"

I thought I told her that both vehicles were mine. "The black SUV in the adjacent spot is mine too. Or I can buy you a smaller car if you want."

"No, I don't need a car. I have a car, just not here."

Noted, don't buy anything extravagant, especially if she already has one. That won't stop me from buying her gifts, but I wouldn't buy a car without her input anyway.

"I can't wait to hear about your meeting tomorrow."

We chat more about Mrs. Waller and Mason, but I don't really know anything useful. I only know her flight schedule—at least, I did. While I plate our food, Noelle grabs two waters, silverware, and napkins. We settle at the outdoor dining table.

"What did Stacy have to say?" She takes her first bite. "This is really tasty, Cash."

"Thanks. So far he found two potential options for us."

She didn't flinch or correct me when I said "us," nor did she blanche when I called her mine earlier. I want to wake up with her in my arms for the rest of my life.

"The first one is in Alaska. It's a much smaller opportunity than I would like. There are limited flights, and the location isn't the best. The second option is in Los Angeles. It's a much better deal, a better opportunity, but it's a big city, which we don't want."

"I gather there isn't a database where Stacy can look to find these deals; it takes a bunch of phone calls and finding the right person to ask to find what a particular client is looking for, in this case you."

"No, there isn't. I chose Stacy because he has contacts in the aviation industry because that's his former profession."

She nods. "I've been giving what you suggested more thought, but I have reservations and concerns. Will you explain how a potential deal would work, one specifically for me?"

"Of course, what are your reservations?"

She pauses a bit too long for my taste. Noelle is thoughtful and careful with her words. I wait for her to speak again.

"Mainly, I feel like I shouldn't rush headlong into anything. Right now, I'm free to go wherever I want and do whatever I want. I would have never considered my own center as an option until I met you. I don't want to make a choice that could jeopardize what you are able to choose. It's unfair for me to suggest you chase your passion, but then make it difficult for you to do it." Slowly, she lifts her eyes to mine.

"*Tesoro*, I have the same reservations about choosing an opportunity for myself."

"Please don't. You need to choose the best option for you. Let's assume I didn't lose my job and you still decided to shift careers. What would be different?"

"I wouldn't be sharing my home with a gorgeous woman who I see a future with."

She opens her mouth to speak, but words fail her.

Yes to every thought crashing through your mind right now. I want you. I want to build a life with you. There will be hardships along the way, but with you, I can handle it all. "The parameters I gave Stacy are the same as they would have been if you were still working."

"I'm confused. You said the Los Angeles deal was better but not what we want. If I still worked there, wouldn't it be perfect?"

"In the short-term, maybe as far as proximity to you. In the long-term, it isn't. We don't want to live in a big city. Did I misunderstand?"

"No. You didn't misunderstand. I don't want to live in a big city, but I will if it's what you need."

That response is precisely why she's perfect. She wants her career, a family, and me, but she's willing to give it up for me as I would for her.

"*Tesoro*, that's the beauty of being able to search for the right opportunity. I don't have to take one that isn't perfect for us." I lean across the table and press my lips to her forehead. We finish our meal in silence—the type of silence that provides comfort. After cleaning up, we cuddle on the couch as I explain the process of how finding her center would work with investors from business plan to opening the doors.

NOELLE

My commute to work with Mason this afternoon has been awful. There has been traffic at every turn. I've considered taking the subway a few times, but Cash nixed the idea swiftly. He's concerned that photographers will hound me if I'm alone, and I'm wholly against having security every single day.

Working with Mason has been wonderful for both of us. I've been able to see him grow and develop. Over the course of the last few weeks, I learned that Mrs. Waller was a teacher for thirty years before retiring. She was impressed with the plan I created for Mason and asked what my plans are for the future. She and I discussed my ideas for a center for students like Mason, but that is about as far as it went.

I agreed to tutor Mason through the summer. Since his mother's death, Mason and I work together every day from nine to one. Mrs. Waller is looking for a home outside of the city within driving distance to a preschool that is willing to work with a private tutor provided by Mrs. Waller to make sure Mason continues to thrive.

Cash turned down three opportunities that Stacy found so far. Alaska, LA, and one last week located near an air force base in Texas for various reasons. I just hope he doesn't get frustrated waiting for the perfect deal. Is it even out there?

I've started working on a business plan for my center, but I keep getting stuck on the location aspect. I can't make that decision until Cash finds his opportunity. For now, I'm just looking forward to a quiet weekend with Cash at home. Other than dinner with his sister tonight, and a date night out tomorrow, we have no plans. Last weekend, I spent the entire time alone in the house. While I missed Cash, the quiet and peace of his home is glorious. I slept in and relaxed, reading two Claire Kingsley novels. I also made major inroads on my business plan. The more information I have, the easier it will be to research the location. As I park, my phone chimes.

Kate: How are you? I miss your face.

Me: I'm well. What about you? How is Keyton?

Kate: I'm good. Keyton is amazing! When are you coming home?

Me: I don't know if I am. Why don't you come here for a long weekend?

Kate: I'll think about it. Are you getting your mail?

Me: Yes, thank you. Do you want my condo?

Kate: I can't buy it, but I could rent it from you. I'll think about it.

Me: I miss your face too. Love you.

Kate: Love you too.

I smile and step out of the car. There is an older man standing near the elevator. I've never seen him before. I scurry around him to ride upstairs. The moment I step inside, the intercom is ringing.

"I have a Mr. Warren Morgan to see you, miss."

"I don't know who he is. He'll have to visit when Cash is home." I text Cash to see where he is.

"He insists he wants to speak with you."

Me: I think your father is here. He wants to talk to me.

Cash: I'm on my way. Please have Arthur keep him in the lobby.

Me: Okay.

"Arthur, Cash will be home in a little bit. Please ask Mr. Morgan to wait until he arrives."

"Thank you, miss. I'll let him know." Once I hang up, I consider making it look like I haven't been living here but decide against it. I don't care what Cash's father thinks.

Less than thirty minutes later, Cash and the man come through the door. Cash follows his normal routine, tugging off his tie and jacket on his way to kiss me hello. Today's is a bit more brief than usual, likely due to our unannounced guest.

"Noelle, please meet my father, Warren Morgan."

"It's a pleasure to meet you." I extend my hand to him. He shakes it firmly. After he releases my hand, Cash slides his arm around me. It's comforting and disconcerting at the same time. Why is he concerned about his father being here? Cash defined their relationship as strained, but he's clearly concerned for my safety, or maybe it's possessiveness.

"What do you need, Father?"

"The rumor mill—aka your mother—has been spinning out of control lately. Her stories range from you're engaged or married to having a baby in the next few months. Judging by her appearance, the latter isn't true. I needed to check on you personally."

"Noelle and I are fine and none of your business. Is there something else? I'm sure you didn't come down here to ask about my relationship status."

"I'm concerned about your choice to change careers with regards to your trust as well as your younger brother's foolish plan to open a restaurant. Does he realize the failure rate?"

I hide my reaction to his questions well. What is he talking about Cash's trust? Mr. Morgan glances over at me to gauge my response. I clearly passed because he seems impressed with my poker face. Cash moves his arm from around me and threads his fingers with mine as he answers.

"Nothing I have set into motion goes against the terms of my trust. Even if it did, I would make the change anyway," Cash replies with conviction. There are apparently more layers to his family drama than I'm aware of.

"I see. What about August?"

"Father, you agreed to give him access to his trust to chase his dream of opening a restaurant. That also means you have to be willing to let him fail as well."

I just fell a little deeper in love with Cassius Morgan. Not only is he standing up for himself but his brother as well, just as he supported his sister after her accident. His protection of his siblings and fierce loyalty reminds me of me and mine.

"Have you spoken to your sister?" Mr. Morgan asks, as if reading my mind.

"As with every other time you inquire, Mina is fine. That's the only information you are getting from me, Sam, or Auggie. Leave her alone. She has made her position crystal clear. Whether she decides to let you and Mother back into her life is solely up to her. I will not be a middleman. I'm surprised she allows us to share even that much."

I'm sure Cash is trying to hurry his father out of here so he doesn't run into Mina when she arrives.

Mr. Morgan nods. "It was a pleasure meeting you, Noelle. I hope to see you at the gala."

"Nice to meet you, Mr. Morgan."

"Son."

"Have a nice evening, Father."

Mr. Morgan exits the door. The moment it closes, Cash whips out his phone to check on Mina's arrival. After furiously tapping and reading her response, he lets out a deep breath.

"Thank you for coming home so quickly. I wasn't sure what to do," I confess.

"I will always come for you." Cash presses his lips to mine, kissing me breathless.

"How is Mason?"

"He's well. Making progress. I'm working with the director of his new daycare center to make sure he has the support he needs in the fall when they move to their new home."

"That's fantastic! I'm so happy for him and for you!"

"How was work? Do you want to change before your sister arrives?"

"Fine, boring. Yes." He guides me to the bedroom so he can change.

Billie arrives near six with two garment bags. After greeting Cash, she turns to me. "It's so great to see you again. I have your gown for you to try and something my brother requested." She yanks me into the bedroom to show me my dress for the gala.

Oh, Cash. What have you done this time?

Billie pulls the dress for the gala out of the garment bag. She took what I asked for and turned it into the perfect gown.

"It's gorgeous. Thank you so much!"

"Try it on."

I step into the bathroom and pull on the dress. It fits perfectly. I step out to show Billie.

"Holy crap! You look stunning! Is anything pulling or tight?"

"It's flawless."

"Take this one with you and try it on too." The second bag has a navy sheath dress with split straps and a low-cut back.

"Gorgeous," Billie says when I return to the bedroom.

"Thanks. Do you know what he's up to?" I slip back into the bathroom and change out of the dress.

"No. I just know he asked for a second dress for you. What was in the box he gave you in Maine?"

"Are you sure you want to know?"

"Yes, just don't share any private details."

I'll have to figure out where that boundary line is at some point. How much information is too much for Billie? "The box had a complete set of lingerie from La Perla. It was gorgeous."

"Their products are amazing. It was the only luxury splurge I allowed myself when I first left New York."

"Your brother is… I don't even know what to say to this."

"As I told you, my brother has a huge heart, and he gave it to you. Protect it and him. I've never seen him this happy, and that's because of you. Thank you."

I smile because words fail me.

We move back into the living room where Cash is putting the finishing touches on dinner. I offer to help, but he sets wine in front of both of us and orders us to sit. The three of us eat his delicious meal and chat until near ten when Billie leaves for Sam's. She has a wedding tomorrow evening and a styling appointment on Sunday before returning to York Beach.

CASSIUS

When I return from a punishing hour with Evan at the gym, I find Noelle practicing yoga on the terrace. Her hair is in a high ponytail, and she's wearing fitted yoga pants and a sports bra. Either she doesn't realize I'm back or she's ignoring my presence.

"I feel you staring at me," she says without breaking her position.

"You're mesmerizing."

"To you."

I leave her and grab waters from the kitchen and check my messages to confirm dinner tonight. Instead of stepping into the shower, I decide to watch Noelle. It drives her crazy, but deep down, I know she loves it.

"Thanks," she says after I hand her a fresh water.

"How is Evan?"

"I think today was evenly matched. No stinging uppercuts today."

"Good. I was thinking about something you said about finding the right opportunity and perfection. I'll be right back." She scurries away and comes back with a stack of papers and her laptop.

"I want to open a center with the ability to focus on a child with Mason's developmental issues. I drafted a business plan." She hands me one of the thickest plans I've ever seen.

"How long have you been working on this?"

"Since I've been talking to the director at Mason's new school and Mrs. Waller."

"What caused you to decide to go for it?"

"Putting the plan I created for Mason into action and finding a receptive director to help me keep him progressing."

"Can I read it?"

"Of course. I want your opinion on the plan as well as if I should wait to have someone start looking or start now. Your statement about waiting for the right opportunity stuck with me. It wouldn't hurt for me to have someone looking for options."

"Fair enough." I open the plan and start skimming the pages. "How much research did you do?"

"Tons. Not only on how to write the plan, but on resources for the students and how readily available they are specifically for low-income students."

I skim through the sections of her plan. It's engaging, thorough, and more in-depth than it needs to be.

She rises from her seat and moves inside.

"Where are you going?"

"I'm hungry. Keep reading, I'll make some breakfast." I nod and dig back into her plan. She has even looked at recent sales of daycare centers across the country. I'm so engrossed in her words that I barely notice she's finished cooking and set a heaping plate of French toast, fresh fruit, and sausage before me.

"This is amazing, sweetheart." I dig into my food and savor the first bite. Apparently, I was hungry too.

"Thanks. It's just food."

"I meant your plan. This is over the top thorough."

She smiles.

"Do you want to teach or have the ability to connect other center owners with the resources they need like an education plan or properly educated teachers?"

"Both I think. As I researched I realized there's no way there would be enough kids in any given area who need this type of support. Given the age of the students, a boarding school like scenario won't work."

Every day I learn something about her that makes me love her more. She's ambitious and willing to help her students reach their full potential.

"How do I get around the location issue?"

"You have two distinct business options here. Yes, they overlap, but you have a consulting part and the brick and mortar part. Can I write on this?"

"Sure."

"If you split this section and this section"—I highlight the two parts—"you could start forming the consulting aspect right now while searching for a center to purchase when you're ready."

A shocked look graces her face.

"You seem surprised."

"I don't know how to do any of that, Cash."

"You said you didn't know anything about business plans too, yet here is one of the most detailed ones I've ever seen. You did this on your own. You can do anything." I lean forward, kissing her softly. "I may not want to work in venture capitalism for much longer, but I do know my way around a deal as well as a bunch of people who can help you with the parts I'm not great at."

"What do I need to do?"

"Really?" I ask only because I don't want to push her, but her plan is outstanding, even if she doesn't yet believe it herself.

"Yes, really. I should follow my own advice, right? I pushed you to take a leap of faith; I should too."

Rising from my seat, I round the table and pull her into my arms. "I'm so proud of you. First, we're going to get ready for our date night. Tomorrow we can polish this up and figure out a time for you to come to my office and meet with an advisor next week."

"Works for me. Where are we going tonight?"

"Don't you worry. Everything is all set. We need to get moving though so we aren't late for the first part."

We move around the bedroom, dressing for our dinner date. It's still early, but we need to drive a bit to our first stop. I catch myself more than once watching her as she gets ready. Her beauty is effortless. She doesn't fuss with tons of makeup or whatever else women do to get ready for an evening out. Her "take me as I am" attitude is captivating. As she is, she's everything I've ever wanted.

"You need to put that dress on, or we'll be very late," I plead as she steps out of the closet wearing the lingerie I bought for her. She's breathtaking.

"Fine, but watching you squirm is entertaining." She steps into her dress, wiggling it up over her hips. Moving toward her, I grip her waist and turn her around to zip the dress. Despite my desire to push it back down over her hips and caress her smooth skin, I gently pull the zipper upward.

I finish my Windsor knot and move to get my watch. Noelle is rummaging through a small pouch on the bureau.

"What are you looking for?"

"I'm looking for a necklace to wear."

"I was going to wait until later, but I might be able to fix that for you." I open the top drawer and pull out a gift I bought for her.

"Cash, you don't have to buy me gifts. I don't need things. Things aren't important to me."

I know what she means. She learned early that life isn't about stuff. It's about love and living each moment to the fullest.

"I know. It's about what the thing says."

Reluctantly, she takes the box from my hand. Everything I have purchased for her says how I feel.

"What did the roses mean?" she inquires.

"The yellow roses with red tips mean I'm falling for you. The red means love."

She takes a step closer to me. "And the spa day?"

"I wanted you to relax and be taken care of. I love that you're independent, but I want to take care of you too."

She moves closer so her chest is barely grazing mine. "And the lingerie?"

"That was twofold. You deserve to have the best of everything. I can give it to you, and I want to. You look hot on any given day, but that set makes you look ravishing, and it feels luxurious under my fingers."

"And this?" She tilts the box in her delicate hand.

"*Tesoro*, I want you in my life. I care about you. Let me show you."

She opens the box. Inside is a floating diamond necklace from a local jeweler in New York.

"Cash, it's beautiful. Thank you." Noelle hands me the necklace to secure it around her neck. Brushing my lips along her shoulder causes a sharp inhale. "How important is the first stop in your evening?"

"It only serves to give Auggie time to prepare our dinner without us here."

"Your brother is cooking for us?" A big smile spreads on her face. "I'm excited to meet him and try his cooking. Did I just ruin the surprise part of tonight?"

"Yes."

"I'm sorry. Where were we going that we're late for now?"

"A winery."

"Are we too late?"

I glance at my watch and quickly calculate the driving time. "Yes. Finish getting ready, and I'll make a few calls."

I walk away to salvage some of the date I planned for her. After a few minutes of thinking, I create a new plan. I place two calls and gather the items I need from home. "Ready, *tesoro*?"

Nodding, she threads her fingers in mine.

NOELLE

Normally, I can read Cash well. After ruining his surprises for tonight, I'm not so sure. He's tight-lipped as we make one stop on our way to whatever he has planned as a stand-in for our winery visit. A young man comes out from a specialty shop with a large basket and two canvas bags.

"I'm sorry I made us late and ruined your surprise."

Cash takes my hand, kissing the top of it. "Don't be. We can always go another time."

After a short drive, short in distance, moderate on time, Cash parks in a docent spot near a large house. We're greeted at the door.

"Mr. Morgan. Miss Barnett. It's a pleasure to have you join us this afternoon at the Bartow-Pell Mansion Museum. If you will follow me." The young woman guides us around the mansion to a tented area near a fountain.

"Thank you," Cash replies after she escorts us to the tent. There is a small table with two chairs. The panel is pinned up so we can see the gorgeous grounds.

"You weren't kidding. You can make things happen."

"No, I wasn't. This didn't take very much effort though. I'm a member of the conservancy, and I got lucky that no events were happening today."

After our escort walks away, Cash opens the basket of goodies we picked up on the way. There are two bottles of wine, glasses, an expertly prepared antipasto tray and the necessary additions. We talk about my plan and what changes we need to make tomorrow over a glass of wine and the appetizers. As Cash regales me with the history of the mansion and the family that owned it, we stroll through the grounds. Retaking our seats, we talk more before returning home.

We chat with Arthur in the lobby before heading upstairs. A host of amazing fragrances tease my nose when the door opens. Not only is Cash's younger brother here, but there is also a woman. Auggie looks just like Cash, only thinner. The woman is beautiful. She's average height with curly, jet-black hair and curves reminiscent of Marilyn Monroe.

Auggie washes his hands and hugs Cash.

"Hi, I'm Auggie. You must be Noelle. It's a pleasure to meet you. This is my best friend, Caroline." He extends his hand to me.

"Nice to meet you both."

"Dinner will be ready in about twenty minutes. If you want to start on the salads, I can bring them out for you?" Auggie asks Cash.

"Sure, that works."

Cash reaches for my hand and leads me to the terrace. The terrace is special all the time, but Auggie added string lights and a few lanterns for dinner. Both add a bit more ambiance than without them.

"What's the deal with Auggie and Caroline? She's beautiful. Does she know he loves her?"

"Yes, she is. How do you see that? No, she doesn't, and Auggie isn't prepared to fight for her like she deserves, so he's waiting."

"Fair enough. How long have they been friends?"

"Since boarding school, I think. He's four years younger than me, so our social circles didn't really cross that often."

Auggie sets our salads on the table while Caroline fills our water and wine glasses.

"How did you rope him into cooking for us?"

"I didn't exactly. He needed guinea pigs to practice on before his final exams in a few weeks. I would have said yes to him cooking before he started culinary school. He was always experimenting in the kitchen with Salma."

"Who is Salma?"

"She's my parents' maid and cook. She and her husband, Henry, have been working for my parents since I was a child."

Auggie brings out the main course of shrimp risotto with mascarpone. He explains the dish and waits for us to try it.

"This is melt-in-your-mouth wonderful, Auggie. It's creamy, not sticky or heavy like most risotto recipes I've had before."

"Thank you, Noelle. Cash?"

"Bro, this is amazing! You will ace your exams in the next few weeks."

"Thanks. Enjoy. I need to finish dessert." Auggie hurries away while I attempt to slow down my rate of consumption. I'll easily polish off every bite and work on Cash's since he's is only halfway through.

I glance toward the kitchen and see Auggie prepping something on the island. He may not want to pursue a relationship with Caroline right now, but the looks she's casting his way indicate she will be receptive when he changes his mind. I feel the heat of Cash's gaze on me.

"What are you thinking, *tesoro*?"

"Nothing you don't already know." I may not have said it out loud, but I almost did earlier. He leans forward, dragging his lips across mine.

Caroline comes out to check on our drinks. "Are you ready for dessert?"

"Whenever Auggie is ready is fine for us. We don't want to keep you longer than necessary," Cash replies.

A few minutes later, Auggie sets a light dessert in front of us. "This is a cherry clafoutis. It's a light and airy sweet dessert perfect for summer."

Cash slides his fork into the piece on his plate, taking almost half. "It tastes like fancy pancakes."

I reach over and smack his arm. "Seriously, Cash!"

Auggie drops his head, shaking it from side to side.

"Auggie, don't mind him. It's sweet and delicate. The cherries are the perfect balance of sweet and tart."

"Thank you. Cash, she's perfect. Put you right in your place. Don't mess it up!"

I smile and lift another forkful to my lips. Two siblings down, one to go. The four of us chat for a while during cleanup. After promising to get together for dinner and exchanging numbers, Cash and I snuggle in bed to watch a movie.

When I wake, Cash's spot is cold. Contorting to find a clock, I see it's near ten. I haven't slept this late in years, even on vacation. Slipping into my robe, I pad to the kitchen and find a note from Cash saying he went for a run. Armed with coffee, I settle on the couch to enjoy the morning sunshine.

I happen to glance up when the front door opens. Holy hell! I've seen and touched every inch of him, but post-run Cash is hot! Sweat drips over the ridges and planes of his chest and abs. It takes restraint not to follow one or two of the beads with my eyes. The way his throat moves as he chugs the water is oddly arousing.

"You can't stare at me like that."

"Like what?" I ask innocently, as if he didn't catch me red-handed ogling him.

"Like you want to devour me."

"What if I do? If I'm yours, that makes you mine, right?"

"Yes."

"Then I'll look at you however I like." Rising from the couch, I stalk over to him as he drops his shirt to the floor. Holding his hand, I tug the sash of my robe.

"*Tesoro*, I didn't realize you have a naughty streak."

I have nothing on under my robe. "Only with you."

"I love the sound of that." He drags his fingertips from the hollow of my collarbone, down between my breasts, and outward to the point of my hip, sending tingly sensations coursing across my skin. I push his shorts to the floor. I'm still taken by the sight of him from his threaded arms to his powerful thighs. Releasing the sash, he grips my hip and turns my back to him. After brushing my hair over my left shoulder, he grasps it, tugging to expose my neck. I can't contain a deep moan.

"You like that?" he asks, sounding surprised.

"Didn't know until right now."

Frankly, I have never been comfortable enough with myself or my partner to just feel in a moment like this.

"I'm fascinated that I'm the only man you can be completely honest with," he whispers near the shell of my ear. Cash pushes the robe down my arms to the floor, and the luxurious silk pools around my ankles. He skims his hands up my hips before palming my breasts. Lifting my arms, I thread my fingers into his damp hair as he plucks one nipple between his fingers and rolls the other, sending spikes of need through me. Heat pools between my thighs as I clench them together, attempting to quell the continuous need I feel for him.

"Let me take care of that ache for you, *tesoro*," he murmurs in my ear, making my core throb even more. Slipping one hand down over my belly, Cash teases my nub with his fingers. I open for him, setting my foot on the ottoman. Cash plunges three fingers into my folds, curving them into the perfect spot.

"Cash," I rasp out while piercing his legs with my nails.

He twists, turns, withdraws, and advances his fingers until I shudder with pleasure against him. His shaft is rock-hard between my cheeks. Moving slightly adding some space between us, Cash shifts, bringing his shaft between my thighs. He teases my core, moving forward and back against my folds while his fingers tease and rub my clit.

"Holy hell, that feels good!"

"Come again, sweetheart," he commands.

Pleasure spiraling from my head to my toes, I shatter.

He brushes his lips across my shoulders before lowering my leg and guiding me forward and setting my hands on the ottoman. My feet remain on the floor.

"I need you to tell me if you're uncomfortable."

Looking over my shoulder, I nod, noting his eyes are heavy with heat.

With his tip grazing my core, he says, "Words please."

"I will. Now, Cash." After my definitive words, Cash thrusts forward until he's fully seated. "Holy fuck!"

"I love hearing you curse."

"I can feel you deeper inside me. I'm full. It's—"

He effectively cuts off my words when he moves. My walls tighten around him before he pulls out before plunging forward repeatedly with deliberate strokes. My release swirls in my abdomen as Cash pulses inside me. Just when I feel I've reached the peak, Cash touches me and I fall deeper with more tantalizing sensations rolling through me. I crest the edge, bucking against him as he empties in hot bursts.

Cash slowly lowers us onto the couch with me in his lap. I lean against him, recapturing my breath with his arms wrapped around me.

"Should I be concerned if you don't curse while I move inside you?"

Turning to look at him. "No, of course not."

"A blush looks sexy on you," he says against my heated skin. Standing slowly, I lead him into his huge shower.

CASSIUS

There is something about a woman who knows what she wants. No woman has even been raw with honesty both in and out of the bedroom like Noelle. After tangling up the sheets after our shower, Noelle and I made changes to her business plan. She's genuinely excited about having her own center. I sent an email to Mallory to set up a time to talk with her tomorrow. After dinner, we sit on the terrace until sleep calls us both.

Lately I have been waking before her. Today is no different. I study the curves of her face, the dip of her collarbones, and the freckles that mark her shoulder.

"I can feel you staring at me," she mumbles without opening her eyes.

"You're beautiful. I love waking up with you. Plus, you're mine, which means I can stare whenever I want for as long as I want." I watch her brow wrinkle as if she doesn't believe she's beautiful. Her ambivalence to her beauty makes her even more attractive to me. "We need to get moving or we'll both be late for work."

"Fine." She exhales and turns to get up.

Pulling her back down to the mattress, I kiss her hard, making my head spin. She sighs against my mouth before cautiously dragging herself up again. "I'll make the coffee while you take a shower."

"You could shower with me."

"Then we will absolutely be late. Go." She presses her lips to mine again. As I shut off the water and step out of the shower, Noelle hands me coffee before turning the spray on. It takes restraint to refrain from stepping into the steamy shower with her.

While Noelle showers, I make a second cup for her. When I return to the bedroom, I set her cup on the bureau. As I secure my tie into the perfect Atlantic knot, I watch her, raptured by her graceful movements.

"Cash." Her voice pulls me out of my head.

"Yes."

"Do you want a cup to go?"

"No, I'll get one at the office."

We bustle around the kitchen and out the door. As we arrive at the lobby, we greet Arthur and go our separate ways for the day.

Myles updates me as I walk from the elevator at my office. "Mallory stopped by already. She'll give you a few options on Wednesday or Thursday in the afternoon. Do you have the plan for her to review?" he asks.

After handing him Noelle's plan, I drop into my office chair and tackle the day.

When next I look up, Mal is standing at the threshold to my office.

"You want to invest in a daycare? Seems a bit odd for someone who flies planes in his spare time."

"Good morning to you too, Mal. I don't; my girlfriend does. Noelle needs the consulting aspect set up as soon as possible. She can do that from anywhere. Then an actual location."

"Back up. Your girlfriend? How long have I been out of the loop?"

I smile. "Long enough."

"Does she explain your improved demeanor?"

"Yes." I have never been happier, and she is the sole reason.

"I have available appointments on Wednesday at two or Thursday at three."

"We'll take the Wednesday at two. Do you need anything else before then?"

"Just a standard new client information sheet."

"No problem. I'll have her fill it out tonight. Thanks, Mal."

"She lives with you?"

"Yes. Why?"

"Just surprised. When you jump in, you opt for the deep end. I've never seen you like this. I'm happy for you, Cash. The four of us should have dinner sometime."

"Dinner would be great."

Mal doesn't realize that wherever she finds a center for Noelle will be my home too. I don't want the circle to be any bigger yet. I message Stacy for an update and plow through my day.

In a blink I'm meeting Noelle in the lobby of my office for her meeting with Mallory on Wednesday afternoon.

"Hi, *tesoro*. How is Mason?" I kiss her softly. I'm all for everyone knowing she's mine; I just don't plan to make a statement doing it. The chatter will be about her anyway.

"Hi. He's great. Making progress each day. It's all I ask of him. One of his neighbors, Elizabeth, is great. She walks each morning. We joined her on a walk today, working on finding things in nature and naming them. It also helps him with handling having people around other than me and his grandparents."

I escort Noelle to Mal's office, and we take a seat.

After introductions, Mal gets right down to business reviewing the information sheet and discussing all the options for the consulting aspect of the business. Noelle answers her questions carefully and thoroughly. She's amazing. As much as she doubts her ability to make this business successful, she looks confident and ready to take this challenge on. I know she can handle it; plus, I will be there to help whenever she needs it. I doubt she'll need help, but the offer is there. I note an extra number of passersby during the meeting. Stacy, Myles, and even Kip meander past Mal's office door. None of them have a reason to be anywhere near this side of the office. Only an office-wide meeting would necessitate coming over here for the largest conference room next door. There is no meeting today. I smile inwardly and focus on Noelle.

Noelle chooses the structure for her consulting business, and they move on to the physical center location. She narrows it down to the same areas I did without a second thought. Mallory tempers her expectations about a time frame for finding a location and an interested investor, indicating it could take a few months to almost a year.

"Thank you, Mallory. I'm excited for this." Noelle shakes her hand.

Threading my fingers in hers, I lead her to my office. Myles follows us in. I officially introduce them and take my messages before chatting with Noelle a bit about her meeting with Mal.

"How are you feeling about all of that?"

"I'm nervous, but there's no reason for me not to give my dream job a shot, right?"

"None at all. I'm so proud of you."

"Thanks. I'll let you get back to work. I'll see you at home after you spar with Evan."

Did she just say "home"? I love that she feels like my home is hers now.

"Okay," I reply, rising from where I was leaning against my desk. Sliding my hand to cup her cheek, I pull her against me. It doesn't matter how often I'm able to do it, it still feels like the first time. Her luscious curves in my arms are unmatched. I kiss her tenderly. "You should go.

There isn't a lock on this door, and I want to strip that dress from your body and have my way with you on my desk."

"You have a desk at home, don't you?"

Well, isn't she adventurous? She continues to surprise me daily.

"In fact, I do. Perhaps we should put it to use, and soon."

"We should. Get back to work. I'll see you later."

While I should focus on something unappealing, I watch her walk to the elevator. As the door closes, she smiles at me. Every day with her is exactly what I want.

Evan was in a mood tonight, his pace frantic instead of measured like normal. When I asked, he shook me off. Kip and Stacy took a few jabs at me in the locker room after our gym sessions.

"How did you manage to land her?" Kip asks.

"I have the same question, but however you managed it, I'm happy for you," Stacy chimes in.

"Thanks, guys. Don't worry, Kip. Whenever you're ready, you'll find the right one for you. I decided I was ready and that she wasn't in New York. I would say fate stepped in a tiny bit, but except for that, it was all me."

I hurry out of the locker room and head home to my woman. I don't know what the rest of this year looks like for us, but I do know I want her in it every single day.

"Hi, honey. I'm home," I say with a laugh.

Noelle steps into the living room wearing one of my dress shirts. It hits high on her toned thighs. If my hunch is correct, she isn't wearing a bra. It's hard to tell if she's wearing panties though.

"Hi. How was boxing?" She moves in front of me, pressing her lips to mine.

"Good. Evan was off today though. Do all of my clothes look better on you?"

"Probably." She smiles as she moves into the kitchen. "Go shower. I'll cook something."

With ingredients from the fridge, Noelle puts together an amazing meal. We talk about her new businesses and discuss my update from Stacy.

"Did he find another opportunity?"

"Possibly. One of the owners of the airfield in Portsmouth is looking to sell his stake, just not right away. Overall, the opportunity could be great, but I may not be able to make my deadline of this year if I move forward. The other drawback is it isn't for the whole business, just 60 percent."

"What would it mean if you don't finish it by this year?"

"I don't want to only have income from flying coming in, but that might be the case if I take the deal."

"But there are advantages too, right?"

"Such as?" I'm intrigued how she sees this deal.

"You would be closer to Billie, out of the city, in charge of your schedule, and you would have your dream job."

I take in her words and let them settle. The only drawbacks are the timing and that I'm not the sole owner. There is no such thing as a perfect deal; I know that. This one has almost everything I want. Everything we want.

"What if you ask Stacy to approach the other owner to see if they are willing to sell to you as well?"

"You're a genius." I hop up from my chair, take her hand, and lead her into the office to email Stacy. Perched on the edge of my desk, she watches as I type. "Will you review it?"

"Me?"

"Of course, this involves you too."

She twists slightly forward to read the draft. While I wait, I skim my fingers up her calf and thigh. Briefly she closes her eyes as my hand slides north. Before I get close enough to determine if she's wearing panties, she answers me.

"It's perfect. You should send it before you continue moving your hand any higher."

I press send before sliding her in front of me, leaving her ass perched on my desk. "Are you naked under my shirt?"

Her eyes widen before she whispers, "Maybe you should find out."

Grasping the hem of my shirt, I consider slowly unbuttoning each one. Instead, I send buttons off in every direction, baring her gorgeous body.

"You're a bit vixen, Miss Barnett." Shimmying out of my shorts, I rise from the chair.

"Only with you, Mr. Morgan."

Pressing my lips to hers, I set her further back and climb on top of her. I plunge into her in one thrust, taking her hard and fast on my desk. Panting, I look down at her. Her skin is flush, her breath ragged, and her walls are still pulsing around me. I've fallen for this woman, and I'm ready to build a life with her. Even if Stacy can't get me the rest of the ownership stake, I'm going to take this huge leap. Then I'm going to marry this spectacular woman and we're going to have a huge family.

NOELLE

Since Mrs. Waller isn't travelling to California to see Mason, Cash is flying a bit less. Unfortunately, he's flying this weekend. My preordered new releases will download tonight at midnight, so tomorrow after work, I'll have something to keep my mind occupied.

I don't like that he's on edge leaving me alone. I don't plan on going anywhere alone this weekend. Tomorrow after work, I'll stop for baking ingredients, and then I'll stay put until Sunday.

Snuggling deeper into Cash's arm, I hear him sigh. "*Tesoro*, we don't have time before you need to leave for work."

I groan loudly. "Can't I be a little late, just this once? I want to stay here naked with you."

It doesn't help when Cash drags his tongue along the slope of my neck, chilling beneath my skin. "As much as I want that too, you can't. Mason needs you to meet your own expectations."

I sag against him knowing he's right. Throwing the covers back, I pad to the shower. Once I'm dressed, I find Cash in the kitchen plating scrambled eggs and toast.

"Thank you, but I don't have time to eat that."

"You do. I'm going to drive while you eat. I'll run back and then get ready for work."

"There is no point in arguing with you, is there?"

"No, let's go. Plus, it gives me at least twenty more minutes with you and another kiss to hold me over until Sunday."

"Sweet talker." I slip my arm through the handle of my tote before grabbing the plate and utensils. While I eat, Cash drives to Mrs. Waller's. He parks in the small lot behind the building with eight minutes to spare. "Travel safe. I'll see you on Sunday."

Cash leans toward me, dragging his thumb across my lips. He kisses me softly at first, but then it turns possessive and needy.

"I'll be fine."

"How do you know I'm worried?"

"It's in your kiss. Whatever went through your mind, I can handle it. Your 'she's mine' protective instinct goes into overdrive when you leave. I'll be fine. Please call me when you land. Where are you going anyway?"

"Florida." He presses his lips to mine again before handing me the fob. We walk to the entrance where Cash kisses me again. The next few days are going to be boring without him.

"Go," I whisper, forcing myself to step away. I take another quick peek as he runs away from the staircase, his perfect ass in motion as his pace increases.

"Good morning," Elizabeth says in her normal chipper tone. She's a bit later than usual. Generally, we chat a bit on the stoop before I go in. Today she is just coming down the stairs. "Who is he?"

"My boyfriend."

"Good for you, honey. Have a wonderful day."

"You too."

Mason is in a great mood today and the day flies by. On the way home, I stop by the market close to home to procure a bottle of wine and the ingredients for the clafoutis recipe that Auggie left from our dinner. I'm nowhere near as capable as Auggie, but he said it was simple. I'm going to change the fruit, but otherwise it'll be the same. At home, I peel off my work clothes and dress in another one of Cash's shirts. Luckily, he has enough shirts for both of us to wear. I snap a quick photo and send it to him before attempting the recipe.

An hour later, I pull my peach clafoutis out of the oven and snap a photo.

I text it to Auggie and realize I won't have enough milk for breakfast. I decide against going out now. I'll take a walk first thing in the morning.

Grabbing my Kindle, a full glass of wine, and a bowl of popcorn, I settle onto the couch on the terrace. As I sit, my phone chimes. I know it's too early for it to be Cash.

Auggie: It looks perfect! Great job!

Me: Thanks. I'll let you know how it tastes.

Auggie: See you at the gala.

A few chapters in, I decide to soak in the hot tub. I slip out of Cash's shirt and drop into the scalding water. It's glorious, especially with the stars twinkling above and the peacefulness of this space. I don't mind being alone. He'll be home on Sunday, but I miss having him near me. I know that sounds sappy and a tad over the top for the length of our relationship, but I don't care. He feels right. We feel right. It may seem fast to others, but to me, it's perfect.

Climbing the steps, I surround myself with the towel. Cleaning up, I set my glass and bowl in the sink before retrieving my Kindle and Cash's shirt. With my phone plugged in, I burrow under the covers with my Kindle. I hear my phone ringing in the haze of sleepiness.

I fumble to answer the video call.

"Hi, *tesoro*. I'm sorry it's late. We had issues before takeoff."

"It's fine. I'm glad you called anyway. Thank you."

"You're welcome. Are you naked?"

"Maybe."

He knows full well I sleep with the least amount of clothing possible. "Why must you torture me?"

"Why must I put on clothes when you're not here when I don't wear them when you are?"

"Fair point. It's just unfair that I can't touch you right now."

"I agree, but you'll have to deal with it until Sunday like I do."

"Sleep, *tesoro*. I'll call you in the morning."

"Good night, Cash. Sleep well."

I curl into the bed, inhaling Cash's scent from his pillow.

Near seven, I pad to the kitchen for a cup of coffee, short on milk. Once the caffeine hits my soul, I throw on some jeans, tie Cash's shirt at my waist, pull on tennis shoes, and head out the door.

After a quick trip to the corner market, I round the corner with my groceries and see a large crowd of people at the front of the building. I walk straight toward the front door.

As I approach, I hear:

"How are you handling Brittany's pregnancy?" one reporter calls out.

"Where is Cash?"

"Will he submit to the paternity test?" another shouts.

"Will he be present when the baby is born?"

Opening the door, I enter the lobby and lean against the column to regain my composure.

"Miss Barnett, are you okay?" Arthur asks with concern in his voice.

"Hi, Arthur. Yes, I'm fine. I knew this day would come. I was just hoping for a bit longer. When did they start congregating?"

"About thirty minutes ago."

"Is this the first time they have been hanging around?"

"No."

"Does Cash know?"

"Yes, I told Mr. Morgan when it started. Generally, I've been able to get them to leave. Today they weren't accommodating."

"I doubt they will be accommodating going forward as they just saw me enter the building this early on a Saturday. It also doesn't appear that they know who I am yet either."

"Who are you, Miss Barnett?"

I laugh. I appreciate his jovial nature at this tense time. "I'm not anyone. Ellis Barnett is my older brother." It dawns on me that Arthur may not know who Ellis is.

But I am someone. I'm in love with Cassius Morgan, one of New York's most-eligible bachelors, and he wants me. Unfortunately, the press doesn't know that yet. They just think I'm some woman Cash slept with last night. For now. I cross the lobby and motion for Arthur to join me. "See that billboard for the upcoming movie?"

"Yes," Arthur replies.

"He's my brother. However, their questions were only about Cash. Not about my brother, his new wife, or the new movie."

"I see. Do you have any plans to go out again today?"

"No, I don't. Eventually another story will break, and they will leave. Nothing interesting will happen here today or ever for that matter. When I need to leave, I'll drive going forward. Thank you."

The moment I enter the house, my phone starts ringing with a video call.

"Are you okay, *tesoro*?" The background is some nondescript hotel room.

"Arthur called you?"

"Yes. I asked him too. You didn't answer me."

"I'm fine, Cash. This isn't my first run-in with photographers. They don't know who I am yet. They were only asking about you. Nothing about Nicholas or Kelly."

"So, it will get worse," he opines.

"It will. I can handle it. I'm not some fragile flower."

"I know you aren't, but maybe you should take your brother up on his offer of security."

"No."

"*Tesoro.*" The deep, growly tone is arousing. It shouldn't be, but it is, nonetheless.

"I don't need security to follow me around. The only place I go alone is Mrs. Waller's, and I drive. They won't follow me there."

"*Tesoro*, be reasonable. I care about you. I don't want you to feel trapped in our home." *Our home.*

"I care about you too. I don't need personal security, Cash. If it starts to bother me that I can't go out when you aren't here, I'll talk to Nicholas about setting up a schedule to have Maia or Connor here when you fly. It just seems like an unnecessary expense."

"No expense is unnecessary if it pertains to your safety. I just found you; I can't lose you." He's in this as deep as I am.

"Cash." They won't hurt me. Potentially, they could scare me, but they won't hurt me.

"Sweetheart, please promise me you'll stay in until I get home tomorrow."

"I promise."

"*Tesoro*, I have no reason not to trust you, but I need to know you will stay put. I'm terrified something will happen to someone else I...." He drags his hand down his face.

"I don't want to have this conversation over the phone, Cassius. I will stay here, I promise."

"We will have this conversation face-to-face tomorrow."

"Okay."

"I need to go check out a beachfront location for a client. I'll call you later."

After ending the call, I can't hold it in anymore. A few tears streak down my face. Swiping them away, I curl up on the couch, staring out the terrace doors. It isn't long before I decide against wallowing in my feelings and flow through some yoga to de-stress a bit. I consider whether Cash has a point and I should take Nicholas up on his offer. How much worse will it get when they realize that Hollywood's First Sister has taken New York's most-eligible, uber-rich bachelor off the market? My heart squeezes in my chest knowing I will tell Cash how I feel and soon. I just don't see the point of having security when I only leave to go to work. It's boring for them to hang around all day while I teach.

As I finish in warrior one, Arthur calls.

"Miss Barnett, Mr. Morgan is here to see you." That didn't take long.

"Which one?"

"Auggie and Sam," he replies.

"Thank you. You can send them up." I hurry into the bedroom and pull on a tunic top over my workout top.

"Hey, good to see you again. I would have preferred different circumstances," Auggie says, hugging me.

"You weren't exaggerating, Auggie," Sam says.

"Not even a little," Auggie replies, setting a bag on the island.

"Hi. I'm Sam. Pleasure to meet you. My brothers weren't exaggerating when they said you are gorgeous." He extends his hand to me. Sam is the oldest. He's handsome like Cash, but he has an air of sadness around him. His smile doesn't reach his eyes.

"Nice to meet you as well. Thank you." I consider arguing with him, but it isn't worth it. "Who called, Cash or Arthur?"

"Both. Arthur called because he knows Cash is flying. Cash called as soon as he finished talking with Arthur. I called Auggie just because I know you already met him," Sam explains.

"I may not have met you in person, but Cash told me all about each of you. The relationship the four of you have is remarkably similar to my brothers and me. They would drop everything for me. Even if he's filming, Nicholas would come."

"Filming?" Auggie asks.

"Cash didn't tell you who I am?"

"No. He said, and I quote, 'my woman needs to be checked on because of paparazzi,'" Sam replies.

I smirk before responding, not only at the "my woman" part, but at the air quotes Sam used. "Ellis Barnett is my brother." The brothers exchange a look and take a seat.

CASSIUS

The timing of this flight is a disaster. I knew this day would come, but I was hoping I would at least be in the same borough when it did. The woman I love is trapped in our home because she's stubborn and wholly against personal security. I want to share my feelings, but I refuse to have another serious conversation over the phone.

Once I finished speaking with Arthur, I called in the cavalry. Just like Ellis would for her, my brothers will show up for me. The bigger question is whether I reach out to Ellis or not. If it were Billie, I would expect a call. Yet Noelle and Billie are quite different. Noelle is fiercely independent, and she'll be pissed if I alert Ellis. Plus, if he acts, she will not only be angry with him but me as well.

During the walkthrough for my client, my mind is working on all the angles for whether to talk to Ellis. Is it possible he will just take the information and not act if I ask him to wait? Maybe. Should I wait? Also, maybe. The shop owner is detailing the specifics, but my head and my heart are in New York. After finishing up with the owner, I take the packet and mentally add reviewing it to my list of things to do first thing on Monday.

Despite all the arguments against it, I call Ellis on my walk back to the hotel.

"Good afternoon, Ellis."

Before I can say anything else, he asks, "Is she okay?" The edge on his tone is almost as sharp as mine.

"She's fine." I explain in detail everything that I learned from Arthur, Noelle, and even a covert update from Sam. I also request that he give me more time to talk to her about having personal security when I fly.

"I sent my brothers over after I spoke with her earlier. I asked them to stay with her, but she's persistent. She will make them leave tonight. My building has round-the-clock security, and my approved guest list is extremely short, just my brothers and my sister. In fact, you aren't on it. I'll remedy that as soon as I get home."

"She said no to personal security when I suggested it earlier. I gather her position is still the same?" Ellis asks.

"Yes. I'll work on it when I can talk to her in person. I don't want to have another serious conversation with her over the phone."

"Another? Never mind, I won't pry."

"Ellis, I care about Noelle. No, it's more than that."

"I think it's time for you to call me Nicholas. Cash, I have a small circle of six people in my life that I love and trust completely. Three women occupy that circle—Kelly, Noelle, and Mabel—and three men—Noah, Jacob, and you. I'm trusting you with my sister. My family is everything to me. I'll wait to talk to Jacob again until either Noelle or you contact me. Please take care of her."

"I will as long as she will have me." I hope he hears the underlying message.

"Thank you for calling. She'll be angry with both of us if she knows you called me."

"You're welcome. Yes, she will. I'll try my best to get her to accept some type of security when I travel."

"Thanks, Cash."

"You're welcome, El—Nicholas." I end the call feeling a bit better.

Nothing will be completely better until I can hold her, check she's okay physically, and tell her I love her. Grabbing some takeout, I return to my room. The next eighteen hours are going to be hell. I have done everything I can from here. Sam and Auggie will stay with her if she allows them too. I feel like a caged animal unable to protect my woman. Protect my future. Instead of eating, I change and hit the gym. After more than an hour of punching a stationary bag, a quick run, and a shower, I collapse onto the bed. I don't even bother heating up the takeout.

Near eight, I call Noelle with video because I need to see her beautiful face.

"Hi."

"Hi. How was the storefront? Will it work for your client?" She acts as if what happened today is normal, is okay, or is something she should have to handle. Not on my watch.

"It will be fine for what he wants, but I have deep-seated doubts about his overall plan, and I told him as much. Do you really want to talk about my day?"

"Yes, because I don't want to talk about why your brothers are here and won't leave. Don't get me wrong, they're great. I appreciate them for coming. Sam is kind of broody and a tad grumpy, but Auggie is funny and knows his way around the kitchen."

"Auggie is there too?"

"Yes. Sam invited him because he didn't want to show up alone because he and I have never met."

Leave it to Sam to make sure Noelle is comfortable. He always puts others before himself, even Meghan. She died before they could get married because he wanted her to finish school.

"Thank you for not turning them away."

"You're welcome."

"I don't want to talk about it over the phone, but how are you?"

"I'm fine. They weren't rude, nor did they impede my progress into the building. It isn't anything worse than I've been through before."

"What else is wrong, *tesoro*?"

"Nothing."

"I don't believe you. What happened to complete blunt honesty?"

"I appreciate that I can't hide anything from you even through the phone."

"You forget that I can see you. Do I have any clean shirts left?"

She looks hot right now wearing my shirt buttoned just high enough to be classy with her hair piled on top of her head and wearing her glasses. The glasses aren't a good sign. Either she doesn't feel well, she's upset, tired, or all the above.

She smiles. "Yes, you do. The anniversary of my parents' death is coming up soon. I get nostalgic and sometimes moody, especially when my life keeps moving without them." She has handled so many things without her parents, like graduation and getting her first place. There are so many more to come, such as starting her own business, our wedding, and having children.

"I'm sorry. Thank you for sharing with me. Is there anything I can do?"

"You're welcome. No, but thank you. I haven't had anyone except Kate to deal with me at this time each year. What time is your flight home tomorrow?" Her question is laced with anxiety—anxiety that seems to fade away when I can hold her.

"Early. I should be there before dinner."

"Sleep, Cash." There is a long pause at the end as if she wants to say something else.

I love you more.

"You too, *tesoro*." I end the call and pack my bags before falling asleep. The sooner I sleep, the sooner I can look into her eyes and tell her how I feel.

After landing in New York, I hurry through my postflight checklist and rush to my car. I consider stopping for flowers but decide against increasing the time it will take for me to get to her.

"Hello, Arthur. Thank you for your help yesterday," I say, stepping into the lobby.

"Good afternoon, Mr. Morgan. You're welcome. She handled herself well. Your brothers left a few hours ago."

"Thank you."

"Pardon me if I'm overstepping. Present circumstances notwithstanding, she's good for you. You have never been happier in the time I've known you." That's saying something. I moved here five years ago, and Arthur has been here since day one.

"Yes, she is. I'm thankful I found her."

"Have a good evening, sir."

I hurry into the elevator. As I enter my apartment, I lean my bag against the island and go searching for Noelle. It's near three. I check the living room, terrace, and our bedroom but don't find her. Where else could she be? A shred of fear grips me. Did she go out alone? No, she said she would stay here. The BMW is in its spot. I inhale deeply and walk around again.

Finally, I find her sound asleep with her Kindle against her chest, glasses askew, in the chair in my office. Either she was up worrying, upset about her parents, or sleeps better with me. It could even be all three.

I decide to let her sleep and fulfill her challenge from our second date. I will cook her an amazing meal on my own. I scour the fridge and find leftovers from Auggie. I will not cheat. Undeterred from acing her challenge, I gather all the necessary items and get to work. As I put the finishing touches on the table, I see her leaning against the wall. Even just waking, she's beautiful.

"Hi, *tesoro*."

"Hi. Why didn't you wake me?"

"It gave me a chance to cook for you. Plus, you don't normally nap, so I figured you needed the rest." I pull her into my arms and kiss her like I'll never be able to again. "I missed you."

"I missed you too. What are you cooking? It smells delicious."

"Pasta with sausage, greens, and beans. Sit. It's done. I was coming to wake you."

"Thank you." I set two dishes on the table and sit beside her. After a few bites, she asks, "This is delish, Cash. Is there anything you can't do?"

"Protect you properly." She sets her fork down and starts to rise from her chair. I set my hand on her forearm. "I don't want to argue with you. I just want to talk."

She settles back in her chair. I refuse to move my hand. Touching her is calming for me, especially with this topic of conversation.

"I don't want personal security, Cash. I don't think it's necessary. Yes, there were photographers camped out when I came back from getting milk yesterday. They were respectful, just doing their jobs like Jimmy."

"They may not always be respectful." My gut tells me I may not make any headway with her, but I need to try. It'll ruin me if something happens to her, especially since I can afford to protect her.

"I know. I only drive to Mrs. Waller's or your office. They won't follow me to work. I won't walk anywhere alone. Mason and I won't walk during the day anymore. There are only a few weeks left anyway."

"You may not think it's necessary, but I won't recover if something happens to you." She lifts her eyes to mine. I can only hope she sees what I'm trying to convey.

"Cash, I only drive to work. I don't need security."

"You don't understand. It's about you, not whether you're walking or driving. Photographers chased Billie when she left the gala because she refused to pose and answer their questions. A driver with no connection to the paparazzi crashed into her. She doesn't remember any of the accident or the moments leading up to it. For that I'm grateful. The photos are horrific. It took them almost eight hours to repair the lacerations to her face. I can't go through that again. I can't handle something happening to you because of me. I want to be with you every single day. I need you. I love you more."

"I love you more."

Standing from my chair, I pull her up to me and kiss her breathless. I might just make some progress after all.

NOELLE

After dinner, Cash and I have an in-depth discussion about my security. I agree to have a member of Jacob's team with me when he flies until we leave the city, as well as at the gala. Only due to the remaining length of my commitment with Mason did he relent and agree to drive me himself.

My sessions with Mason this week have been wonderful so far. Midweek, Mrs. Waller asks me to stay later so we can discuss a few things. I have one week left before they move and Mason starts school with a specialized development plan that I created. The director at his new school has been instrumental in assisting Mrs. Waller to make sure Mason's progress continues while at the center.

We enjoy iced tea on her terrace while Mason plays with Legos on the floor.

"Noelle, I'm so glad I reached out to you for Mason. He has made amazing progress. We owe that to you."

"Thank you. Initially, I was surprised you called."

"A dear friend of mine, Blythe Ellerbee, and I were discussing Mason and how her grandson may require the same type of intervention. I would like to give her your contact information."

"Thank you. I appreciate it."

"Have you made any decisions about your future?"

"Yes, I have. Cash introduced me to Mallory, a coworker of his who set up a consulting company for me. Also, I'm actively searching for a center to purchase."

"That's wonderful. Good for you. Did you always want to own a center?"

"Truthfully, yes, but I never thought it was possible. Cash pointed out that I could make it happen with some hard work and Mallory's help."

"You two remind me of myself and my husband, Gerald. You're lovely together."

I feel my cheeks heat up. "Thank you. Speaking of which, he's probably here to pick me up." I set my glass on the table and wave to Mason.

"I will speak with Blythe later today. Please expect her call."

"Thank you again. I'll see you tomorrow." Scooping up my tote, I hurry down the stairs. Him driving is a compromise, but I don't like making him wait for me either. As I round the banister and swing open the door, Elizabeth is entering the building.

"Have a great afternoon, Noelle."

"You too!" I pull the entry door closed and skip down the steps. When I round the building, I see Cash waiting for me.

"I hope you weren't waiting long," I say as I settle into my seat.

"Not at all. What is going on? You have a huge smile on your face."

"Mrs. Waller has a referral for me."

"That's great, sweetheart." Cash leans over and kisses me. The drive home is quick today. Parking in his spot, Cash hops out to open my door.

"Why did you park?" He's been pulling into the garage since he started driving me, but he doesn't normally park. He has been dropping me off and returning to the office.

"I'm working from here the rest of the day." He kisses me quickly and follows me inside.

I change into comfier clothes and filter through my email and texts while Cash makes some calls.

Kate: How are you? I miss your face.

Me: Hi. I'm doing well. You?

Kate: Same. I hate to admit it, but you were right. Having a man in my life is awesome.

Me: I tried to tell you.

Kate: You did.

Me: I'm so happy for you.

Kate: Thanks. Gotta go back in. TTYS.

At least Keyton is a man of his word. He said repeatedly he would treat her right, and he does. I should talk to Cash about my condo. He turned down the opportunity in LA, so do I need to keep my condo for us? Plus, I should get my stuff and my car. Maybe I should sell my car and buy a new one here rather than transporting it here. As I ponder these issues, my phone rings.

"Hello, this is Blythe Ellerbee. Georgia Waller gave me your contact information."

"Hi. She briefly explained your situation. How can I help you?"

Mrs. Ellerbee describes in detail the needs of her grandson and asks for my assistance in creating a plan for him. I agree to send her an information packet, and once I have it back, I'll get to work. Then I send a quick email to Mallory to verify that everything is set up for me to take on a client.

Grabbing two waters, I pad to Cash's office. He is animatedly talking on the phone with his back to me.

"Yes, I'm sure. I appreciate your assistance." Turning slowly, he smiles and ends his call. "Hey. Thanks." He sits in his chair and opens his arms to me.

"Do you have anything planned this weekend?" I ask after curling into his lap.

"Just spending time with you, why?"

"I want to get my clothes and some other personal items from my condo. Also, I want to sell my car and buy a new one rather than ship it here."

"A weekend away with you sounds perfect, even if it includes packing. When do you want to leave?" This man is too much. He'll do anything for me, as I will for him.

"Does Friday afternoon work for you?"

"Sure, I'll make the arrangements. What else?" If it were anyone else, it would bother me that he can read me so well.

Inhaling sharply, I ask, "At the risk of breaking the traditional norms you love so much, do I need to keep my condo available for us to use?"

"Do you want to keep it?"

"I don't want to spend money on a mortgage each month if no one is going to use it. The mortgage is small, and any amount of rent will cover it easily. Kate wants to move in because it's closer to her job and the beach, but it'll mean you can't use it whenever you fly to Los Angeles."

"Now I understand. Was I unclear when I said every single day? *Tesoro*, will you move in with me... permanently?"

"Yes, I will." I lean forward and kiss his soft lips.

"There's more. Enlighten me."

"I spoke with Mrs. Ellerbee, the referral from Mrs. Waller, already. She's going to send the paperwork back, and I will start my first client. I contacted Mallory just to make sure everything is set too."

"That's great!"

"What about you?"

"I'm going forward with the deal in Portsmouth, even though it will take longer than I would like."

"Wow! I'm so happy for you! What about the other owner?"

"Stacy is working on it. Either way, we're moving to Portsmouth."

"I'm so excited for you! How are you feeling about it?" I don't really give him a chance to answer because I pepper him with congratulatory kisses.

Breaking away, he replies, "I'm only concerned about the timing. If Stacy can negotiate with the other owner and secure the other shares, fantastic. If not, everything else is as close to perfect as I can get." The moment he finishes talking, I leap up from his lap.

"Where are you going?"

"I need to email Mallory right now."

"Why?"

"I need to change where she is looking for me."

"Not right now, you don't."

"Why not?"

"We need to celebrate."

Celebrate we do, for the rest of the night.

CASSIUS

Early evening on Friday, we arrive at Noelle's condo. We have a ton of work to do before we return to New York and a lot of decisions to make going forward, but for now she's keeping her condo.

Instead of getting to work, we recreate the latter part of our first date. Walking along the pier hand in hand is not only fun but nostalgic. I don't know when or if we'll be able to come back here again. We play a few games at the arcade before buying tickets for the carousel. Tickets in hand, I feel a tug on my shirt.

"Mr. Cash, Miss Noelle, what are you doing here?"

We crouch down to speak to our interrogator. Tonight, Annaliese is wearing a pink romper and white sandals. She throws her arms around Noelle's neck and whispers something I can't quite make out. Whatever Annaliese said made Noelle smile after a brief flicker of sadness.

"Hi. How are you?"

"I'm good. Mom brought me to get rid of some energy."

Noelle chuckles. "Sounds fun. Where is your mom?" Annaliese turns and points to her mom about five yards over on a bench watching us. Noelle waves just for good measure.

"Did you take my advice, Mr. Cash?"

"I did. Thank you very much."

"You're welcome. You two are perfect!"

"What is she talking about, Cash?" Noelle asks with a wink.

"Annaliese suggested that I ask you to be my girlfriend."

"Well, thank you, Annaliese," Noelle says, fixing her sandal strap.

"You're welcome. I knew I was right about him. I need to go. It was nice to see you. Bye." Before leaving, she hugs me and then Noelle again. Once she's safely back to her mom, the adults wave and go our separate ways.

Like the last time we were here, I surround her in my arms in line. I see her admirers, but I don't care. Before we were just getting to know each other; now we are building our future together. They can look all they want. I'm going to have her by my side for the rest of my life. Noelle opts for the unicorn again, and I ride next to her. After our ride, we stroll along the beach and watch the sunset. We're sitting on the sand like we were on our first date. The only difference is she's closer to me. On our first date, she was in my arms, but it was tentative, less intimate. Now, there is no question she's mine to anyone who may pass by. After the sun falls below the horizon, we walk slowly back to her condo.

We slide under her covers until daybreak after a few hours on her terrace, and I stare at the ceiling for a while before deciding to get up. Noelle is still peacefully asleep. Slipping out of bed, I lace up and run to the shore and back. As I round the corner to Noelle's, there is a tall guy wearing cargo shorts and a T-shirt hovering near her steps.

"Good morning, Mr. Morgan. Care to comment on your relationship with Miss Barnett?" I need to give him credit, it's crazy early West Coast time to be on the clock, especially on a weekend. I suppose gossip never sleeps.

"Jimmy, right?" I extend my hand to him. He shakes it before handing me his card.

"Yes."

I skim the card to verify that he is indeed a reputable reporter. "Do you live nearby? It's early on the weekend to seek a story if you live far away."

"Yes."

"Noelle indicated you were a stand-up guy and never made her concerned for her safety like other reporters. I appreciate that, as does her brother. I'm also sure you were the first person to see the connection between her and me. I'm going to make a deal with you. I'll give you an exclusive about our relationship if you're willing to wait until Saturday just before the gala for the arts to publish. I'll provide you with a photo and answer any questions you have, including my lack of relationship with Brittany Templeton."

"I can work with that," Jimmy replies. I use his pen and jot my work number and email on the back of a card.

"Please email your questions to this address, and I'll answer them. I reserve the right to refrain from answering for her safety. Otherwise, I assure you, I will be honest with you. This agreement only pertains to her and me, no one else."

"Understood. Have an enjoyable day, Mr. Morgan. I look forward to your responses." He shakes my hand and walks away.

I toe off my shoes and grab a water from her fridge. It reeks. We need to clean that out today. After chugging the water, I consider brewing coffee, but decide against it because the milk is sour too. With another water in hand, I move to the patio.

I consider when I should share my news with my siblings. I don't want to get anyone else's hopes up, but I don't see the deal going south either. Enjoying the morning sun, I smile inwardly, knowing I'm where I should be and it will only get better.

"What has you so deep in thought?" Her voice warms me from the inside out.

"You mostly. Sit with me."

"Did you go run already?"

"Yeah, I couldn't sleep with the time zone change. I saw Jimmy when I got back."

"Oh, do I need to call Nicholas?"

"I don't think so. I made a deal with him. He's going to break the story of our relationship next Saturday before the gala. I agreed to answer his questions and provide him with a photo so we can control the story."

"That was nice of you."

"You're not angry?"

"No. I know we're racing against the clock. The moment the guest list is released, everyone will know about us."

"He has been respectful of you and never made you concerned for your safety, and I appreciate that. Plus, he was the first one to figure it out. He deserves the exclusive. He's going to send me some questions by email."

"Okay. Anything else on your mind?"

"What is your plan for packing? Where do you want to start?"

"I need to disassemble my bedroom, and the movers will be here at two for transportation to New York. I rented a storage unit until we have a place to live. Then I need to pack my clothes and personal items. I'm going to leave the rest of the furniture and the dishes for Kate, except for a few teacher gifts. The only thing of importance is my bedroom set."

"Why, sweetheart?"

"It's from my childhood."

I nod and pull her close despite my sweat-soaked clothing.

After talking a bit more, Noelle makes a quick trip to the coffee shop while I shower. A latte and breakfast sandwiches later, we start disassembling her bed and emptying her bureaus. Near two, the movers arrive and remove the bedroom furniture.

"Do you mind if Kate and Keyton stop by later?"

"No, of course not."

She responds to Kate's text and gets back to filling boxes. She's methodically going through her clothes while I empty her closets. After finishing the bathroom and the linens, I move back into her bedroom. As I'm moving each album carefully into her luggage, one box falls off the shelf and photos, newspaper clippings, and small mementos scatter all over the floor.

"*Tesoro*, were these in a particular order?"

She turns, surveys the mess, and instantly tears fall from her eyes. I surround her with my arms. Sobs wrack her frame as I hold her tightly against me. Feeling helpless, I scoop her up and carry her to the couch, holding her snug against me. Soon her sobs lessen, and she looks at me. Her face is puffy, her eyes red and bloodshot.

"I'm sorry. I didn't mean to upset you."

She shakes her head. "It's tomorrow."

"I know your birthday is tomorrow."

"Yes. No, the anniversary is tomorrow." She buries her head into my shoulder. The sobs and heaves resume. Dumbfounded, I process what she just said. That's awful! My heart just shattered for her.

"They died on your birthday? Is that why you didn't tell me it was your birthday?"

She nods. "How did you find out?" she asks between heaves.

"It was on the client form for Mallory." She shakes her head against my shoulder. "How can I help?"

"Just hold me," she replies, her lips against my neck.

"As long as you will have me."

NOELLE

My parents, Edward and Josie, died in a car accident on their way home picking up my seventeenth birthday cake. I have not enjoyed my birthday since. Every therapist I have ever spoken to indicates I should move on—either party hardy or celebrate my birthday early or late. Neither one of those options work for me. I have tried both. Celebrating on my actual birthday isn't going to happen. When I celebrate the day before, I feel disingenuous because it isn't my birthday. Celebrating the day after isn't pretty either, considering I just lived another year without my parents. After six years of attempting every option, I choose to avoid celebrating. Even Nicholas and Noah support my decision. We agree to send a memory to one another via text or email and never mention the fact it is also my birthday.

"I don't celebrate my birthday anymore. I have tried so many ways to get around the facts, but I can't. While my therapists have warned me, it isn't the best choice, it works for me."

"What should I do with your gift?"

"You bought me a gift?"

"Of course. I didn't know the true reason you didn't share your birthday with me."

"I don't know. Can you just hold on to it for now? I can't. I just can't."

He nods and tightens his hold on me even more.

After some time passes, I turn in his arms and kiss him tenderly.

"Thank you."

"You're welcome. Why don't you sit here, and I'll go clean that up?" I nod wondering if that's the right response. Would steeling myself and sharing the photos be better? I'm not sure. As I consider my options, Kate and Keyton arrive.

"Hey." Kate pulls me into a bear hug. Looking me in the eyes, she asks without asking because she knows. It's impossible to live with someone for four years and not share most of your closely guarded secrets. Plus, I started sharing a dorm room with Kate just a year after they died. Content that I'm okay, she walks into my bedroom.

"Keyton, nice to see you outside of Kiely's," I say to welcome him.

"You as well. Kate mentioned she's going to move in."

"Yeah. It shortens her commute and I'm staying with Cash."

Cash and Kate return and we order some takeout. After we eat, Kate and I move into the kitchen and talk about her lease.

"I'm going to miss you," Kate chokes out.

"I'll miss you too. You're my bestie and I'm grateful you were assigned as my roommate all those years ago." I'm holding in tears, but I'm happy as well.

"Me too."

Knowing I have a lot more work do to, Kate and Keyton leave once the guys finish cleaning up.

"Don't be a stranger. You're both welcome here anytime you find yourself on the left coast." She hugs us both and whispers something to Cash. He nods.

We finish packing and sorting near nine. The last thing to clear is the kitchen. An hour later, we've emptied the cabinets and fridge. Exhausted, we collapse on the air mattress and sleep until morning.

Our flight is early, so after making one more trip around my condo, we leave for the airport as the sun comes up. I'm not selling it quite yet, but I don't imagine I'll be back again.

After spilling one of my deepest, darkest secrets to Cash, I feel a bit lighter. It's not as if I was hiding it; he knew my parents died. However, he certainly didn't know all the facts. Thankfully, we flew here on a private jet, so my extraordinary amount of luggage won't be a problem.

As we take our seats, Cash interlaces his fingers with mine and presses his lips to the top of my hand.

"Please tell me, Cash."

He simply shakes his head before speaking. Probably because I can read him as well as he can read me. I know his brain is working out an issue or a problem by the look in his eyes. "I can't possibly imagine how the last decade has been for you without your parents. Mine may be difficult, but at least they are here."

"Thank you. Keep going."

"How many birthdays have you not celebrated at all?" he asks. He has a plan, no doubt.

I consider his question. "Four, I think."

"Will you make a deal with me?"

"I'll hear you out."

"Fair enough. I would like to celebrate with you for four hours today. I agree to set aside six o'clock this evening for remembering your parents. We can set that hour aside every year for the rest of our lives if you want, but we should celebrate you as well."

Either Kate told him the time or he read it in the clippings in the box from my closet. I appreciate the effort.

"What do these four hours look like to you?"

"Once we get home, I would like to get you a meal and maybe a cake. I would love for you to share some of the memories that your brothers have shared or one of your own. Perhaps you would be willing to peek at your gift."

Before answering, I consider the huge step he is asking me to take, along with all the others we plan to take together. "Can we start smaller? Say two hours for me and one for them."

"We can."

"'Thank you' doesn't cover what I need you to hear. I have never shared this truth with anyone. I never wanted to. No one truly ever saw me before you." I lean over to kiss him tenderly.

He brushes the single tear away with the pad of his thumb. "I will move a mountain for you, *tesoro*."

My heart clenches in my chest. I unbuckle us and lead Cash to the couch to curl up in his arms.

Luckily, Cash drove the Rover to the airport on Friday. These boxes wouldn't fit in the car. We made a stop at a small bakery on the way home. I opt for pizza instead of eating out. The knot in my stomach keeps getting tighter as we get closer to home. The sheer terror of the notion that I will celebrate today makes me nauseous.

We move the boxes up to the lobby and then into the elevator with Arthur's help. Cash orders the food before we set the boxes into the guest room. I'll go through them and move clothes as I need them. I sorted them as I packed and labelled each box. I won't need my shorts much longer as fall is rapidly approaching.

All the mantras from therapy keep resurfacing. *You can do this. They would want you to be happy. Life goes on.* The list is endless. All sage words no matter which way you look at it. I steel myself and resolve to handle these three hours. Next year, I'll do four if this goes well.

The food arrived just a few minutes ago, and we sit on the terrace and eat. The pepperoni pizza quells the nausea a bit. Wherever we move must have an amazing outdoor space like this one.

"Will you tell me a memory that Nicholas has shared with you?"

"Yes, but when did you start calling my brother Nicholas?"

"I talked to him last Saturday." He lets his words hang, probably expecting me to lash out.

"Nicholas only texted to check on me. You made a deal with him, didn't you?"

"Depends. Will you be angry if I did?"

"Not necessarily."

"I knew he would learn about the photographers, so I reached out to prevent him from sending Maia or Connor without at least hearing you out first."

"He texted but didn't mention anything. Apparently, you got through to him. You didn't answer my question."

"By calling and risking your wrath, his words, I basically put it out there that I love you. He indicated that he trusts me and that I should call him Nicholas."

I nod and share Nicholas's favorite memory of our Labrador digging up my mother's garden and our failure of reconstructing it.

"How do you normally remember your parents today?"

"I usually spend most of the day alone and quiet."

"Do you want me to go, or can I sit here with you for at least the next hour," he says in a whisper, opening his arms to me. I snuggle into his warm body and steal every ounce of comfort he's offering me. I would never ask him to go.

Cash chose a chocolate cake with a Nutella mousse filling. I don't recall telling him chocolate is my flavor of choice. Just past seven, with one candle to symbolize starting birthday celebrations over, I make a wish for the first time in a decade.

"What would you like to do now?" he asks as we clean the dishes.

"Thank you for holding me up today. It may not seem like much, but I made noteworthy progress today. Please don't take my next statement personally. It's about me. I can't accept your gift today. I can't balance getting gifts with the loss I still feel."

Rounding the island, Cash pulls me into his arms. "Whatever you need."

I decide to call it a night.

CASSIUS

While this weekend wasn't exactly how I planned. I took the curveball and went with it. It's unfathomable that her parents died on her birthday. To make matters worse, they were out getting a cake. The pain in her eyes is unbearable. I never saw it before yesterday. When she mentioned the anniversary was coming, I wasn't prepared for this level of sorrow.

Noelle's response is vastly different from Sam's loss. Sam retreated and has yet to fully come out again. I see any time she's willing to focus on herself as a win. The time to reflect on her parents is important. Allowing me to get her a birthday cake was a gigantic step. I'm grateful she let me to do it. They may not be here, but they have profoundly affected her world view and how deeply she loves. Thankfully, she loves me.

After dropping Noelle off at work, I stroll into my office and take my messages from Myles. I have emails from Mallory, Stacy, and Jimmy. I'll handle Jimmy's questions after I pick up Noelle from Mrs. Waller's.

"Hey, Mal," I say as she steps into my office. Face-to-face works just as well, I suppose.

"Hi, Cash. How was your weekend?"

"Good. Yours?"

"I was going through Noelle's information and noticed a discrepancy on her paperwork."

"What?"

"She listed her home address as California. I thought she lived with you." I exhale silently. It isn't that I distrust Noelle. Momentarily, I was worried this error could affect her new business endeavor.

"Just habit would be my guess. She just moved in with me permanently last week." I don't need to explain the changes that have occurred in the last few weeks. "Is that all?"

"Yes. I gather she has her first client set up. Good for her."

"She does. Thank you for working with her. Taking this leap was a big deal for her."

"You're welcome." Mal hurries away after her cell rings, and Myles announces that Stacy is early for our appointment.

I indicate that I need a few minutes before the meeting. I need to settle my nerves. All the pieces of my life are starting to fall into place, and I couldn't be happier.

"Good morning, Stacy. How are you and Jocelyn?"

"Morning. We're doing well. Let's get this started. She and I have a meeting with a potential birth mother this afternoon."

"That's wonderful. I hope it's the perfect match."

He nods. "There are two distinct parts to this deal. First, Graham Edson is the majority shareholder of Edson Avionics. He answers to a board comprised of his four children. They own the balance of 24 percent of the company. They have signed off on the sale. He's looking to sell his 60 percent stake of Pemberton Airlines, and he has accepted your purchase offer. However, he refuses to expedite the timeline and the closing is set for January 15."

While I hoped he would be amenable to an expedited time frame, I prepared for him to balk at that part of my offer. I want his shares of Pemberton.

"Here are the preliminary reports. I didn't find anything that concerns me other than the time frame. I don't see a legitimate reason why he wouldn't expedite the sale." Stacy hands me a box full of documents.

"He's thorough. I'll give him that. And the second part?"

"Second you asked me to look into the minority owner of Pemberton. Cecil Elliott is an older gentleman who owns the remaining 40 percent of Pemberton Airlines. He would like to meet with you in person to discuss your terms."

"Do you see that as a good thing or bad thing?"

"All the information I could find on Mr. Elliott leads me to believe he's old school. Prefers to deal face-to-face rather than via email."

"Okay, did he give you times he's available?"

Stacy nods and hands me a list of open appointments and Mr. Elliott's assistant's contact info.

"I'll set this up today. Thank you for your help on this. I don't trust anyone else with our life."

"Our?" Stacy asks with keen interest in my use of pronoun.

"Yes, our."

"She's good for you. I'm happy for you. I'll miss you here and in the ring."

I reply in kind, and Stacy leaves me with a stack of paperwork to review and a meeting to schedule. Before clearing off my desk for the day to pick up Noelle, I reach out to Nicholas regarding security for the gala and a consultation request with Jacob for our new home, wherever that may be. I will share my news with my siblings after I meet with Mr. Elliott.

On the ride home, Noelle and I discuss Jimmy's questions and our responses. While I drive, she types out the answers on my phone. For some reason, there is traffic today.

Rather than slave away in my cozy home office, I opt to work on the terrace. Noelle is finishing up some things for her new client, including a call with the director of his school and a second referral, this one from the director of Mason's school. My plan is fine until Noelle decides to catch some rays, clad in her red bikini, her long tresses piled atop her head, and huge sunglasses. I'm no longer focused on the reports cast before me. Instead, I'm focused on her toned abdomen moving rhythmically as she breathes and the curve of her heavy breasts straining against the thin fabric.

"Do you need me to go inside?" she asks, turning her head in my direction.

"Not at all." That's a bold-faced lie. Although I should move, not her.

"Are you sure? I can feel you memorizing me instead of those reports."

"Yes, I'm sure. At this point, it doesn't matter if I'm here or in my office. I'll be thinking about your curves more than these reports. We should talk about these reports anyway."

Her turning on her side offers me a different view of the luscious curves I burn into my mind each time I touch her.

"Are those for your deal?"

"Yes. Stacy gave them to me this morning."

We spend the rest of the afternoon talking about the two deals, along with a host of other related options, like where to live and when to share the news with our families. Noelle plans to share her new business and plans for a center at the same time I do. Despite my desires otherwise, I stay far enough away so I can't touch her. The moment I touch her will be the last I work today.

During our discussion, I field calls from Nicholas, Jacob, and Esther, Mr. Elliott's assistant. I schedule a meeting for Thursday afternoon to return on Friday. I sent a quick text to Billie to make sure her condo is empty.

When we finish reviewing most of the reports and talk more about our ideal place to live, I gather everything and bring it into the office. As I return to the terrace, Noelle is stepping into the hot tub sans bikini.

"Care to join me?"

I have never stripped off my clothes faster.

NOELLE

Sadness overtakes me as I get to work at the end of this week. Cash left in the wee hours this morning to meet with Mr. Elliott about purchasing his stake in Pemberton. When I took the position to tutor Mason, I was grateful to have something to do with my time as well as the opportunity to use my plan. Not only have I been able to help Mason make considerable progress, but it also assisted me in starting my consulting company.

Yesterday I conducted a teleconference with Mrs. Ellerbee and her grandson, Jeremy, after receiving his assessment. While I don't like to compare my students, Jeremy isn't as far behind as Mason was. I believe that my work with Mason and Mrs. Waller's referral will assist Jeremy earlier. I'll create a plan for him within the next week and work to implement it with the director of his preschool.

"Good morning, Miss Noelle."

"Hi. Mason. How are you today?"

"Good but sad."

"I'm sad too. It's okay to be sad. Your grandmother said you can call me anytime you want or write as often as you would like. I'll make sure she has my address and phone number."

"What are my tasks for today?" Mason asks, eager to learn. I don't normally pat myself on the back, but he didn't have that eagerness before. I instilled that in him. I just hope his new center allows him to continue to flourish. I have set up a quarterly conference with the director to review his plan and make changes as necessary. I will follow the same procedure for Jeremy after his plan is in place.

"Your choice."

A huge smile spreads across Mason's face. He opts for reading, sight word practice, and dramatic play. After a funny rendition of *Beauty and the Beast* with cardboard puppets, Mason takes a quiet break in his room. While he takes some time, I check my messages.

Billie: I can't wait to see you tomorrow. The gala is a wonderful event.

Me: I'm still surprised you're going.

Billie: I'm more than comfortable with my life to see my "parents."

Me: Good for you. Are you coming in with Cash tomorrow?

Billie: Yes. Maybe I'll stop by.

Me: Perfect.

After hearing about Billie, her parents, and her learning about her biological father and half sister, I wouldn't want to be in the same room as her mother. Unfortunately, her mother is Cash's mother, so I don't have a choice.

The memories I have of my mother are wonderful and preserved in my head. I recall times where I was grounded or in trouble for something or other, but nothing rises to the level of anguish that Billie must feel for the lies and betrayal.

Cash: I just landed. I'll call you tonight. Please be aware of your surroundings when you leave. Please don't go out alone. I made sure there is milk, ice cream, and that dark chocolate you love at home. I love you more.

His overprotective streak almost had him pushing this meeting off until next week so I wouldn't be alone. While I love the growly possessive vibe he has, I couldn't allow him to put off this meeting. It's two commutes. No big deal. On Saturday when Jimmy publishes his story, it will be different. Hence why someone from Jacob's team will be arriving early Saturday to attend the gala with us.

Me: Good luck. I'll be fine. I will. Thank you. I love you more.

I toss my phone into my tote and move to rouse Mason. After a soft knock, I find him balling in a comfy chair in the corner of this room.

"What's wrong, sweetie?"

Between gasps and sobs, he says, "My mommy died."

"I know, sweetie. Mine died too."

"Really?" Mason asks softly.

"Yes, my mom and dad died about ten years ago." I hear footsteps outside Mason's door. Mrs. Waller is there, but Mason isn't aware of her presence.

"Is it hard?" Mason mumbles against my arm.

"What?"

"Having no parents?"

"It is. I'm not as lucky as you, though. You have an amazing grandmother who can take care of you. I didn't have that."

"Who took care of you?" Mason asks.

I can see the disconnect in his eyes. To him I'm an adult. I don't need anyone to take care of me like he does. I don't know the situation with his father, but in his mind, it seems he never had one.

"For about a year, my big brother took care of me. After that I was an adult and I took care of myself."

"I'm sorry, Miss Noelle."

"Thank you, Mason. I am too."

Mrs. Waller enters the room and declares schoolwork done for the day. The three of us bring a drink to the rooftop and absorb some sunlight. Tomorrow is my last day with Mason. He'll be moving on. The director at his new center is competent and willing to work with me for him. Either way, I'll miss seeing him every day.

After driving straight home, I change into comfy clothes and edit my draft of Jeremy's education plan. I hope to get it finished tomorrow afternoon before Cash gets back from Portsmouth. Saving the latest draft, I close my laptop to answer the intercom.

"Miss Barnett, there is a Miss Caroline Waterman here to see you."

I pause before answering. "Good afternoon, Arthur. Does she have long, dark hair, average height, and she was here with August Morgan a few weeks ago?"

"Yes."

Good. Otherwise, I had no idea who she is.

"Please send her up." I consider changing quickly but decide against it. I wonder what she needs. Cash wouldn't send her. He would send Sam to check on me. As she steps inside, I greet her. "Hi, Caro. How are you?"

"I'm well. How are you?"

"Pretty good." I move into the kitchen. "Drink?"

"Water, please."

I grab two waters and lead her outside. "What's up?"

Dressed in leggings, a tunic, and a light sweater, she looks much younger than she did when I first met her. Auggie better not wait too long or someone else will scoop her up. She's gorgeous, and the details I know about her are extraordinary.

"I'm here for my little brother, half brother. Auggie mentioned something in passing about your company. He was short on details, so here I am. If you can't help Cooper, no problem. If you can, that would be wonderful for my family."

"Do your parents know you're here?" She nods. "Tell me about Cooper."

I listen to Caro explain the issues with Cooper and his school. Then I explain the process for my services, how I determine if my services can assist Cooper, and my fees.

"What do you need me to do?" she asks with a bit of excitement in her voice.

I hand her a piece of paper "Jot down contact information for you and your parents. I'll send over my intake sheet to see what, if anything, I can do."

Caro throws her arms around my neck hugging me tight. "Thank you. Thank you. I'm hopeful you can help."

We trade our water for wine and chat for the next hour or so. She leaves, indicating I'll see her at the gala.

I consider her visit. Part of me is sad that her brother is going through so much at school, but the other part of me is giddy knowing I may be able to help another student reach their full potential. I have Cash to thank for that. As if he heard me, my phone rings with a video call.

CASSIUS

"Hi, *tesoro*. How was Mason today?"

I can tell something is off. Generally, she's full of rainbows and sunshine after she works with Mason. Also, Mrs. Waller is also a great sounding board for her and her business endeavors.

"He had a small breakdown about his mom. When I explained that my mom died too, we talked more in depth."

"Was that hard for you?" I wonder if anyone has ever cared enough to ask that question, a therapist maybe.

"Honestly, it was hard at first, but then I realized I could be for Mason something I didn't have—a sympathetic ear."

"What else happened today?"

"I got another referral, and Caro stopped by about me possibly helping her brother. What about you?"

"Wow! That's amazing! I didn't know her brother had developmental issues." I'm not sure I knew Caro had a younger brother either.

"Did the meeting go poorly, Cash?"

"No, not at all. I'm still wrapping my head around it. I was with Mr. Elliott until thirty minutes ago. I want to have a third of his energy at eighty-five years old. He's a spry guy and funny."

"Cassius Morgan."

Holy hell! That's arousing even through the phone. Not only her saying my full name, but the bit of fire behind it.

"Say that again."

"Cassius Morgan. Tell me!"

"That is so fucking hot, *tesoro*!"

A fierce blush appears on her face. "Cash, do you want to sleep on the couch?"

"You wouldn't dare kick me out of my own bed." It's my bed. No, it's *our* bed. I love this fiery side of her.

"If you don't start talking, I will."

"After Stacy processes the paperwork, I will be the proud owner of Mr. Elliott's shares of Pemberton by the end of October."

"Really! I'm so happy for you! I wish you were here so we could celebrate."

"Me too." I kissed her thoroughly before I left this morning, and it wasn't enough. It'll never be enough. I need her. I'll be home soon, but I have a breakfast meeting with Jacob at Rick's regarding security concerns for our new home. "What time is your spa appointment tomorrow?"

"I'm going straight there after working with Mason. I'll need something relaxing. Plus, I want cute toes for the gala."

"I should be home for dinner. I just need to pick up my tux from the cleaners." I need to pick up jewelry to match her gown too. I asked Billie to pick out the perfect jewelry. I love that she's willing to help.

"Good night, Cash. I love you more."

"I love you more." I end the call and sit listening to the ocean sounds through Billie's French doors. Near the water would be perfect. Now to find a location that will make Noelle happy. That's all I need.

When I arrive at Rick's, Jacob nods from a corner booth along with another equally imposing man. I'm a fit guy, but Jacob and whoever is sitting with him would worry me in a dark alley.

"Good morning, Cash," Jacob says as I near the table.

"Jacob."

"This is Connor. He's a member of my team and usually works on Kelly's detail. He'll be attending the gala tomorrow, so I thought you would like to meet beforehand. He and Noelle have met before."

"Pleasure to meet you, Connor." I extend my hand to him.

His huge hand takes mine. "You as well."

A server approaches the table. After a moment's pause, she takes our order and leaves. It wasn't until Noelle that I notice people gawk and stare at her, but me as well. Pair me with these two, and the stares from the staff and patrons are comical.

"What can I do for you, Cash?" Jacob asks.

"Noelle and I will be looking for a property in the area soon. Are there areas or property types we should avoid, or is it case by case?"

"Are you looking for a general assessment or on-site security?"

"Noelle is adamantly against personal security. She has agreed for the gala because it'll be our first public event as a confirmed couple. A reporter we trust will be releasing a vetted story and photo tomorrow, which necessitates having Connor present. She also agreed to have security when she's alone in the city on the weekends I fly. I don't believe on-site security will be necessary after we leave New York. I need an assessment of the property and installation or creation of a complete security system if we build."

"Let me know when you narrow it down and send me the property sheets. I can make a cursory assessment. Once you narrow your choice to one or two, I can come and walk the properties with you. Griffin Harbaugh is a discrete local realtor. He caters to clients like you, including Kelly and Nicholas, in the purchase of their home."

I nod and dig into my breakfast. After eating and discussing a few more details for tomorrow, the three of us part ways. Hustling to the airport, I hurry back to the city, along with my sister and Peter.

Pulling into my parking spot, I note that Noelle is home. As I step inside, she isn't in the kitchen or living room. After a brief search, I find her sitting at my desk tapping away on her laptop with AirPods. Leaning against the door, I watch her. Her long legs tucked under her, wearing one of my shirts, her hair tied in a loose braid over her shoulder, her lower lip trapped by her teeth, she's focused. Her brain makes her even sexier than her smoking-hot curves.

Me: Are you ignoring me?

I send the text and wait. As her phone lights up, she glances over and then looks up. A huge smile brightens her features as she moves into my arms.

"No, I was trying to finish this before you got home."

I scoop her up, and her legs wrap around my waist as I carry her into the bedroom, my mouth against her smooth skin.

"I don't like being away from you even for a day," I confess.

"I'm not a fan either."

"How was your last day with Mason?" I ask, continuing my quest to taste every inch of her tonight.

"Good but sad as well. Do you really think—" A moan falls from her lips.

Setting her on the edge of the mattress, I unfasten the top two buttons of my shirt while marking a southward path with my tongue.

"I'll be able to answer your quest—"

Moving downward along the column of buttons, I open my shirt completely, exposing her perfect, lush breasts and a small triangle of lace barely covering her center.

"—while your mouth is on my—"

I feel the surrender when she fails to finish her sentence.

As I drag my tongue up her rib cage, nipping the underside of her breasts while pinching her nipples between my fingertips, she trembles under me. When I feel her heat through my pants, I purposely move back so I can take my time savoring her. The pout of her plump lips is almost enough for me to speed up.

Hooking the sides of her thong, I draw it down her toned legs. Kneeling on the floor, I start with her freshly painted toes and kiss a path upward from the top of her feet to the apex of her thighs. Pushing her legs apart, I hold her still before gliding the flat of my tongue from bottom to top, flicking her clit. I may have pushed off her release, but she's teetering on the edge again. Lapping and sucking her folds has her arching off the bed. Holding her still, I continue feasting on her until she shatters from my tongue.

"Cash, I need you."

"I need you, but I'm not finished memorizing you yet." My response coupled with my mouth travelling along her hip elicits a groan.

Not content with my answer, she reaches for my belt, unhinging it with one hand. Moments later, her delicate fingers wrap around my shaft. Pumping up and down, she makes me lengthen and harden even more.

"Noelle," I grit out. Determined, I continue my exploration of her body with my tongue and fingers. Releasing me, she attempts to push my pants off. I take advantage and pin her arms above her head and grab her pink point between my teeth.

"Cash, I need…. Let go of my hand."

Gripping tighter, I slide my hand between her breasts, over the curve of her belly, and thrust three fingers deep into her heat. I plunge in and out of her slick channel, watching her body writhe. Seeing the effect of my hands on her—the flush of her skin, the bounce of her breasts as she vibrates with need and pushes against my hand, the strain of her abs as her release coils inside her—is a heady feeling.

"Let go, *tesoro*."

As if my words are a catalyst, her walls clench around my fingers and milk them as she writhes beneath me. Before the throbbing around my fingers ends, she yanks her arm free and pulls me on top of her.

"Off! Your pants need to come off!" she commands.

Honestly, I didn't plan on exploring any longer, but her words arouse me even more. I hover over her as she pushes my pants and boxer briefs down. Instead of using her feet or allowing me to remove them, she slithers under me, her taut nipples grazing my skin, her mouth marking my chest as she moves down. As I struggle to free my feet, she draws her tongue along my cock before swirling around the tip.

"Not happening right now, sweetheart! Get back up here!"

I hear a soft giggle as she moves up, drawing a circle around my nipple before making a path up my neck to my lips. When she finishes wiggling her way up, the desire in her eyes is unmistakable.

"I need to feel you deep inside me."

I align my shaft at her entrance.

"How do you have this much self-control?" She whines at my pace.

I push forward a mere inch.

"Deeper, Cash."

In one motion, I watch her center swallow me whole. I withdraw and thrust forward. The sounds of pleasure falling from her lips spur me on. I'll never tire of making her shatter in pleasure from my body. Hard and deep, I thrust into her sheath. Her walls clench around me, her fingernails pierce the skin of my back, and her mouth marks my shoulder as she shudders around me. With another plunge into her heat, I pour myself into her. She's every fantasy I have ever had come to life. I plan to spend every minute of that life showing her how much I love her.

Turning slightly, I lower myself next to her while kissing her deeply. "How does that keep getting better?"

"I don't know, but we should keep doing it to find out," she murmurs against my lips.

"Yes, we should."

Forgoing dinner, we fall into a deep slumber.

NOELLE

As if last night wasn't enough, I wake to Cash pressing soft kisses to my shoulder blade and the back of my neck. The feel of him hard against me isn't unwanted either.

"Mmmm, good morning to you too."

"Morning. How much time do you need to get ready?"

"An hour or less, not including breakfast. Why?"

"I need to know how much time I have to worship you again." Cash presses his mouth to the cap of my shoulder and starts to move down my arm.

I squirm under his mouth before succumbing to his fingers and body making mine sing again.

A few hours later, we stumble into the kitchen foraging for food. After filling up on a tasty breakfast, I pad into the shower before Cash. He steps in while I dry my hair. The brush stops moving through my hair almost immediately. Instead, I'm focused on the water running down his hard, naked body.

"You should pay attention to your hair, not me," he says, catching me staring.

"You're no fun," I pout.

"That's a bold-faced lie and you know it."

I chuckle and resume drying my hair. When Cash steps out of the enclosure, it takes restraint to keep my hands to myself.

"*Tesoro*, as much as I would like to peel that luxurious silk off of your body, we can't be late."

I pull my lower lip between my teeth just to get a reaction out of him.

"You need to fight fair." He slides his hand around my neck before kissing me. The heat of his kisses ticks up rapidly, and the next thing I know, I'm sitting on the vanity counter and his towel is on the floor. His erection pressed against my heated core.

"Fighting fair doesn't work for me."

"As much as I want to feel you wrapped around me, we don't have enough time." He grabs his towel off the floor and tucks it at his waist. Even still I'm still drooling over his bare chest. With a quick, chaste kiss, Cash leaves the bathroom.

My dress is gorgeous. Billie created a fitted gown with a scoop neck in an emerald green silk. The back is open except for two strands of gemstones attached at the top of my shoulders. Faintly I hear the intercom as I'm dressing. The next time I see him, I'm sliding on my shoes.

"What's wrong?" I ask when he steps into the bedroom.

"You're stunning."

I feel heat seep across my skin. "It's the dress. Your sister is gifted with design and fabric."

"No, it's all you."

"Thank you. You look hot yourself. I was right about the tux; it's better than the suit, and you look damn good in your tailored suits."

"Did you stick with your other plan?"

I smirk. He remembered the "no panties" plan. "I'll never tell." I wink and move to spritz on some perfume.

"I want to strip that dress from your curves and find out right now."

Heat pools between my thighs, and the ache I feel for him intensifies. "You'll have to wait until we get home."

He hangs his head before removing a box from his top drawer. "Billie said this would work with your dress."

I simply shake my head and take the box from his hand. "There's no way for me to stop you from buying me gifts, is there?"

"Probably not."

Inside the box is a gorgeous tennis bracelet. I must admit, his gift choices thus far have been on point. Gaudy jewelry isn't for me. As Cash clasps it around my wrist, I wonder what he got for my birthday. He reaches into the bureau and pulls out a small box.

"Are you inside my head?"

"Maybe a little." He gently wipes the tear from my cheek. "You deserve all of this and more. Maybe next year, you can accept it on your day. Don't cry. I love you more, *tesoro*."

Nestled inside the box is a pair of diamond solitaire earrings.

"These are…. I love you more."

Before leaving for the gala, Cash has Connor take a photo and send it to Jimmy. He replies instantly and thanks Cash for trusting him. Cash replies in kind. We probably have thirty minutes before our phones start exploding. The line of limos is around the corner from the Plaza Hotel. I sit beside Cash, fidgeting with the clasp of my clutch.

He takes my hand to slow my fidgeting and shaking. "*Tesoro*, I won't leave your side."

I nod and stare deeply into his dark, loving eyes. I'm not sure what I'm worried about. We set it up to control the release of our relationship and put any other rumors to rest.

I inhale deeply as the car stops at the entrance to the gala. *Here goes nothing.* Connor steps out, followed by Cash. After buttoning his jacket, Cash reaches down for my hand. Looking up at him, I see my future. I also see that this is temporary. We won't be here much longer. I can handle this for him. I slide my trembling hand in his, and he tucks it around his arm. The questions pelt us the moment my Louboutins touch the red carpet.

"Is she pregnant too?"

"What about Brittany?"

The type of questions shifts the moment everyone realizes they have been scooped by Jimmy. A proud smile creeps onto Cash's face as we walk along the red carpet.

"Where did you meet?"

"How long have you been hiding her?"

"When does Ellis's next movie release?"

"Does your brother approve?"

Yes, but I don't need it. As we reach the door, we turn for the obligatory posed photo. The heat of his hand on my skin makes my heart race. After a full minute, Connor ushers us inside.

Cash leads me over to the side, crowding me against the wall so our conversation is private. Connor stands close enough to prevent a photo, although most of the photographers are busy with the arriving guests.

"I'm fine. Truly, but that was only half of what I need to handle tonight."

"I love you more, *tesoro.*"

"I love you more, Cassius."

After a kiss promising more sexy time later, Cash taps Connor on the shoulder and we walk toward the ballroom. As we approach, Billie rushes up to us, pulling me into her arms.

"Billie, your dress is phenomenal!"

"Thanks, but I think your perfect frame has something to do with it too."

I smile and chat with Billie while Cash and Peter catch up. Connor is standing dutifully beside me, even though Cash hasn't let go of my hand. We sit with Cash's siblings, but not his parents. As we take our seats, I chat with Billie, Caroline, and Sam's assistant, Savannah. She's is breathtaking. Her flawless skin, dark hair, and piercing blue eyes compliment her sharp wit. She started working with Sam about four months ago and reluctantly agreed to accompany him tonight.

Dinner service starts promptly, and we dine on the delicious food. Even Auggie seems to be enjoying the meal. That's certainly saying something.

After the first two courses, the ladies and I take a trip to the powder room to gossip a bit. Connor dutifully follows me after I assure Cash repeatedly that I will be fine with his sister and future sisters-in-law. He smirks at that part. It might be a dream on my part, seeing Auggie and Caro together in the future. As dinner wraps, a few couples take to the dance floor.

"Will you join me on the dance floor? It's the only place I'll be able to hold you against me and it won't be frowned upon," Cash whispers so only I can hear him.

"I want nothing more than the heat of your hands against my skin," I reply near the shell of his ear. I love that I can make him squirm. Cash leads me onto the dance floor, pulling me against him. His big, warm hand grips the exposed skin of my back.

"Are you going to tell me or let me wonder?" he asks, sliding his hand lower on my back.

"I'm going to keep you guessing until we get home. It wouldn't be any fun if I simply tell you. Would it? Plus, that hitch in your voice is quite sexy."

"You think I'm sexy?" Cash's eyes bore into mine.

"You are everything I never knew I needed in a hot, sexy-as-hell package."

"I love when you curse. Do we need to get out of here right now, Miss Barnett?"

"We can't leave yet, Mr. Morgan, but I love where your mind is."

Cash spins me away from him and twists me back, holding me even closer. After a few more ballads, the pace of the music increases, and Cash leads me off the dance floor. As we walk toward our table, I catch a glimpse of Mr. and Mrs. Waller.

CASSIUS

"We should say hello to Mrs. Waller," Noelle suggests, and I dutifully follow her.

"Noelle and Cash, it's wonderful to see you," Mrs. Waller says as we approach. She looks lovely in a tailored, sequined suit. Mr. Waller looks unhappy to be in attendance, but his suit makes him look dapper, nonetheless.

"You as well."

The four of us chat about Mason and their upcoming move and how Noelle was instrumental in helping Mason cope with his mother's death. Her fingers tighten around mine as Mrs. Waller heaps on the praise. Nothing Noelle does for herself, me, or her students is for the praise. It's for the betterment of the person or relationship. She's the only truly selfless person I have ever met. That reason alone is why I plan to put her first every single day for the rest of my life.

"Son," my father bellows from behind me to the left. Mr. and Mrs. Waller discreetly walk away. My distaste for my parents is held by the Wallers as well.

"Father." I try my best to keep the edge off my voice.

"Miss Barnett, a pleasure to see you again."

"Mr. Morgan," she replies with a fake, tight smile. When Noelle smiles, truly smiles, her warmth affects everyone around her. She's weary of my father. It's understandable given what I've told her. I slide my arm around her, guiding her close to me. The tension in her body relaxes but only slightly.

"I want to speak with you about your trust. Our attorneys have reviewed the provisions, and arguably you have skirted violating the employment rules. Your mother and I don't approve of your latest endeavor. However, she is hell-bent on stopping the payments. She will once she finds an appropriate means to do so."

"As I said before, I'm making this career change either way. If you and Mother feel the need to cut me off from my trust, so be it. I don't need the money." Noelle tightens her grip on my fingers. "Here she is now."

My mother joins our tidy group. Noelle's fingers clench my hand so hard I think she may break my fingers. The tension has returned tenfold. I glance over at her and see fire in her eyes.

"Cash."

"Mother."

"Aren't you going to introduce me to your lady friend of the moment?" My mother knows nothing about my personal life. I highly doubt she would remember any date I've been on before her dreadful setup with Brittany.

"Mother, please—"

Before I get a chance, Noelle interrupts me. "I genuinely thought your wonderful children were exaggerating. Not having had a mother figure for the last ten years, I thought there's no way you're as evil and manipulative as they suggest. Yet you are. They may have even been sugarcoating you a tad. How dare you pretend you've never met me before while pretending to be someone else."

I shiver at Noelle's words and look between her and my mother, neither woman giving any ground. It's hot as fuck that my fiery woman is going toe to toe with my mother.

"Mother, what is she talking about?" I'm giving her the opportunity to back out of her lie.

"I have no idea."

Resolute, Noelle continues. "What should I call you, Mrs. Morgan? Margaux or Elizabeth? You stalked me. You invited me and my student on walks in the park. For what? To what end?"

"You aren't good enough for my son."

"You don't know me."

"I don't need to know you. I know your type—beautiful, orphan, gold digger. As soon as you can, you'll quit your job and bleed my son dry."

Enough.

"Mother, your behavior is unacceptable. She should bring charges against you, although I'm sure you failed to step over the line for criminality. Have a good evening."

"I will cut you off, Cassius."

"You do what you need to do." I turn with Noelle and walk away from my parents. I'm fuming. I knew my mother's required level of civility barely rises to the level of hatred, but this is over the top even for her. We approach our table, and Noelle grabs her clutch. I nod to Connor who is calling for our car.

My phone is incessantly vibrating in my pocket. I'll deal with it later. As we approach the door, my father impedes our exit. I turn, effectively sandwiching Noelle between myself and Connor.

"Son, I was unaware of your mother's subterfuge. I will address her actions later. If you would like to petition for the release of the corpus of your trust a bit early, I'll support it."

Maintaining my poker face proves difficult. He would break ranks with my mother? Color me intrigued. It makes me wonder what other misdeeds my mother has committed aside from adultery and betraying my sister. Is there more? My stomach roils at that thought.

"Miss Barnett…."

Noelle steps to her left only enough to see my father's face.

"I apologize on behalf of my wife. Her actions are unacceptable. I would have hoped that our daughter effectively cutting us out of her life would be enough for Margaux to change her ways. That doesn't seem to be the case. I sincerely apologize. I have never seen my son happy until he met you, and for that I'm grateful." My father extends his hand to me, and I take it. As I release his hand, I note that my siblings and their dates are standing in a line at the top of the staircase. Margaux is noticeably absent.

Connor bids us farewell once we arrive at home. I thank him for his assistance. I'm glad he was with us, even though it turned out to be unnecessary, a fact I will dispute to Noelle until I die.

Noelle is pacing on the terrace barefoot with a glass of wine in her hand. Occasionally she stares up at the stars. I could stand here and watch her indefinitely, but I prefer to hold her in my arms.

"I'm sorry, sweetheart. I didn't know."

"You have nothing to apologize for. You warned me. You said your parents were…. It's a fault that I see only the good in people, that I fail to see when I'm being played. Honestly, I feel used. Luckily, I didn't share anything with her. I just can't understand what she would gain, other than a breakup."

"Your 'fault,' as you call it, is nothing of the sort. It makes you, you. That is where I get caught up as well. Sharing my life with you shouldn't matter in the slightest. It has nothing to do with the turbulent relationship I have with my parents. That's on them, mostly her."

The intercom rings, and I move to answer it. I return to her, kissing her thoroughly before the door opens. "I will need to wait to determine if you are wearing panties a bit longer."

"Why?"

As I start to respond, my siblings and their dates step into our home for an unplanned afterparty because I failed to check my phone.

"Apparently, they need details tonight."

I grab more glasses and a few bottles of wine. Auggie and Caro sit side by side on the couch. Billie curls up on Peter's lap on the love seat. Savannah is sitting on the couch adjacent to Sam's chair. After a brief chat about what went down with Margaux, I declare the subject closed. We drink, laugh, and dance for a few hours on the terrace instead of the Plaza ballroom. It's fantastic.

As she sets the last glass to dry, I move behind her, drawing my fingertips from low on her back to the curve of her neck. Goose bumps materialize as my fingers rise.

"You really shouldn't do dishes in a custom silk gown," I murmur against her bare skin while sliding my hands over her body to determine if she followed through.

Turning in my arms, she responds, "Perhaps we should address that," before wetting my lips with her tongue.

Slowly and purposefully, I dance her to our bed to spend the night pleasuring her.

NOELLE

Near one in the afternoon, we stumble to the kitchen for food. At least we got some sleep. I lost count after three mind-numbing orgasms. The intensity of us increases each time we make love. Our first kiss has nothing on us now.

As Cash rushes out the door to the office, I start my yoga practice in the living room. Yoga in the rain is not a fun endeavor. My goal for this week is to set a schedule, complete the plans for my five clients, tweak the intake form a bit, and reformat the fee schedule.

Even though I no longer work with Mason, Cash has been working at home in the afternoons before boxing with Evan. I try not to entice him to stay home. He'll miss the guys when we move.

Midweek, as I sit to get started on my plans, I check my phone for texts and emails. There are a few texts and an email from Mallory with an update. Unfortunately, there is nothing to report on the brick-and-mortar center currently. I scroll through my texts.

Kate: Hey there! Your condo is fantastic! How are you?
Me: Hey! It is! I'm glad you love it there. I'm well. You?
Kate: We're good. Really good. I miss being able to drop in on you.
Me: I miss you too. Say hi to Keyton for me. Love you.
Kate: I will. Love you too.

I would like to say it was hard leaving California, but it wasn't. Sure, I miss Kate and my cute condo, but the plan was never for me to stay there as long as I did. Who knew I would be looking to move closer to Nicholas again?

Nicholas: Hi. I saw your press release. Well done.

Me: Thanks. That was all Cash. At least we aren't a story anymore.

Nicholas: Just be vigilant in the city. Out here, it's much easier.

I consider disclosing Cash's plans, but he wants to tell everyone at once. He hasn't indicated how he plans to pull that off, but I bite my tongue.

Me: I will. I need to get back to work. I love you lots.

Nicholas: I love you lots more.

My phone rings with an unknown number, yet I answer anyway.

"Good afternoon, Noelle speaking."

"Yes, this is Shelly Coulter. I'm the owner of the Bright Horizons Center. Jeremy Ellerbee is one of my students."

"Hi, how can I help you?"

"During our daily meeting, my manager, Ivy, was raving about you and your plan. She also mentioned that you were looking to purchase a center in addition to your developmental plans."

I refrain from doing a happy dance, just barely.

"Yes, she is correct. Are you looking to sell yours?" It would be perfect! It's within commuting distance of the airport for Cash. I wouldn't need security when Cash flies. Let's add in the fact that

Nicholas and Kelly are nearby, along with Billie and Peter. Plus, the Nubble, the Perk, the inn, and Dunne's are all within a reasonable drive.

"I am. I would love to set up a teleconference with you. First, though I would like to send you the information for the center—budgets, curricula, staff, etc."

We discuss the best way for her to send the information, and I end the call, indicating I would get back to her soon. As I press end, Cash strolls into the house.

"Hi, how was your morning?" I greet him as he tugs off his tie.

"Not too bad, you?"

"What will happen if I stumble upon a center that is for sale? How would that work?" Reeling in my giddiness is difficult. I watch as he processes my words.

He moves to me, wraps his arms around me, and spins us in a circle while he asks, "Really? Where? How? That is fantastic!" He presses his mouth to mine while lowering me to the floor. After some seriously early celebratory kissing, Cash pulls back slightly. I answer all his questions, and he answers mine. Armed with his information, I email Mallory and let her know about the opportunity.

Over a delicious spaghetti dinner, we discuss a host of subjects from when to tell our siblings, where to live, a car, and when we want to move.

"I would prefer to be near the water, but I don't want to sacrifice land. If we could have an acre or two near the water, that would be perfect." I state my preference.

"Do you want to be near Nicholas?"

"I don't need to be next door, but I wouldn't be opposed to it either. I would be able to have dinner with my brother on occasion and you could with Billie. Anything less than a flight would be ideal." We talk more about budgets, how many bedrooms, etc.

"I'll send some options to Jacob to get his initial opinion on security concerns."

"Can I pry a bit?" I ask. "You can decline to answer after you hear the question."

"You can ask me anything."

"What's the deal with your trust? Why do both of your parents keep attempting to use it as leverage?"

"I'll answer you. First, I know you don't care about my money. As I told you before, if I thought you did, you wouldn't be here now. If you had to rank my net worth and Nicholas's, whose would be higher?"

I consider my answer carefully. "I would say they are close to equal, bearing in mind that the last balance sheet I saw of Nicholas's was two movies ago."

"Fair enough. I agree. My parents created a trust for the four of us at birth. My siblings and I receive a set amount of money each month. There are strings attached to the money, such as gainful employment, never tarnish the Morgan name, and acting with class in public when requested as a family like the gala. At age thirty, we can request the corpus be turned over to us for investing on our own."

"Okay. You are gainfully employed, and you will be as the owner of Pemberton too. What am I missing?"

"Margaux believes that certain professions are beneath a Morgan. Anything in the service industry or something that requires creativity is not an acceptable profession."

"Yet Billie is a fashion designer and Auggie is a chef who wants to run a restaurant."

"True, but Billie is a separate case because she's no longer subjected to the terms of the trust. When she learned about mother's affair, she essentially walked away from the family, including her trust. To bring her back, my parents sold her loft, liquidated her trust, and turned the money over to her, no strings attached. To date, Billie hasn't touched any of the money, nor has she spoken to my parents."

"She was at the gala though?"

"Billie and Peter met at the gala three years ago. Her attendance is about their relationship. She didn't speak to our parents at the event. My parents allowing Auggie to draw from his trust for his restaurant is a step in the right direction, but deep down they believe he'll fail. Thus, proving their point that service jobs aren't good enough."

"What about you?" I ask contemplating his words.

"My parents believe that Sam and I rely on our trust to survive, that he and I party and squander our salaries from our jobs. That is wholly inaccurate. We have taken our trust payments, pooled them, and invested wisely for the last eight years. We will offer to pool Auggie's once he starts earning a living."

"Why not just have it out with your parents?"

"I haven't foreclosed the idea yet. My mother's treatment of you was abjectly evil, and I won't tolerate it. However, my father's apology as we left has made me pause. He has never stood in opposition to my mother about our trusts or our relationships. They were always a united front until the gala. Sam and I intend to talk about it tomorrow in more depth."

I ponder his response and realize it's up to him and Sam. I don't need him to have it out with Margaux. My words spoke for themselves.

CASSIUS

I'm tense since I struck my deal with Mr. Edson and Mr. Elliott. I'm meeting with Stacy to finalize both deals. Unfortunately, I'll be waiting an additional two months for Mr. Edson.

Noelle: Where are you flying this weekend?

Me: Portsmouth. Do you want to come?

Noelle: Yes, if there's room.

After three hours reviewing and signing. I have set in motion two deals for my dream job, thanks to my perfect woman. Without her, I never would have fathomed taking this leap. This weekend we will tell our siblings and search for a home.

After our flight, we huddle around the computer in Billie's condo waiting for Noah to log on.

"Are you pregnant?" Billie asks.

"No," Noelle replies.

"Show me your ring?" Kelly asks.

Noelle flashes her bare left ring finger.

Not for long, tesoro.

Finally Noah logs in.

"Hi, everyone. Thank you for joining us. To recap, we're not engaged nor having a baby. However, we're both making some changes."

I explain my two deals and Noelle's acquisition and consulting gig. The questions are fast and furious, but I ignore them.

"Lastly, Noelle and I are moving near Pemberton as soon as possible."

Cheers erupt from Billie and Kelly.

"The girl gang just got bigger!"

"Woohoo!"

I have no idea what those two are talking about, but Noelle is grinning from ear to ear, so she must have some idea. After ending the call, we snuggle up on Billie's terrace.

"That went well."

"It did," she agrees. "Are you going to keep your penthouse?"

I hadn't really thought about it. "If Sam doesn't want it, I may rent it out. Why?"

"Just wondering."

I see something cross her gorgeous features. "*Tesoro*, do you want me to keep it?"

She sighs deeply. "Keeping my condo is one thing, small in comparison to your place. It's not practical, but…."

"Complete bare honesty, sweetheart."

"I don't want you to sell it because it's part of us. I know long-term it isn't reasonable to keep a multimillion-dollar home that we won't use often."

"If that is what you want, I'll hold on to it." There must be a deeper reason she wants to hold on to these places, but I'm not sure what it is. My penthouse is paid for, so keeping it won't cost too much. Eventually, I'll understand why she wants to keep two pieces of real estate that we may never use again.

I sent four property sheets to Jacob. He eliminated one for security reasons. We'll see the other three today with Griffin. While Jacob recommended him, he is also a friend of Peter's. He helped Peter find Billie's dream home and one for Nicholas and Kelly. I have been assured of his discretion.

"Sweetheart, if you want to stop at the Perk, we need to go." Noelle hustles out of the bedroom, throwing her thin sweater over her shoulders, making me ask, "Do you move that fast for other things?"

"Just you." She kisses me hard.

Kelsey, one of Billie's friends, owns The Perk. When we arrive, there is a short line. As we step up to the counter, a young, bubbly girl named Becca asks, "Welcome to the Perk, what can I get for you?"

We place our order and hurry to meet Griffin at our first potential home.

"Miss Barnett. Mr. Morgan. It's a pleasure." Griffin extends his hand to her.

"Please Noelle and Cash," Noelle says, closing her door.

The first option is a piece of land with a few acres close to the airport. There is an ocean view, but a street sits between the land and the shore. Unfortunately, the street is busy. That's not something that the property sheets indicated. Nor will it work in the future with our children. I should be listening to Griffin, but I can already tell from Noelle's reaction. This isn't the one. "Shall I give you two a minute?" he asks after explaining the property.

I nod at Noelle. "No, we are ready to move on." He provides us with the address of the next property, and we follow him there.

We drive up to a massive house with a wraparound porch. The two-story foyer is gorgeous. Griffin is rattling off the stats—six bedrooms, six and a half bathrooms, home gym, and even an inground pool.

"What do you think?" I ask, already knowing her answer. She will say something like "it's nice but not it."

"It's huge. Enough room for all five kids, but it isn't the one."

I heard Griffin choke on the "five kids" part. "You have five kids?"

"Not yet, but we might someday," I reply with a huge grin on my face.

"On to the next, please," Noelle says, lacing her fingers with mine.

After a short ride, we stop at a gate. Opening the gate, we follow along a wooded driveway. I watch her face. So far, she hasn't moved this one into the no column. To be honest, this is my pick of the three, at least from the property sheet and photos online. The house is a newer construction, only a few years old. The current and only owner used it as a summer home and has recently decided it's too much home for the three weeks his family spends here in the summer. Her silence leads me to believe this one may be the one. There are six bedrooms and at least as many baths in this house. The kitchen is modern with white cabinetry, Carrera marble countertops, and restaurant-grade appliances. The living room has a large fireplace. On the rear wall of the house is a large office with a water view. The entire rear façade is a wide porch.

It's an exceptionally good sign that Noelle is climbing the wide staircase. There are two master suites. The larger one has double walk-in closets and an insane bathroom including a huge shower and claw-foot tub. Aside from the plentiful bedrooms, this property sits on three acres and abuts a nature conservancy. No one can build to the left or behind the home.

"What do you think?"

"It's perfect."

Leading her onto the terrace, I point over to the right. "Do you see that beach straight ahead?

"Yes."

"The house comes with access to that secluded beach. It's shared with three other homes on this street."

"Really?"

I smile. "There's more." I tap my finger on my lip, waiting for the reaction I'm bound to get. First, I love teasing her, and second, my name falling from her pouty lips makes my chest tighten.

"Cassius," she whispers, knowing what it does to me and to make me answer.

I kiss her cheek quickly before asking, "See that house two doors away?"

She shrugs.

"That is Nicholas's house."

"Really?"

"You didn't know?" I ask.

"No. I've never been there before. I never made it to the house when I came to visit because they were in Paris." Her eyes widen before she jumps into my arms. "Do you love it too?" Her lips descend on mine before I can answer. After kissing her thoroughly in what will be our bedroom, we walk downstairs to put in an offer.

After handling some details with Griffin, we decide to stop by to see if Nicholas and Kelly are home.

"It's so good to see you," Mabel says as she opens the door. She pulls both Noelle and me into a huge hug.

"Come in. I'll get them for you."

Kelly and Nicholas come out from what looks like an office. We greet them and chat over drinks and snacks that Mabel brings out. The girls are chatting about the gala, girls' night in, and Noelle's necklace. Nicholas motions for me to follow. I rise from the deck chair and follow him around the house.

"Thank you, Cash," Nicholas says as soon as we are out of earshot of our women. We walk down the lawn toward the shoreline.

"You're welcome. I didn't do anything."

"You did. You make her happy."

"She does the same for me. I realize you aren't her father, but you're the closest family she has. Nicholas, I love your sister. I want to build a life with her. At the risk of adhering to a traditional norm she loves to break, I would appreciate your blessing to marry Noelle." I extend my hand to him, and he takes it.

"You have it. Welcome to our family."

We discuss my plans a bit more before returning to the patio with Kelly and Noelle. On our trip back to Billie's condo, Noelle fills me in about her chat with Kelly, including details of her recent trip to Paris, the newest film she's working on, and what's coming up for Nicholas. Honestly, I'm only half listening. I have never felt this way before. Not only did Nicholas give me his blessing, but I have no doubt we'll be happy for the rest of our lives.

NOELLE

During our glorious weekend in Maine, we shared our news with our families, found the perfect home for our future, and shared a filthy, dirty evening on Billie's terrace. Now my nose is deep in paperwork working on my students' plans. Never have all the pieces fallen together for me. Every moment since I spontaneously kissed Cash has pushed me toward complete blissful happiness—happiness not only with him and my career but with myself. No man has ever completely listened and understood my need to ignore my birthday. Yet Cash makes me see that day is more about me than a reminder of losing them.

Glancing at the clock, I realize I'm late. I hurry to Cash's office to see Mallory.

"Noelle Barnett to see Mallory—"

"Hi, Noelle. Come on in," Mallory interjects. I follow her into the office late in the week. "Do you want me to call Cash?"

"I peered into his office. He was on a call. If he can stop in, he will." Mallory and I spend the next forty minutes going over the finer points of my deal to purchase Bright Horizons. The only provision that gives me pause is Shelly, the current owner, wants a stipulation that I will maintain the staff for at least one year. There are a few exceptions allowing termination, but basically the staff remains for at least a year.

Despite Mallory's insistence this isn't absolutely abnormal, I want to discuss it with Cash before agreeing. Armed with a draft sales agreement and a few more documents, I move toward Cash's office.

"Miss Barnett, Cash asked me to have you wait. He should only be a few more minutes."

"Thank you, Myles." As I take a seat outside Cash's office, I note a steady flow of guys walking past me. "Is it always like this?"

"Not at all. That is about you."

"Me? Why?"

"I can readily admit you're gorgeous despite my desire to bed someone who looks more like your boyfriend. Every other guy in the office is intrigued by the woman who could capture his stone-cold heart."

"Nothing about Cash is cold, Myles." I'm surprised his coworkers see him that way. He isn't cold to his siblings. Cash certainly isn't that way with me. He's loving and doesn't refrain from showing it as often as he can. Does he temper his displays of affection based on our surroundings? Of course. So do I.

"Frankly, we've never seen him like he has been for the last few months during the time he has been with you."

I open my mouth to respond, but when I do, Cash emerges from his office and invites me in.

"Hi, sweetheart. How was your meeting? I'm sorry I couldn't join you."

"No, problem. Mallory's great. I do have a few questions to go over with you tonight."

"I'll be home in a few hours." Despite our audience of one, Cash kisses me more deeply than he normally would. I wonder what that's about.

After a brief chat with Arthur, I fall into his office chair and review the paperwork from Mallory more thoroughly.

"Hi," Cash says, standing at the door later that same afternoon. He looks shell-shocked. Distraught. Heartbroken even.

"Who is hurt?"

"Mr. Edson."

It takes me a few moments to recall who that is. This can't be good. I unfold my legs and move to him.

"What happened?" I ask, wondering how it will impact Cash's purchase.

"He died."

Taking his hand, I guide him to the supple leather couch in his office. Setting his hands in my lap, I tug at his tie, loosening the expertly tied knot. He truly is off. Normally he has already peeled off his jacket and tie by the time he gets to me. I push his jacket off his shoulders and lay it on the arm of the couch behind me. I retake one hand in mine and slide the other along his sharp jaw, drawing my thumb along his cheek. A day's worth of stubble prickles against my skin. A million questions float through my mind, but I don't have the answers to a single one. Even though I'm working through the process with Mallory for myself, I have absolutely no clue what will happen now.

"What does that mean for your deal?"

"I don't know."

Has this ever happened before? To date, I have never seen Cash in the position of not getting his way or delaying getting his way, I hope.

"What can I do?"

"You already are." He slides his arm around me, pulling me into his lap. I kiss him before resting my head on his shoulder. The emotions pouring off him are intense, almost as intense as when he kisses me. He's tense and angry. His foot is tapping a hard, fast beat on the plush area rug.

"What is your plan?" I ask quietly. If he answers, great. If not, I'll just ask again later.

"Don't really have one yet. Stacy is working on it. If it were my client in this situation, I would reach out to the board. In this case, that's his children. As far as I know, his four children were on board with the sale. The worst case is I will have to renegotiate with the children. That will cost us time. Best case, in my opinion, is the kids agree to honor this agreement, but that will likely also cost us time as well."

The last thing Cash wants is to spend more time in New York, not only because we will be apart but because he sees his passion becoming his career.

"Maybe we should wait to hear the board's response."

The tension in his neck and back eases a tad. While his arms are still holding me securely against him, the anger vibrating through him has lessened as well. He sighs deeply before kissing my hair. "Tell me about your meeting. You're concerned about something in the agreement, right?"

"It isn't important, Cash. We can talk about it later."

"No, we can't. My crappy news doesn't in any way diminish the dream you're chasing. Your good day is equally as important as my mediocre or possibly atrocious one."

He is just so.... No one except Nicholas has ever put me first, but Nicholas is family. I have never felt so loved as I do right in this moment. Even though his dream is absorbing a potentially crushing blow, Cash is still interested in hearing about mine.

"Mallory gave me the draft sales agreement and a few more documents, including the staff report and inventory. The only provision that concerns me is keeping the staff for at least one year. What do you think?"

Before answering, he kisses me deeply. Each time his lips touch mine, the intensity is impossible to ignore. Despite what I thought, it doesn't diminish. It keeps gaining strength.

"Let's talk while we make some dinner," he says, pressing his lips to my forehead before setting me on the floor.

CASSIUS

Hesitantly, I decide to go into the office today. It'll give me more access to Stacy and the status of my deal. I even beat Myles in today. That's rare. Armed with a third cup of coffee, I filter my emails and calls. Surprisingly, there is a voice mail at work from my father. I just missed the call while I was getting my refill.

"Good morning, Cash. Thank you for returning my call."

"You're welcome." I figured getting it out of the way made the most sense. I won't ignore my father simply because my mother's behavior was abhorrent. Yesterday, Sam and I discussed my father's offer of releasing the trust corpus early. We decided, if his offer still stands, that I should take him up on it for a few reasons. First, it will give me more control over my portfolio, and second, it'll give me more liquidity for my Pemberton deal.

"I want to reiterate that I wasn't aware of your mother's actions. Lying to Miss Barnett to, I don't even know what, was unacceptable. I apologize again on your mother's behalf."

"Thank you."

"As you know, my marriage to your mother was a business deal. I never wanted that for my children, despite how it looked last year with Mina and young Mr. Thomas. I have never seen you peaceful and content in both your career and your life. I suspect Miss Barnett is the catalyst for those things. I'm genuinely happy for the both of you. You both deserve an apology from your mother. However, I question my ability to make that happen. Additionally, at least in the short-term, I doubt Miss Barnett nor you would be willing to be in the same room as my wife."

I'm floored. "Thank you. Nothing Noelle has ever done or ever will do warrants mother's behavior. She puts everyone before herself and cares for everyone she meets. Not only characterizing her as a gold digger but throwing her parents' death in her face was despicable. Margaux is nowhere near the pillar of humanity everyone thinks she is."

"I agree. It's my understanding that you're purchasing Pemberton Airlines. I assume you're moving as well."

"Yes on both accounts. My plans are not public knowledge; please keep them to yourself. The last thing I need is Margaux telling the world before I resign officially."

"I understand. What is the time frame, if you're willing to share?"

"Up until yesterday, I would have said by the end of this year. However, Mr. Edson passed away, so that put a wrench into half of the deal. I'm waiting on my broker for an update."

"Thank you for sharing. I will keep this information to myself."

"You're welcome. I would appreciate that. Very few people know of my plans. I need to keep it that way for a bit longer."

"I have spoken to our attorney regarding your trust. I can release it to you without your mother's consent. The offer still stands."

"Thank you. I will take you up on your offer. Please let me know what you need from me."

"Very well. Thank you for listening, Cassius. I hope your deal works out and that you and Miss Barnett continue to be happy together."

"You're welcome. Have a wonderful day, Father." I end the call and immediately inform Sam of this development and my plan to add most of the corpus to the fund we created. His response via text was simply "Wow!"

I have never heard my father take a stance in opposition to my mother. Now he has done it twice in the last week. Since I found Noelle, I can't understand how a loveless marriage could work long-term. Just before lunch, I stop by Stacy's office for an update.

"I have some good news and some great news," he states as I take a seat.

"Mr. Elliott has requested to expedite your deal for his stake in Pemberton. He would like to close in two weeks if that is acceptable to you." Joy, elation, and downright trepidation pulse through my veins all at once.

"I would appreciate expediting the purchase. Please set it up. Let me know where I should send the funds."

Stacy nods. "The good news is Mr. Edson's children would like to keep the deal in place as it is. Luckily, his will leaves everything to his children in equal shares. However, they need to admit his will to probate in New Hampshire to obtain the necessary power to re-execute the sales documents on behalf of his estate."

"How much additional time do you think that will be?" I ask hesitantly.

"It might not be longer than the original closing date. It simply depends on the court and the speed of their probate attorney."

"Thank you, Stacy. I appreciate all of your arduous work on this."

"Of course. I'm thrilled you found what you are looking for both in your career and in your life."

"Thank you. What about you?"

His face drops as he shakes his head.

"I'm sorry. The perfect baby will come along for you and Jocelyn." I hear my words and cringe, hoping that was the right thing to say.

"Thank you."

My emotions are mixed as I leave his office. I'm ecstatic for me and Noelle. While this deal will take longer than I would like, it's happening. On the other hand, I'm sad that Stacy and Jocelyn have been unable to find a baby to adopt.

I hurry home to share the great news with Noelle. As I search for her, I shuck my jacket and tie. I find her tucked in the chair in the corner of our room with her laptop balancing precariously on her lap. As I fill her in, she closes her laptop, setting it aside. I explain everything that Stacy shared with me as well as my call with my father.

Rising from the chair, she says, "I'll be right back," before hurrying from the room. Moments later, she returns with a bottle of champagne and two glasses. After setting it down, she retrieves a gift bag from the closet.

"What's all this?"

"I have some news too." Before continuing, she pours two glasses of champagne and hands me the gift. "Mallory said not only is my deal ready to close in a few weeks, but two female investors who wish anonymity have fully funded the deal."

"Sweetheart, that's spectacular. You could have led with that."

"Your wins today are just as important as mine."

Palming both glasses of Taittinger, I reach for her hand and lead her to the bed. She follows with the gift in her other hand. I settle in the middle of the bed and draw her close, her legs over mine. I hand her a glass and we toast our new endeavors.

"What's in the bag?" I ask.

"It's for you."

"You didn't have to get me anything."

"I know. It took some time to figure out the right gift. Honestly, you don't really need anything, which makes it immensely hard to find something special. I was super close to asking Billie for help, but I found this before getting her input."

I peer into the bag as if something will jump out of it. Inside is a small, heavy box. I haven't the slightest clue what it is. I open the box and find cologne, but it isn't a brand I've ever heard of.

She laughs. "You look confused."

"I am a bit. I've never heard of this company before."

"It's a company based in New York. They create a personalized cologne for you based on a quiz on their website. I entered all the information I could find and researched the cologne you use and created one personalized for you."

I open the box and inhale the scent. It's perfect. Fresh, clean, and spicy—it's completely me.

"It's fantastic! Thank you."

"You're welcome. I'm glad you love it. It's hard finding gifts for you."

Before I can lean forward to kiss her, she pushes me back to the duvet, kissing me with abandon.

Over dinner, we discuss when she's moving to Maine and how long she'll be alone in our new home. Thankfully, I'm less worried about her security thanks to Jacob and his team. They met us at the house to explain our new system and the security measures of our property. There is one additional aspect that I plan to put into play. It will be available soon. It also helps my piece of mind that Nicholas and Kelly are a few doors away and Kelly has a member of Jacob's team with her at work. If Noelle needs help, it's nearby.

NOELLE

A fresh cup of coffee in hand, I curl up on our porch. I wish Cash were here. It's an odd feeling. When we first met, I only saw him over video chat and on the weekends. Then I moved into his home and spent every, single, possible minute with him. Now we're apart again. I know it's temporary, but the whole point of buying a home was to be together.

It hasn't even been long since he was here. Last weekend he was here finalizing the modifications to the basement gym. He also wanted to assist with the furniture delivery. It isn't as if the furniture company would have let me place the pieces myself. His protective streak came out again in full force. I'm not sure why.

I push away thoughts of Cash and finish dressing for work. I closed on my center three weeks ago, and I have loved every second of being the director of Bright Horizons. My consulting business is thriving. I spend each morning at the center handling my director duties and have each afternoon scheduled for handling my education plans. If there is an event at the center, I swap the time frames. So far, that system works. Today I'm heading to the center first. Later I'll join the girl gang, as Billie affectionately calls us, for a girls' night in at Kelly's.

Unlike when I worked with Sheila, running the center is pleasant and the staff competent. After a staff meeting, I head home for the afternoon. Before finishing the last few new intakes I have for this week, I change and settle myself with some yoga on our balcony. Everything about our new home is perfect. I keep reminding myself that being apart is temporary, just a few more months. I can handle it. We can handle it. I just don't like it one bit.

Once Mallory created the consulting aspect of my business, I've had a steady stream of referrals. So far, I have been able to handle them in a timely manner on my own. At some point, I may need to consider hiring someone for the center or assisting with these plans. It's a problem I'm grateful to have.

Near six, I walk along the private lane to the front of Nicholas and Kelly's house. As I round the house, Mabel descends the front steps.

Pulling me into her arms, she asks, "Noelle, how are you?"

"Hi, Mabel. I'm great. I would prefer that Cash didn't have to stay in New York, but he'll be here soon enough."

"I'm so happy for you, my gorgeous girl."

"Thank you, Mabel."

After another tight hug, Mabel drives away. The front door swings open and Jacob and another huge guy step onto the front porch. I notice Jacob looks back inside once more. He isn't looking at Kelly though. He's looking at a gorgeous, tall brunette, Kelly's sister, I think. I don't readily recall her name. The longing in his eyes is unmistakable.

"Good evening, Noelle."

"Hi, Jacob. Pleasure to see you again."

"This is Christoph. He works for me."

I'm taller than most women, but even I need to look up at him.

"Nice to meet you." I take his hand and note it dwarfs mine even more than Cash's. A heaviness takes residence in my chest. Holy hell, I miss him so much.

"Have a nice night with the girls." Jacob states as he and Christoph walk to their car.

I nod and step through the front door.

Kelly is to my left in the kitchen. "Hey, Noelle. What can I get you to drink?"

"White wine please."

Billie approaches and pulls me into a huge hug. "Hi, how are you?"

"I'm hanging in there. I know this is temporary, and I'm not one to complain, but I feel a bit lost. I don't like being away from Cash."

You would think it would be weird for me to drone on about my love life to Billie, especially considering Cash is her brother, but that isn't the case. If I stay on the just enough side of intimate details, Billie and I can talk about Cash.

"I don't like when Peter is away for work either. I completely understand. When will he be back again?"

"Next weekend he'll be here. He's flying this weekend. I didn't even ask where. It doesn't matter."

"Have you met everyone yet?"

I shake my head, and Billie introduces me to Kelsey. I have heard so much about her and spend plenty of money at her bakery. She's beautiful, and if the way she's shielding her belly is any indication, she's pregnant but hasn't told anyone. Maggie is a tiny little thing holding a small baby named Caleb in her arms. The baby boy looks to be about six weeks old or so.

Finally, she introduces me to the woman that Jacob was looking at. Then I remember meeting her briefly at the wedding.

"Pleasure to see you again, Norah." I take her extended hand.

We all take a seat near the television, and Kelly selects *Sweet Home Alabama* as background noise. We chat about Kelsey's bakery and her upcoming events. Maggie discusses the latest wedding at her job where the bride's mother objected during the ceremony despite footing the bill.

Norah moves into the kitchen to refill our drinks while Kelly brings over more snacks.

"How is the house?"

"It's perfect, Kelly. Too big for just me, but eventually it will be fine."

"Are you?"

"No, we just plan on having a bunch of kids when we're ready."

"Are you?" I can't wait to be an aunt.

"Not yet but we're trying."

"Yay!" Maggie rises, handing me her son so she can go to the bathroom alone. It isn't unusual for women to hand their children to me, especially if they know I work in childcare. Kelly and I continue chatting about her newest costuming project and a custom dress she's making for Lynn Smith, the lead in Nicholas's last movie.

When Maggie returns, I suggest she eat something in peace. The baby is cooing and happy swaddled in my arms. After a brief pause, Maggie walks to the kitchen for food.

CASSIUS

Arriving at the house, I peer into the window and see my woman cradling a baby in her arms. I imagine when that will be our child. Once my heart beats again, I open the door. Our puppy escapes his leash, barreling into the house. Awws and reactions of cuteness surround me. As if we're moving in slow motion, a woman takes the baby from Noelle and she leaps into my arms.

"What are you doing here? I missed you so much." She kisses me so deeply it borders on inappropriate given we aren't alone. Her toned legs wrap around my waist, pressing the heat of her center against me.

"I need you. I can't be away from you any longer. I love you more." I reply.

A chorus of sighs erupt from the ladies in the room. She pulls back slightly before kissing me once more and unhooking her legs.

I whisper, "I'm sorry for crashing girls' night, but I need you to come with me."

After hurriedly saying goodbye to the girl gang, she follows me out the door.

"Can you hold him?" I ask her, setting the furry bundle in her arms while I secure his collar around his neck again.

"Why am I holding a puppy?"

I set our unnamed dog on the ground, take her free hand, and lead her around the house. Intertwining my fingers with hers, we stroll along the private lane past our home toward the beach.

"When everything was coming together, I looked into getting a dog for security reasons. I realize the security issues are significantly less here, but I knew you would accept a puppy as company. In my mind, a trained dog made me feel better about you being alone."

"He's for me?" She stops in her tracks.

"Yes, and he needs a name." I can see her confusion with my presence dissipate as we start walking again. It could be because I'm still concerned about her safety or it could even be that I bought her another gift. That is never going to change.

"What are you doing here? I thought you were flying this weekend?"

"I did. I flew here, but I'm not flying back to New York."

She stops again as we reach the edge of the beach. There is a tent with a large blanket and pillows with a small table spread out on the sand. "Cash, what is going on?"

"I had this set up for us and a bonfire for later."

"While I appreciate this, that isn't what I meant, and you know it. Why are you here?"

"You don't want me here?"

"I need you here more than anything, but there are at least three more months before that is a reality."

"I can't do three more months away from you. I signed the paperwork for my deal with Mr. Elliott this morning. The probate court approved the Edson portion of the sale yesterday. I'm waiting for a time to sign the paperwork. Stacy is going to bring it to me here. I gave my notice to the firm two weeks ago."

"You did?"

I nod.

"Why didn't you tell me?"

"I wanted to surprise you."

"You're staying here?"

"Yes, and for every night after tonight." I lead her into the tent that is setup on the beach. We settle onto the blanket and pillows on the sand. The furry little monster curls up in my lap and promptly falls asleep. Despite the furball in my lap, my nerves are all over the place. I was nervous on our first date; it's only natural to be nervous now.

"This is for you."

"More gifts, really, Cash? Don't you think a trained dog is enough for one night?"

"Clearly not. Open it."

I watch her open the box. Inside is a bound book that opens as large as a map. On the map is every place we visited marked with a pin and a number. Along the side, there is an explanation and a date. There is a pin at the airfield in Los Angeles where I met her to bring her to Nicholas's wedding, a pin at the hotel where she kissed me, the café near her condo, the pier, the beach, and her condo. I even put a pin in her old center for career day. Every location we have been together, including our new home and this moment right now.

"This is amazing." She leans forward and kisses me deeply. I set the sleepy dog on the blanket and pull her up to her knees facing me.

"When you kissed me at the hotel, I was taken aback. I have never felt intensity so strong ever before. On our first date, we shared a second kiss more mind-blowing than the first. You make me a better man. Without you, I never would have considered chasing my childhood dream of owning a plane, much less an entire airline. I spent almost three years looking for you. I knew my forever was not in New York."

"Cassius…." she whispers as I dry a single tear falling from her eyes. I move so I'm on one knee.

"*Tesoro*, you are my swan. I want to spend forever with you. Will you be my wife?"

"Yes, I will marry you." She captures my mouth, sliding her hands around my face as I cup her jaw. If every kiss is better than the last, this one adds a few notches for the next one to meet. I will thank Nicholas every day for the rest of my life. One favor for him led me to her, my forever.

"Can we wait until tomorrow to tell anyone?"

"Some of them already know."

"Who?"

"Nicholas and most likely Kelly. I didn't swear him to secrecy. I assume he told Kelly about my plans."

"You asked Nicholas for permission to marry me?"

"I did." A fresh batch of tears fall from her eyes. "Don't cry, *tesoro*. I know how much you love breaking tradition, but that one deserved to be honored. If your father were here, I would have asked him."

"Thank you."

Nodding, I pull her ring out of my pocket. As I slide my Asscher cut ring with an eternity band on her finger before pressing my mouth to her hand.

"It's...."

I'm sure her instinct is to say it too expensive, too much, or any other "I don't need this" expression. The truth is she deserves the world, and I intend to give it to her and every tiny human we create together.

"What shall we do now, almost Mrs. Morgan?"

"We should celebrate, Mr. Morgan."

I kiss my fiancée and lead her straight to our bedroom.

EPILOGUE

My stunning bride stands barefoot on the edge of the sand arm in arm with her brother Nicholas. Her custom, lace gown created by Kelly and Billie is perfection. It clings to her curves and dips low in the back with a mermaid fit, so I'm told.

"Who gives this woman to be wed?"

I see my future wife inhale sharply.

"With the blessing of our parents, I do." Nicholas kisses Noelle on the cheek. He whispers something else to her that I can't quite make out before shaking my hand.

The entire time our officiant is talking, I gaze at Noelle, recalling every moment of our life together thus far. Knowing that from this point forward, it'll only get better with her as my wife. As she slides a platinum band on my finger and I slide a matching eternity band on hers, I whisper, "Thank you for being my swan. I love you more, *tesoro*."

"Thank you for being mine. I love you more, Cassius."

"I now pronounce you husband and wife. You may kiss your bride."

He doesn't have to tell me twice. I kiss Noelle tenderly before dipping her as a small group of friends and family look on. Cheers erupt as we walk hand in hand down the fabric runner on the sand of our beach, and I feel truly whole.

When we first discussed what our wedding would look like, we talked about a huge wedding in the city. Realizing our home is here, we chose our beach. Adorned with round tables for our guests with white linens and chairs, our beach looks spectacular.

Kelsey acted as our event planner. She even created a memory table, including photos of Noelle's parents. We had a dance floor constructed for today as well as a small stage for the DJ. Kelsey took everything Noelle wanted and made it happen, from the centerpieces right down to the cannoli cake with two intertwined swans on the top tier.

Auggie enlisted some of his classmates to create the menu for our big day. He has been cooking up a storm in our kitchen for the last few days. As we try to escape for a private moment, our progress is slowed by Nicholas and Kelly.

"Welcome to the family, Cash. Congratulations." Nicholas shakes my hand. I hug Kelly gently. I don't want to squish my future niece or nephew.

"Congratulations, Cash and Noelle," Stacy says as we approach him, Jocelyn, and their new baby girl, Joy. The glow on their faces is a welcome sight. I'm glad they found a child to complete their family.

"Congratulations to you as well. She's beautiful," Noelle says, taking Joy's hand in hers. I can't wait to see her round with my child.

Lastly, my father is standing on the edge of the aisle.

"Congratulations to both of you."

"Thank you," we reply in unison. My mother is notably absent, as is his wedding band. I opt to leave that observation alone for now. I appreciate my father's presence and his renewed interest in our lives.

My wife and I make our way to the dance floor for our first dance. Sliding my arms around her, I pull her lush curves against me. "I love you today and always, Mrs. Morgan."

"I love you today and always, Mr. Morgan."

The opening bars of our song, "From this Moment On," a duet of Shania Twain and Bryan White, begins. Despite her difficult childhood, Noelle loves fiercely and completely. I'm grateful every day she chooses me to share her life. Our siblings and their significant others join us on the dance floor, surrounding us in a tight circle. Our lives are better with them.

After our dance, we dine on an exquisite menu. We endure toasts from Nicholas, who stood up for Noelle as her man of honor, and Billie who was my best woman. All our siblings stood with us as we took our vows. Laughter and tears, both from sentiment and levity, fill the evening. Along with our guests, we dance the night away.

Against Noelle's wishes, Nicholas and I set up a brother-sister dance. The DJ dutifully called them to the dance floor to dance to "My Wish" by Rascal Flatts. I watch in awe of her, knowing her fierce heart matches mine. I will lay it all down for her as she will for me. After our final guests make their way off the beach, Noelle and I sit at the shore and enjoy the intoxicating peace of the ocean.

"Do you want your gift now?" Noelle whispers.

"I already have it."

"I may have held one back."

I turn to look at her and see her fingers forming a heart over her lower abdomen. I tear up, set my hand over·hers, and kiss her deeply. I wanted a fairy tale; today I have it.

EXTENDED EPILOGUE

NOELLE

THREE YEARS LATER

"Josie, can you get your daddy for me?"

"Sure, Mommy." As she runs off, I move to finish the salad for our barbeque later this afternoon.

"I'm here to help. What can I do?" Kelly asks, stepping into the kitchen with Nick in tow.

"Hi, Auntie," he says, throwing his arms around me, or at least tries to.

"Hi, bud. Why don't you find Jules and play outside?"

He nods and runs off.

Kelly and I finish the tossed salad and start on the potato salad before setting it to chill. Cash bounds into the kitchen with Ellie, our niece, gripping on his forearm. Setting her on the floor, he kisses my temple.

"What can I do to help?"

"Nothing. I need a kiss." Even with Kelly standing there, Cash kisses me thoroughly.

"Gross. Seriously, there are other people present," Nicholas bellows as he enters the kitchen.

"Leave them alone. It's cute they still can't keep their hands off each other," Kelly admonishes, coming to our defense.

"She's still my sister. Still not a fan of his hands all over her even after a few years, a few nieces, and one more on the way," Nicholas replies.

I laugh. As Cash and Nicholas walk away, I have a contraction. I've been through it before, and I shake it off. It's too early anyway. Greeting the rest of our guests, Kelly and I join the guys outside. Everyone who lives nearby is here and even a few who took a weekend to hang out, like Auggie, Caro, Sam, and Warren.

Cash is chatting with Connor at the grill. Our daughters, niece, and nephew are running circles around Peter and Nicholas. As I lower myself into the chair, I feel another contraction and my water breaks.

"Cash," I call, but he doesn't hear me. "Cash." He's laughing. I decide to pull out the most powerful weapon I have. "Cassius." Instantly, everyone turns to look at me. Just like the last time, he's frozen with fear.

"Noelle, is your bag ready?" Kelly asks.

"Yes, it's in the bedroom. Left closet on the floor."

As Kelly scurries away, Cash moves to my side.

"It's early." Cash whispers.

She's ready a month early. Who am I to argue? "Cash, everything will be fine. We did this once already for twins. We can do this for one baby." Even so, I still see fear in his eyes. Josie and Julianna were no treat to deliver, so I understand his concern.

After prepping Josie and Julianna, I change, and we leave for the hospital. Less than four hours later, our third daughter, Josephine, joins our growing family.

"I thought we would have all boys," Cash quips.

"We may need to renegotiate if we keep having girls."

COMING SOON

Two new stories are coming soon!

A York Beach Novel
My Once in a Lifetime (Norah and Jacob)

The Morgan Brothers
Until I Kissed You (Samson and Savannah)

MY BOOKS

Did you love *One Unforgettable Favor*

Thank you for taking the time to read it. I hope you loved it!

If you liked this book or another one of my books, please consider

posting a review.

A short line or two will be perfect!

I appreciate your support and feedback.